Praise for the Joe Pickett Series

"Raining here, but I've got a cup of hot tea and a Joe Pickett novel, so who has it better than me?"

—Stephen King, via Twitter

"Joe Pickett, the conscientious game warden in these rugged novels . . . shows the tough-and-tender qualities that make him such a great guy to have on your side." —*The New York Times*

"Picking up a new C. J. Box thriller is like spending quality time with family you love and have missed. . . . It's a rare thriller series that has characters grow and change. An exciting reading experience for both loyal fans as well as newcomers."

—Associated Press

"Box is a master." —*The Denver Post*

"Box knows what readers expect and delivers it with a flourish."
—Cleveland *Plain Dealer*

"Wyoming game warden Joe Pickett strides in big boots over the ruggedly gorgeous landscape of C. J. Box's outdoor mysteries."
—*The New York Times Book Review*

TITLES BY C. J. BOX

THE JOE PICKETT NOVELS

Three-Inch Teeth

Storm Watch

Shadows Reel

Dark Sky

Long Range

Wolf Pack

The Disappeared

Vicious Circle

Off the Grid

Endangered

Stone Cold

Breaking Point

Force of Nature

Cold Wind

Nowhere to Run

Below Zero

Blood Trail

Free Fire

In Plain Sight

Out of Range

Trophy Hunt

Winterkill

Savage Run

Open Season

THE HOYT/DEWELL NOVELS

Treasure State

The Bitterroots

Paradise Valley

Badlands

The Highway

Back of Beyond

THE STAND-ALONE NOVELS AND OTHER WORKS

Shots Fired: Stories from Joe Pickett Country

Three Weeks to Say Goodbye

Blue Heaven

G. P. PUTNAM'S SONS
NEW YORK

THREE-INCH TEETH

A JOE PICKETT NOVEL

C. J. BOX

PUTNAM
—EST. 1838—

G. P. Putnam's Sons
Publishers Since 1838
An imprint of Penguin Random House LLC
penguinrandomhouse.com

LCCN
2023951956

First G. P. Putnam's Sons hardcover edition / February 2024
First G. P. Putnam's Sons trade paperback edition / August 2024
G. P. Putnam's Sons trade paperback edition ISBN: 9780593331361

Printed in the United States of America
1st Printing

Title-page and section photograph by COULANGES/Shutterstock.com

This is a work of fiction. Apart from well-known historical figures and actual people, events, and locales that figure in the narrative, all other characters are products of the author's imagination and are not to be construed as real. Any resemblance to persons, living or dead, is entirely coincidental. Where real-life historical persons appear, the situations, incidents, and dialogues concerning those persons are not intended to change the entirely fictional nature of the work.

For Parker
and Laurie, always

THREE-INCH TEETH

OCTOBER 14

A man screaming is not a dancing bear.

—Aimé Césaire,
Notebook of a Return to the Native Land, 1939

CHAPTER ONE

Double Diamond Ranch

CLAY HUTMACHER JR., twenty-five, stood knee-high in the Twelve Sleep River, casting for trout with a determined look on his face and an engagement ring in his pocket. He was twelve miles from the town of Saddlestring on the ranch his father managed and that, he hoped, he would take over someday.

It was fall in the mountains of Wyoming, and a day away from the opening of most of the local elk hunting season. Opening day was rife with anticipation throughout Twelve Sleep County, as out-of-state hunters loaded up on groceries and alcohol and gear in town, and locals told their bosses they wouldn't be in to work the next day. In the mountain campgrounds and trailheads, orange-clad hunters were setting up their elk camps and scouting the meadows and timber. For many in the area, tonight would be without sleep.

Clay Junior, meanwhile, had spent the day patrolling the ranch's entrance roads to chase off trespassers. He'd exchanged words with three Missouri hunters, who had refused to move their camp from private to public land, but finally relented when he threatened to call the sheriff and have them arrested. The fact that his GPS proved that they were in the wrong convinced them to pack up. The ten-millimeter Glock semiautomatic handgun on his hip probably helped as well.

IT WAS THE longest and most pleasant fall he could remember since returning to the ranch after a stint in the military and three years in college. Unlike many years, when "fall" was a hard freeze that came out of nowhere and instantly killed all the deciduous greenery, this one had brought out colors he didn't know existed outside of New England. Yellow leaves crunched underfoot and seams of crimson ran up every mountain draw.

The late-afternoon sun dappled the water and ignited the river cottonwoods and buckbrush along the bank with intense golds and reds. It almost hurt his eyes. A slight breeze rattled through the drying leaves and hundreds of them had detached upriver and now floated like a tiny yellow armada on the surface of the water. Above him, a bald eagle in a thermal current glided in a lazy circle.

The leaves on the water made it difficult to see his indicator bobbing along, so Clay Junior retrieved his fly line, clipped off the nymphs he'd been using, and replaced them with a heavy articulated streamer.

A boulder the size of a pickup truck stuck out of the water near the opposite shoreline, and he knew there was a deep pool directly downstream from it. In the summer, he'd seen massive brown and rainbow trout rise from the depths of the pool like pistons and eat trico flies floating along the surface. Clay Junior wanted to catch one of those big fish. Maybe two.

He was outfitted in chest-high waders, a waterproof Simms jacket with a mesh fly-fishing vest over it, and a Stormy Kromer rancher's cap. A lanyard loaded with scissors, spools of tippet, and forceps hung from his neck. A fishing net was attached to the collar of his vest and a wading staff undulated in the strong current from where it was tied off on his belt.

The back of his vest sagged from the weight of the Glock in the rear pocket. The weapon held fifteen rounds and had enough stopping power to take down the biggest of wild-game species. Clay never went anywhere without it.

The wonderful thing about fly-fishing, he'd discovered, was that it was all-consuming. The tactics, the gear, reading the water, the choice of flies, keeping his balance on smooth round river rocks—all of that fully occupied his mind and pushed out other concerns.

Fly-fishing was like sex in that way.

AFTER HE'D RETURNED to the ranch headquarters that afternoon, Clay Junior had thrown his rod and gear into an open Polaris Ranger and drove it straight through the hayfield to the bend in the river.

He particularly wanted to take his mind off dinner that night with Sheridan Pickett. That was when she would see the engagement ring for the very first time.

The ring had been in his pocket for a week. He'd just been looking for the right moment. In his mind, they were already engaged.

Should he ask Sheridan's father, Joe, for permission first? Clay Junior had debated it several times. In the end, he'd decided not to. Joe Pickett was the local game warden, a friend of his dad's, and the father of three daughters. Sheridan was the oldest, and she and Joe clearly had a special bond. Clay Junior wasn't sure her dad liked him all that much, and why risk the remote possibility that the man would discourage him? If nothing else, Clay Junior had confidence in himself.

Star high school athlete; army veteran; conventionally handsome, with broad shoulders, blue eyes, and a square jaw; a future as the foreman of a twenty-thousand-acre ranch that was one of the largest in north-central Wyoming. He had a lot going for him. Why wouldn't he be confident?

Besides, Sheridan had a mind of her own. Too much so at times, he thought. She wouldn't let her father's reservations about him influence her.

Would she?

HE CAST THE big streamer upstream from the boulder, a perfect shot. It *ploop*ed on the surface and sunk fast, and he fed line out so the fly would drift naturally along the side of the rock, looking like a wounded minnow, and go deep by the time it entered the pool. Clay Junior held the rod with his right hand and grasped the line with his left and got ready.

When the line straightened out suddenly, he strip-set the hook by jerking back on the line and raising his rod tip. A fish had taken it, and it felt big. He reveled in the electric connection.

But he gacked it by pulling too hard, and the line went slack. He figured the trout had either thrown the hook or wrapped the line around a submerged branch or rock, but when he reeled in, he saw that the fly was gone and the end of the tippet was curled up like a pig's tail. That meant he'd likely tied a poor knot and that big trout was streaking down the river with a fly hanging out of its mouth.

He cursed and began to attach a heavier leader and tippet, to try again. There had to be more than one big fish in there.

WHILE HE STOOD tying, leaning slightly against the powerful current with his hip, Clay Junior heard a crashing in the trees on the opposite hillside.

He paused and looked up.

Another branch snapped, and he noticed that the top of a spindly aspen jerked and shed dead leaves as something hit it at its base.

At first, he thought it was a rockslide. They happened on the steep canyon wall, and sometimes they gathered so much momentum, they snapped off trees as they tore down the mountain.

He looked over his shoulder at the bank, where he'd parked the Polaris Ranger. He wasn't sure he could navigate across the slick stones fast enough before a jumble of large rocks came his way.

Then a large doe mule deer crashed out of the brush and plunged headlong into the water twenty yards upriver from him. The deer paid no attention to him and he recalled Joe telling him that prey animals didn't fear anything in the water because they knew predators came from the land.

In fact, the doe had her head turned at something behind her. *Fearing* something behind her. As she got to the middle of the river, she struggled for a few seconds, then she began to swim, keeping her head above the surface, bobbing it front to back like a chicken.

The current brought her closer to Clay Junior and he wondered for a second if she'd knock him off his feet. Switching his rod to his left hand, he reached behind him with his right for the back pocket of his vest and the Glock. A shot in the air might make her change course.

And that was when a massive tan bear with a dark brown hump on its back emerged from the trees, roared, and threw itself into the river in pursuit of the deer, hitting the water with a loud splash.

Not a rockslide, Clay Junior thought, but a grizzly bear *more than twice his size.*

The doe regained her footing as the river shallowed and she was able to scramble toward the shoreline just a few feet above

Clay Junior. She was close enough that droplets of water from her thrashing sprayed across his face.

But when she was gone the bear was still there in the middle of the river and moving remarkably fast. Instead of pursuing the deer, the grizzly was coming straight at him. *Swimming* straight at him. It had small, close-set eyes centered in a massive round head. The bear was so large that it produced a wake in the water until it, too, found the floor of the river.

The grizzly closed the distance and rose onto its back legs and towered over him, blotting out the light. He could see its thick coat shimmer as river water sluiced out of it. Long claws were curved like yellow scythes, and the bear was close enough he could smell it. The stink was like wet dog, only twenty times worse. The bear roared at him, and Clay Junior felt his anus instinctively pucker and his limbs go weak. He'd never heard a sound that affected him in such a primal, visceral way.

Scrambling, he stepped back and his boot sole slipped on the top of a round river rock. Losing his balance, he fell back and to the side, and fumbled the Glock into the river. The weapon thumped on the side of his thigh through the waders, then slipped beneath the surface, out of sight. At the same time, the bear dropped to all fours and charged.

Clay Junior wanted to shout, "What the fuck have I done to deserve this?"

His last look at the bear before he went under was its tiny black eyes, gaping mouth, and long, sharp, scimitar-like teeth.

The grizzly lunged on top of him and pinned him flat on his

back to the rocks on the floor of the river, a foot and a half beneath the surface. As the jaws closed around his head, the last sound Clay Junior heard was the awful crunch of those teeth through his skull.

His last thought was:

Would she have said yes?

OCTOBER 15

Are people more important than the grizzly bear?
Only from the point of view of some people.

—Edward Abbey

CHAPTER TWO

Saddlestring

THE NEXT DAY, Wyoming game warden Joe Pickett was feeling all of his fifty-one years when he received a call from Clay Hutmacher, the foreman of the Double Diamond Ranch.

At that moment, he was working his way down the side of a steep mountain on foot, wearing a daypack filled with optics and gear. As he descended, he concentrated on not tripping over a sagebrush or dislodging a rock that would send him ass over teakettle down the slope to where his truck was parked.

Although it wasn't yet noon, Joe was tired. He'd been up since before dawn, and since it was October he'd spent the entire morning in the breaklands and mountains checking hunters in the field. For the last two hours, he'd been glassing hunters and hunting camps through his spotting scope, as well as a herd of elk, a small band of mule deer, and a contingent of pronghorn antelope out on the plains.

He was exhausted, but pleasantly so, and the morning had gone smoothly. He'd witnessed no violations and issued no warnings or tickets and made no arrests. The camps he'd visited were generally clean and the hunters he'd met were friendly and ethical. Their food was hung from trees to discourage bears and no one had reported any large carnivore or wolf sightings. He was still a little surprised by the four young men he'd met early on in his rounds: hipsters from Jackson Hole with long beards and blaze-orange porkpie hats, who were hunting elk not for trophy racks but to fill their freezers for the winter. It was good to meet younger hunters keeping the local traditions alive, he thought. It encouraged him to keep doing what he was doing and knowing it was right.

Since the many elk seasons in his district had expanded over the years, legal hunting was now allowed from archery season in mid-September to limited cow/calf seasons as late as January 31. Joe was busy every day and he'd learned to pace himself. He wasn't getting any younger.

THE DAY BEFORE had been more challenging. He'd encountered three elk hunters from Pennsylvania camped on Bureau of Land Management land a stone's throw from the boundary fence of a big ranch known to locals as the Double D. The Pennsylvania hunters had made it clear to him that they intended to "corner-cross" from the parcel they were on to an adjacent public parcel by means of a ladder they had built specially for the purpose and brought with them to Wyoming. The plan, they explained, was to move across the checkerboard of public lands without stepping foot on private. The hunters showed Joe the extremely accurate GPS mapping apps they'd put on their phones to make sure they stayed legal.

Joe had warned them that corner-crossing was a complicated issue, and a newly contentious one. There were laws that allowed citizens to access all public lands, as well as laws that said that even entering the *airspace* of private land was trespassing. Since there was no way for the hunters to climb the ladder from corner to corner and not prevent any part of their bodies from passing over a tiny slice of private land on the way, they were risking trespassing charges from the county sheriff.

The Pennsylvania hunters were well aware of the dilemma, they told Joe, but they were willing to risk it. It was their land as much as anyone's, they said. Joe had told them as long as they broke no Game and Fish regulations, he'd let them be. But he could do nothing to prevent their arrest by the county sheriff if that office decided to pursue it.

Joe could see both sides of the issue. Legal hunters did have the right to access public land, even if the way they did it was legally dubious. At the same time, local landowners owned huge, and hugely expensive, tracts of "private" acreage that contained squares of public land inside of it. If just anyone could access those inholdings at any time, was the private property actually private?

"Corner-locked" public land was a big issue in the West,

where so much territory was owned by the federal government. There were 2.4 million acres of corner-locked land in Wyoming alone, the same size as Yellowstone Park and the Wind River Indian Reservation. That was twice as much land as Rhode Island, and it was bigger than the landmass of the state of Connecticut.

Someday, Joe hoped, the legal system would rule one way or another in a definitive way. In the meantime, corner-crossing would remain a thorny issue that pitted sportsmen against landowners. And it put him and other game wardens in the middle of the dispute.

When he left their camp, Joe wasn't sure he'd convinced them not to try it.

SO WHEN CLAY Hutmacher's name appeared on his cell phone screen, Joe fully expected to hear the foreman sound off about the three hunters who had trespassed onto the Double D.

Instead, Hutmacher said, "I'm sorry to bother you, Joe, but I'm trying to track down my son. Have you seen or heard from him in the last twenty-four hours?"

Joe paused for breath and leaned against the stout mottled trunk of an ancient ponderosa pine tree. Daisy, his aging yellow Labrador, used the opportunity to rest as well and quickly collapsed near his feet.

"No," he said. "I haven't seen much of anyone this morning except elk hunters. I'm on the south side of Wolf Mountain right now."

"Well, damn," Hutmacher said. "I've been calling his phone since last night and he hasn't picked up. That's not like him."

"Is there an emergency?" Joe asked.

"Naw, nothing like that. He's way too old for me to be checking up on him, but he has the only spare set of keys to one of our flatbed trucks that we need today. Plus, it doesn't look like he slept in his room last night."

Joe thought about that, considering the implications. Clay Junior was seeing his oldest daughter, Sheridan, and the relationship seemed to be getting much more serious than Joe wanted to accept or acknowledge. Sheridan had her own apartment in town, so he and Marybeth didn't always know what was going on with her.

If Clay Junior hadn't slept in his own bed . . .

"I'll keep an eye out for him," Joe said. "I'll check with Sheridan as well."

That was what Clay was asking, Joe knew.

"I appreciate that," the foreman said.

"On another subject, I met three Pennsylvania hunters yesterday who showed me the ladder they intended to use to access your public land."

"Corner-crossers?"

"I'm afraid so."

"You didn't arrest them?" Hutmacher asked.

"Nope," Joe said. "We've had this discussion, Clay."

"Goddamn them. If I catch them on the ranch, they better hope their health insurance is up-to-date."

"I didn't hear that," Joe said.

"The boss has had it with them, you know," Hutmacher said, referring to the wealthy owner of the ranch, Michael Thompson, who lived most of the year in Atlanta, where his telecom firm was headquartered. Thompson and his young wife, Brandy, visited the ranch only a couple of times a year to hunt trophy elk and tour it during the summer months, but when they did he always made sure to harangue Joe about keeping trespassers off his ranch.

"I know," Joe said.

"Where were they?"

Joe described where the Pennsylvanians had camped on the northern border of the Double D, about six miles from the highway.

"I'm going to send a couple of my guys out there on ATVs," Hutmacher said. "If we catch 'em, we'll hold them in place until the sheriff arrives to arrest the bastards."

Joe sighed. It wasn't really necessary to say that the Twelve Sleep County Sheriff's Department might not respond with their best—or at all. Since Sheriff Scott Tibbs had retired seven months before, the office was in turmoil. Two of their best deputies, Ryan Steck and Justin Woods, had resigned and left the state for new law enforcement jobs. An interim sheriff had been selected by the county commissioners: a woman named Elaine Beveridge, a former county commissioner. Unfortunately, Beveridge had made it a habit never to answer her phone or leave her desk. A new election was coming up, and Judge Hewitt had hand-selected a candidate named Jackson Bishop, and he was backing Bishop publicly and financially. At the moment, however, the office was completely and totally adrift.

Joe didn't know Bishop at all. His past relationships with local sheriffs had been . . . rocky. Joe and the rest of the locals were grateful there had been no county-wide crime spree in the interim.

"I gotta go," Hutmacher said.

"I'll keep an eye out for your son," Joe said.

TWO HOURS LATER, after Joe had eaten his sack lunch of cold fried chicken and orange slices in his pickup and had fed Daisy her ration of dried dog food out of a tin bowl, Hutmacher called back. He was in tears.

"Oh my God, Joe," Hutmacher cried. "You need to get out here."

Joe sat up in his seat. He'd never heard his friend so distraught. "What's going on?"

"I found Clay Junior down by the river. Or I should say, I found part of him."

"*What?*"

"I found his leg. I think he got attacked by a bear or a wolf or a mountain lion. I don't know what the hell happened, but it's awful. Get here as fast as you can," Hutmacher said through a choking sob. "It's the most horrible thing I've ever seen."

"Did you call Sheriff Beveridge?"

"That bitch won't pick up," Hutmacher said bitterly.

"I'm twenty minutes away," Joe said.

———

ALTHOUGH HE RARELY activated either his siren or the wigwag lights mounted on the top of the cab of his green Ford pickup, Joe turned on both of them when he fishtailed from the county road onto the interstate highway.

"Hold on," he told Daisy as he rocketed past a passenger car from Montana and an oil-field truck from Casper. The turnoff for the Double D was ten miles south on I-25.

He plucked the radio transmitter from its cradle on the dashboard while he drove and was instantly connected to a dispatcher in Cheyenne.

"This is GF-14," he said, referencing the number that corresponded to his badge number. His warden number had recently changed from nineteen to fourteen on account of two more senior game wardens retiring and three leaving the agency in the last year. "I'm responding to a call from the foreman of the Double D Ranch, who reported a possible large-predator attack on his property."

"Oh God," the female dispatcher said. "Not again. Please, not again."

Joe understood the reason for her breach of protocol. There had been four bear attacks on humans in the last month in Wyoming, more than ever before. Three had occurred just outside the boundaries of Yellowstone Park, but one had happened a hundred and fifty miles straight south of the park. This, if it turned out to be a bear attack, would be the first one in the Bighorn Mountains of north-central Wyoming.

There weren't supposed to be grizzly bears in the Bighorns.

"Please notify the Predator Attack Team to stand by," Joe said. "I'll check in with you when I get there."

"Affirmative. What is your twenty?" she asked.

"Eight miles north of the scene."

THE PREDATOR ATTACK Team consisted of five armed wardens from around the state who were called to respond immediately to large-carnivore attacks. They were a kind of SWAT team, except trained to confront wild animals instead of human perpetrators. Members of the PAT were equipped with tactical gear, high-end optics and communications equipment, armor, bear spray, and semiautomatic rifles. Joe was an alternate member of the team and was called upon if the team was a man down or if one of them was unavailable on a moment's notice.

He didn't relish the assignment because he didn't like the idea of hunting down and murdering a bear.

That, and he was terrified of them.

GOING OFF WHAT little Hutmacher had told him, Joe drove straight through the ranch yard of the Double D to a two-track road that led down to the Twelve Sleep River. The headquarters complex of the ranch was impressive, with a magnificent gabled home built of local sandstone nestled into the side of a hill, surrounded by outbuildings and quarters for ranch employees. The foreman's home was a two-story log structure set down and to the side of the owner's house, but with the same expansive view of the river bottom and the mountains beyond. Joe noticed as he drove by that Hutmacher's pickup wasn't parked in its usual place.

Joe plunged down the hillside on the two-track into a shimmering grove of aspen. Mule deer skittered out from the trees to his right, and three scrappy whitetails came out to his left. He slowed as the two-track made several tight turns in the woods before it flattened out onto a large hayfield and the road dispersed into nothing.

He drove carefully across the hayfield, knowing small irrigation ditches wound their way through it. The ditches were hard to see, and he didn't want to drop his tires into one and get stuck. Ranchers instinctively knew how to navigate their hayfields without roads or markers, but Joe didn't.

Halfway across the wide field toward the river, Joe saw two sets of tire tracks pressed into the dried grass. One set was narrow, the other wide. He used the tracks to lead him across the field toward the high wall of river cottonwoods that tangled the banks. A steep rocky slope rose and dominated the view to the east on the other side of the river. He could catch glimpses of the water through the trunks of the trees.

Two vehicles were parked on the edge of the field next to a barbed-wire fence that kept cattle from trampling the river itself. One was Clay's Ford F-350 pickup with the Double D logo painted on the front doors. The other was an open two-seat Polaris Ranger ATV mounted with a fly rod carrier to its roll cage. Twenty feet from the vehicles was an open wire gate that led to the river through the brush on the other side of the fence.

Joe pulled in behind the F-350 and shut off the engine.

"Stay here," he told Daisy as he drew his shotgun out from behind the seat and loaded it with alternating slug and buckshot rounds.

He closed the door and took a long breath of air that was tinged with cut hay and freestone river. A slight breeze rattled through the drying leaves of the trees and provided a soundtrack like ghostly distant hand percussion shakers.

Joe touched the grip of his .40 Glock as well as the handle and nozzle of the bear spray canister on his belt to make sure they were there. He closed his eyes and visualized drawing the spray, arming the canister, and firing it.

He debated what he would do if he had a close encounter with a bear. Would he deploy his bear spray or start blasting with his shotgun?

Then he called out, "Clay? It's Joe Pickett."

THERE WAS NO response. Joe hoped that the reason for Clay's not answering was because the breeze and the sound from the river had drowned out his query.

He touched the plastic hood of the Ranger as he passed it. Cold. He touched the hood of Clay's F-350. Warm.

Joe racked a slug into the receiver of the shotgun and approached the open gate. It was a three-strand barbed-wire gate and it had been flung to the side. Joe stepped through the opening with his senses on high.

The brush near the river was thick, and the only way to push through it was to use a series of game trails that wound through the eight-foot-tall willows. As he did, the brush closed around him and he felt slightly claustrophobic. He could see nothing beyond a few feet, and he knew that a predator could be tucked away in the tangle and he wouldn't see it until it was too late.

Joe used his left hand to push branches away as he approached the river. He held his shotgun tight to his body with his right so the barrel wouldn't catch on the brush and be jerked aside.

When he cleared the willows and the river opened up before him, Joe stopped and surveyed the scene carefully. There was so much color in the trees and the sun's dappled reflection off the water that, for a moment, it was hard to concentrate. The impressionistic tableau in front of him was like a pulsating, neon Monet painting.

As his eyes adjusted, he saw Clay sitting on a rock on the bank of the river with his back to him. Clay was hunched over, his head in his hands, his cowboy hat upside down near his boots. A large-caliber handgun was poised on a flat rock next to him, near the bottom half of a human leg, still wearing a fishing boot and Gore-Tex waders slashed jaggedly at the knee.

"Clay?"

This time, the man heard him. Clay looked over his shoulder. His face was swollen and his eyes were haunted.

Clay was a big man with ginger hair, dark blue eyes, and a

square-cut jaw that gave him a look of authority. That jaw trembled when he said, "He's gone, Joe. Torn apart. A bear must have got him."

As he said it, he gestured upstream with a wave of his hand, indicating that Joe should follow.

"Is the bear still around?"

Clay shrugged. "I don't know. I haven't seen him. But Clay Junior is over there, or what's left of him."

Joe couldn't yet see the body, but he nodded and picked his way over the jumble of smooth river rocks upstream. Twenty yards away from where Clay sat, Joe paused before a finger of dark mud that sat exposed between the rocks. The bear track was massive—at least nine inches long and over five inches wide. There was a large kidney-shaped impression from the pad of its foot, five toe impressions each the size of a quarter, and five claw marks in front of the toes that looked narrow and deep, like repeated stabs of a knife. All of the impressions had filled with water from their proximity to the river.

There was no doubt to Joe that it had been a grizzly, not a black bear. A black bear track was roughly half this size and was distinguishable by the curved inside digit nearest the body of the animal. Grizzly tracks went straight from the pad of the foot.

The track was aimed at a loose mound of dirt filled with debris—small broken branches, mulch, rotting scabs of bark, and short lengths of pale tree roots that looked like entrails. The mound was about seven feet long and two feet high. It looked like a hastily dug grave and was set against the trunks of the cottonwood trees. Unnatural glimpses of color showed in the soft dirt.

As Joe approached the pile, the wind shifted slightly and he caught a whiff of a musky, rotten odor. It made the hair on the back of his neck and forearms prick.

He scanned the row of trees ahead of him and followed them up- and downstream. If the bear was still there it was hunkered down. Was it watching him?

There were more tracks near the pile. The bear had been heavy enough that it pressed several river rocks into the loose dirt around it. Joe noticed that when he stepped on the same rocks with his boot, they didn't sink farther.

He saw where Clay had dug at the mound earlier, revealing Clay Junior's mutilated face and head. The skin was pure white and mottled gray, his eyes wide open. There was a row of large round punctures across his forehead and beneath his chin, and more gaping holes on the sides of his head around the temples. There was no doubt he was dead.

Joe reached down and touched the collar of Clay Junior's shirt. It was soaked.

Joe stood up and breathed in. His heart beat fast. Death, he thought, must have been almost instantaneous. There was no blood on Clay Junior's face or on the ground around him, so he hadn't bled out in that location. His skull had been crushed by the tremendous force of closing jaws.

Drag marks and bear tracks in the mud leading from the river indicated the body had been pulled from the water and buried in an excavated pit. That would explain the wet clothing.

Joe had never heard of a bear attack taking place on a river and the body cached along the bank. Both were unusual circumstances. Was that what really happened?

If so, did that mean the bear was coming back to feed on the victim? Or at least hanging around?

Joe turned quickly and made his way back to Clay on the riverbank. As he skittered across the river rocks, he shot glances over his shoulders in every direction, looking for movement. Leaves rattled in the breeze and the river flowed with muscle. He felt incredibly vulnerable in the open.

He thrust his hand beneath Clay's armpit and helped him to his feet. Joe pointedly didn't look at the severed leg.

"Come on," he said. "Let's get to your vehicle. The bear might still be around here watching us."

Dazed, the foreman reached down for the foot and Joe pulled on Clay to prevent it.

"Leave it, Clay. I know it's tough, but I need to get you out of here."

Clay stared at Joe with incomprehension. He was in shock.

"The bear cached the body for a reason," Joe said. "Bears do that when they plan to come back. I don't want you sitting here when he does."

"I've got to kill that bear for what he did to my boy," Clay said. "He's my only son."

"I know," Joe said, pulling Clay toward the willows and the open gate beyond them. "I know. I'm sorry."

"He served honorably for his country in Iraq and Afghanistan," Clay said, as they wound through the brush. "He led men and he came back. How can he go through all that and get killed by a fucking bear here at home?" Clay's voice cracked.

Joe had no answer for that.

"We'll get the bear," Joe said. "I've already called in backup. We'll get the bear."

"He was going to be your son-in-law," Clay said.

JOE CONVINCED CLAY to go back to his house while he called the sheriff. They'd need armed backup, as well as the evidence tech and county coroner on the scene, if possible.

"I'll have to tell Mrs. Wheatridge," Clay said. "I'm not looking forward to that."

Clay had been widowed for years and he had raised his son on the ranch with his full-time housekeeper, Mrs. Wheatridge. The woman not only shared Clay's bed from time to time but she'd also been a surrogate mother to Clay Junior.

"She always said I'd get him killed somehow," Clay said. "Now I gotta tell her she was right."

"You didn't get him killed."

"She'll say, 'If you'd let him go and didn't insist on him following in your footsteps, a bear wouldn't have attacked him.'"

Joe had no response to that.

WHEN CLAY WAS gone, Joe leaned against the grille of his pickup with his cell phone in his hand. He'd placed his shotgun within reach across the hood. Inside the cab, Daisy stared at him with her head cocked to the side as if to ask what was going on out there.

He speed-dialed his wife, Marybeth, and she answered from her office in the back of the county library that she managed.

"I've got some very bad news," Joe said.

"What happened?" she asked. It was far from the first time he'd called her with that message, nor the first time she'd asked for details.

"Grizzly bear attack on the Twelve Sleep River," Joe said. "The victim is Clay Junior."

Marybeth let out a gasp. "Is he . . ."

"Yup."

"My God, does Sheridan know?"

"Nope. We just found his body."

"This is horrible, Joe. Just horrible. Did you destroy the bear?"

He surveyed the wall of trees near the river and the rocky slope beyond and said, "No. The bear is on the loose."

As he spoke, he received an incoming call from Game and Fish headquarters in Cheyenne. No doubt, he thought, the word of his earlier call to dispatch had made the rounds. "I've got to take this," he said to Marybeth.

"Call me later when you can," she said. "I mean, Sheridan's coming over for dinner tonight with Nate and Liv. Clay Junior was supposed to come over later, too," she said, her voice rising with the implication of that statement.

"I'll be in touch," Joe said. "Don't wait for me to have dinner. It's going to be a late one."

"I love you."

"I love you, too. I'm worried about our daughter."

"So am I, but we know she's tough."

"Yup."

"Be careful, Joe."

"Of course," he said. While punching off, Clay's words echoed in his head:

"He was going to be your son-in-law."

CHAPTER THREE

Rawlins

ON THE SAME day, at the Wyoming State Penitentiary in Rawlins, two hundred and forty-six miles to the south, WDOC Inmate Number 24886 shuffled down the hallway in his state-issued Crocs, accompanied on either side by Corrections Officers R. Winner and C. Egleston. They were headed toward the outtake room near the front lobby.

The prisoner kept his head down and did not engage with other convicts who watched him pass by. He'd left the pod behind him, but his route included the open doors of the mail room, the law library, and the computer room. His ears were still ringing with the hoots, catcalls, and curses that had blasted out in E pod when Winner announced his name that morning after breakfast.

"Gather up your shit and report to the front desk," Winner had said.

Everybody knew what that meant.

Two newbies saw him coming and reacted by backing up against the hallway walls and not making eye contact. Even though they had just arrived, the newbies knew to avoid prisoners wearing orange who came from E pod. Orange was the color of hardened criminals, and E pod was where they were housed.

"Step aside," Winner said to the newbies with mock gravity. "Here comes Dallas Cates." Then: "Yeah, it's him. The one, the only. Don't worry, he don't bite."

"Except when he does," Egleston said. CO Connie Egleston was new to the facility and had obviously been assigned to shadow Winner to learn the ropes. She was one of only three female COs.

"You don't bite, do you, bro?" Winner asked Cates with mock affection.

Cates didn't respond.

"That was kind of fascinating back there in E pod, wasn't it?" Winner asked. "When I called out your name, you know? It was like a sociological experiment come to life. All their true feelings about you just came pouring out. They didn't even try to hide them anymore. How does that make you feel, bro?"

Again, Cates didn't react. He couldn't afford to. Not on his last day in prison. Not when anything he did or said could be used against him as a reason to keep him there a little longer.

Winner said, "The Brothers in Arms and La Familia, they hate your fucking white-boy guts, don't they? But I didn't see all that much reaction from the Warrior Chiefs. Is it true you WOODS are allies with them now?"

The Brothers were Black, La Familia was Mexican, and the Warrior Chiefs were Native American. WOODS stood for "Whites Only One Day Soon." Dallas Cates was their undisputed leader.

"When the cowboys and the Indians get together on the same side against the Blacks and the browns, that's interesting, don't you think?" Winner asked rhetorically. "Kind of like cats and dogs joining up, right? I guess this is the new Wild West, eh, bro?"

This was why they'd sent Winner, Cates was sure. To goad him, to try and get him to act out. To give the COs a reason to beat him and drag him back to a cell, claiming he'd assaulted them.

Winner was a rare CO, Cates knew. Unlike ninety percent of the other COs and five percent of the do-gooder social worker types, Winner seemed to enjoy the worst parts of his job, especially confrontations with inmates. There was nothing the man would rather do. He was the first to break up a fight, and the first to sucker punch anyone he thought disrespected his authority. He was known to leave a door unlocked when a convict "deserved" a beating from enforcers within the gen pop or the gangs. They had history, those two. Dallas Cates hated Winner, and Winner hated Dallas Cates.

Egleston was dark haired and stout, and her movements were hesitant. Cates thought she was trying too hard to fit in. It was clear she looked up to Winner.

"Give it up, Winner," Cates said as Egleston swiped her card on the mechanism that opened the outtake room. "You can take all the shots you want. All you'll get out of me today is warm feelings and happy talk. Do your best, but I'm loving life right now."

Winner laughed.

INSIDE THE OUTTAKE room, Cates stripped off his orange jumpsuit and let it pool on the floor around his ankles. He now wore only dingy prison briefs. He stood there and let Winner and Egleston take him in. The room was spartan and consisted of slick tile walls and a steel table bolted to the floor.

When his clothes dropped away, Egleston said, "Shit. Look at this guy." Her neck flushed red.

Cates had changed his body over his years in prison. He'd once had the wiry build of a world champion rodeo contestant, an athlete from Saddlestring who'd won both the bull-riding and saddle bronc events at the National Finals Rodeo in consecutive years after taking gold buckles at the Pendleton Round-Up, the Calgary Stampede, and Cheyenne Frontier Days. Since then, he'd added forty pounds of solid muscle on his frame. His thighs were as thick as trunks, his neck fanned out to the tops of his shoulders, his biceps like hams, and his chest a hard cask.

Ink covered his body. He'd only used the best prison tattoo artists, from the serpents that crawled up his thighs, to the bucking bulls across his six-pack, to the all-capitalized *WOODS* done in German Gothic font across his pecs, to the portrait of his mother, Brenda, on his shoulder. The undersides of both forearms and the back of his left hand were covered in newly minted red tattoos that Cates hid by keeping his hands down at his sides and turned inward.

"Let's see your valuable treasure," Winner said as he opened the pillowcase Cates had used to gather his belongings from his cell. The CO dumped the contents on the surface of the steel table.

Cates's property consisted of several packs of ramen noodles, the stub of a pencil, three well-thumbed paperback books, and a two-inch-thick roll of cash.

"Jesus Christ on a biscuit," Winner said. "How did you accumulate all this fucking money?" It was obvious from his sneer that he was personally offended.

"I saved it," Cates said. "I'm frugal."

There was no way he'd tell the CO that the cash came as a monthly tribute from WOODS members under his protection, or that other individuals and gangs paid Cates for leaving them alone or settling disputes. The roll amounted to over eighteen hundred dollars. The outside bills were fives and ones, and the larger denominations were in the middle of the roll.

"Don't touch it," Cates said, quickly retrieving the roll. He knew the CO would have taken it if he'd had any idea it existed before that moment.

Winner fanned through each book to make sure there was no contraband pressed inside. As he did, he said, "*The Art of War.* Interesting. And then we have the Holy Bible and *Wilderness*

Evasion: A Guide to Hiding Out and Eluding Pursuit in Remote Areas.

"Naw," he said, "you won't be needing any of this shit."

With that, Winner swept the items into a trash can near his feet.

Cates bristled at that. A minute before, Cates would have messed up anyone who touched his property. Now he looked at it for what it was: trash. He glared at Winner.

"Those WOODS-peckers of yours are gonna get the shit kicked out of 'em now," Winner said.

"They can handle themselves," Cates said. "But I don't worry about that anymore. It's all water under the bridge. I just want everyone to get along."

"We talk about you," Winner said. "My buddies and I take bets on how long it'll be before we see you in here again. It's your second visit, right?"

Cates said, "And my last."

Winner snorted a laugh.

"I won't be back. Bet on *that*."

"Go get his street clothes," Winner said to Egleston, who left the room.

AFTER SEVERAL QUIET minutes in which neither Cates nor Winner said a word, Egleston pushed through the door with a clear plastic square filled with the clothes Cates had worn when he arrived in Rawlins five years before. There was also a small box with a cowboy hat crammed inside. The CO placed the parcels on the steel table and stepped back.

"You know what to do," Winner said to Cates.

He did. He unzipped the square and removed his Western shirt with the snap buttons, the size 28 Wranglers, the scuffed round-toe Tony Lama boots, and civilian undershorts and socks. All of the items had a plastic odor.

Only the socks and boots still fit. The shirt wouldn't button and the jeans wouldn't zip up. His custom-made pure beaver hat was jammed into the box and completely misshapen. Cates didn't even try to put it on.

Cates piled the clothes back on the table.

"Damn," Winner said, feigning concern. "You can't walk out of here like *that*."

Egleston chuckled.

"You don't mess up a man's hat," Cates said. "And where's my belt and buckle?" He felt his neck get hot. The tooled belt was a gift from his mother. **DALLAS** was stenciled across the back. The huge gold buckle was from his second win at the NFR.

"What belt and buckle?" Winner asked.

"You sure as hell know what I'm talking about," Cates said.

Winner and Egleston looked at each other with practiced wide-eyed incomprehension.

Cates suddenly relaxed his shoulders and grinned at them. "Okay, I know what you're doing. I'm not going to take the bait. Now, where's my buckle? And that belt, it means something to me."

"It means something to him because his mother had it made," Winner said. "I think he has a thing about his mother. You can see her face on his skin right there."

"Kind of unhealthy, I'd say," Egleston responded.

Cates wanted to kill them both with his bare hands. When a senior member of La Familia had commented on the tattoo of Brenda's image, Cates waited for his chance and had pushed the man's face onto a hot stove and held him down until the victim's right eyeball liquefied and acrid smoke filled the kitchen. No one had ever gone there again.

Now Cates closed his eyes and breathed in and out. He discovered he was knotting his fingers into fists and he consciously relaxed them.

"I want my buckle back," he said softly.

"And I'm just sorry about that," Winner said. "I truly am. Things get lost in the storage room, and that's a fact. You probably don't remember signing the property release when you came back here. The release you signed says we have no liability for lost or stolen items while you're incarcerated. Do you want me to go get the release you signed?"

"I want to talk to the warden."

Winner shrugged. "Unfortunately, the brass is away at a conference in Montana right now. Do you want to wait a few days to speak to them?"

Although his heart whumped in his chest and there was a red tinge to his vision, Cates stepped back and shook his head. He said, "I'd like to get out of here now. Get me a white jumpsuit and I'll leave in that."

White was the color for nonviolent offenders. It wouldn't scare the locals as much as his orange one.

"We've done you one better," Winner said with a wink. "Egleston?"

THE OTHER CO left the room and quickly returned with a large plastic Walmart sack. She placed it on the table next to the clothes Cates could no longer wear.

Cates took out each item. He could hear Egleston laugh as he did so.

Bright white skinny jeans two sizes too large, a plastic belt decorated with dinosaurs, and an XXL pink sweatshirt emblazoned with **DON'T LET YOUR BABIES GROW UP TO BE COWBOYS.**

"We took the liberty of dipping into your commissary funds to get you a new outfit to wear into the outside world," Winner said with a chuckle. "We hope it all fits."

CATES STARED AT Winner for half a minute. Finally, the CO broke his gaze and looked away. Cates got dressed in the new clothes and stuffed his old ones into the plastic parcel to take with him. He carried his ruined hat by the brim in his free hand.

As Winner stepped to the side to let Cates walk into the public lobby, Cates paused.

"I just added you to the list," Cates said in a whisper.

"What list?"

"My special list of special people," Cates said. "You know, like for Christmas cards."

"Well, that's darned sweet of you," Winner said. "Unless you're making some kind of threat."

"I'd never do that, Officer. Especially right now."

Winner narrowed his eyes.

"I'll send you my address when I get settled," Cates said. "Then you'll know where to send me my belt and buckle."

"You do that."

"I surely will," Cates said. "And I surely expect to get my property back."

THE SKY WAS gray and overcast and the wind was blowing as it always was in Rawlins when Dallas Cates pushed his way through the double doors toward the parking lot. He deposited the square cube of his old clothes into a garbage can on the way out.

A tumbleweed propelled by the wind hit his left leg as he walked, and he shimmied around it and avoided another one that flew out of the lot into the sagebrush flat to the north.

Cates squinted against the wind and the grit it contained until he saw the white 2015 Chevy pickup in the lot. It was a four-by-four with a topper over the bed, and there was a bloom of primer on the front passenger door. Just as she'd described it. She'd obtained it from a former boyfriend who'd been arrested and sent away on drug charges.

Bobbi Johnson, twenty-eight years old and dirty blond with a gold front tooth, beamed at him and waved from behind the wheel. He headed in her direction and climbed into the cab.

"You look happy," she said.

"I am. I am," he said, gesturing through the front window. "Air, open country, open sky. You have no idea how good this all looks to me. It's like I'm breathing real air again."

"What are you wearing, Dallas?" she asked in her high-pitched voice.

"The COs thought it was funny," he said as he leaned over and grasped her in a bear hug. It was the first time they'd ever touched. The prison's visiting room maintained a strict no-contact policy.

Johnson was bony, but she had large, soft breasts under her hoodie. Her hair smelled like weed smoke and he felt her hand squeeze the top of his thigh. He was instantly hard and he wanted her *now*.

She looked older than she was because her face was weathered from too much time in the sun, too much time in the wind, and too much time mixing alcohol and meth. She swore that she was no longer a tweaker and now relied solely on weed, alcohol, and the occasional Oxy for the pain in her lower back. Cates wasn't sure he believed her.

They'd met online and she'd confessed to him that she'd once been a teenage buckle bunny who liked to hang around rodeos and bed contestants. She'd also confessed that she'd always had her eyes on Dallas Cates, but that he was too big of a star at the time to get close to him.

Johnson had visited him twice in the last two months, and she'd promised to be there to pick him up when he was released.

"After all," she'd said, "you don't have no family no more."

CATES SAID, "LET'S get the fuck out of here."

"Where are we going?" she asked.

He beamed and said, "We're gonna buy a bottle of whiskey and get a cheap motel room. I'm gonna get drunk and then I'm gonna fuck your brains out. Then I'm gonna get drunk again and fuck your brains out again. How does that sound?"

"It sounds good, babe. I've been waiting for this day for years."

"So have I," he said.

Johnson swooned and let out a howl and floored it.

"Don't speed out of here and give 'em a reason to stop us," he said firmly.

She slowed down and said, "I'm wet and I'm literally shaking."

"Me too. Hey—did you buy me a couple of those burner phones I asked you to get?"

"There's three in the glove box," she said. "You owe me a hundred and fifty bucks."

CHAPTER FOUR

Saddlestring

THAT NIGHT, JOE Pickett drove down the county road to his home in the dark. He was bone-tired from the events of the day and dull with trauma. He knew he'd never be able to unsee Clay Junior's face and wounds, or unfeel the jolt he'd experienced when he encountered the fresh grizzly bear track in the mud. His neck ached from looking over his shoulder.

Something primal had infected him—the very real possibility of being mauled and killed by a predator over twice his size and weight. A predator that had taken out a human much younger and fitter than he was.

The cow moose that often blocked the path to his state-owned home on the bank of the Twelve Sleep River didn't show up tonight, and he was grateful. His headlights splashed against the lodgepole pine trees and aspen as he wound down the lane.

With all that had happened, he'd forgotten that Marybeth had told him that the Romanowskis and Sheridan were coming over for dinner. He wasn't reminded of it until he saw the white Yarak, Inc. falcon transport van and Sheridan's midsize GMC Acadia SUV parked in front of their home.

"This is going to be tough," he said to Daisy.

THEY WERE ALL at the dining room table when Joe entered the house through the mudroom. Empty plates sat in front of everyone except for Sheridan, whose lasagna was untouched. Marybeth was at the foot of the table to be closer to the kitchen, and both Liv and Nate sat across from Sheridan. They all turned toward him, and the two house dogs padded over to greet Daisy. Tube, their half-Corgi and half-Lab mix, licked Daisy's face. Bert's Dog, the mixed-breed Catahoula creature, stared at Joe with crazy eyes.

"Not a good day," he said to everyone at the table.

"Did you find the bear?" Nate asked.

Joe removed his hat and shook his head. He sat down in the empty chair at the head of the table and reached out to Sheridan. His oldest daughter had two-year-old Kestrel Romanowski in her lap, and the energetic little toddler seemed content to be cuddled.

"I'm so sorry, honey," he said to Sheridan. In response, she lowered her head and leaned into him. His daughter had red-rimmed eyes and her face was puffy from crying. It broke Joe's heart. As if on cue, Kestrel wriggled free, slid down between Sheridan's legs, and ran out of the dining room into the hallway, her arms flapping at her sides.

"I'll watch her," Sheridan said, following after her.

"We saved you some dinner," Marybeth said, getting up and going into the kitchen. She returned with a pan with two large squares of lasagna remaining.

"Thank you," Joe said. "I think I should be hungry."

"I thought there weren't supposed to be any grizzly bears in the Bighorns," Nate said with a wry smile.

"There weren't," Joe responded.

NATE WAS JOE and Marybeth's longtime friend and now Sheridan's boss. A tall, rangy outlaw falconer with a Special Forces background, he had comfortably glided between both sides of the law throughout his life. He'd married Liv, a striking, smart native of New Orleans, and she now ran Yarak, Inc., a bird abatement business that used falcons to rid facilities of problem pests. Kestrel was their adorable daughter.

"We've got the Predator Attack Team coming by helicopter tomorrow," Joe said. "I'm going to meet them first thing in the morning and take them to the scene."

"Everybody's talking about this on Facebook," Marybeth said.

"It's big news," Joe said. "There was even a camera crew from a Casper television station out at the Double D. The Game and

Fish director is beside himself and headquarters is panicking. All the higher-ups were calling me this afternoon like I didn't know this is the fifth grizzly attack this fall."

"I'm aware of it," Nate said. "I've heard of so many cancellations from out-of-state hunters that it's not even funny. The outfitters around here are looking at another year where they don't get paid. First the pandemic, and now this."

"Is Clay okay?" Marybeth asked.

"No, he's not," Joe said. "A highway patrol trooper volunteered to stay with him tonight and make sure he doesn't go after that bear by himself."

"I can see him trying to do that," she said.

"What about tonight?" Nate asked. "What if the bear comes back?"

"We set up a command center down by the river for the time being," Joe said. "It'll be manned by sheriff's deputies and local cops tonight. They brought out floodlights to illuminate the kill zone like a football field and all of the LEOs are armed up. I set a few leghold snares up by the cache in case the grizzly tries to sneak back for the body."

The snares were designed and built by Game and Fish personnel. They consisted of quarter-inch cable and heavy metal fittings and they were anchored to nearby tree trunks. Their purpose was to hold the animal alive and in place until armed responders could arrive.

"Did Clay Junior provoke the bear?" Nate asked.

"I don't see how," Joe said. "From what I could tell, he was fishing in the river and the bear attacked him. That's not to say maybe something else happened. I guess it's possible he somehow got himself caught up between a sow and her cubs, but I didn't see any evidence of it. No one heard any gunshots or anything, but Clay Junior was down in that canyon, so shots would have been hard to hear."

"Did he use bear spray?" Nate asked.

"Unknown," Joe said. "There's a lot to figure out. Just like I don't know if he was armed, although I assume he was. I didn't uncover his body any further than how I found it because I needed to leave it for the forensics team. I hated to just leave him like that."

"So what you're saying is that there is a grizzly bear out there on the loose," Liv said.

Joe sighed heavily. He wished it was otherwise.

"I think I'll keep Kestrel inside for a while."

"Good idea," Joe said.

"This is going to panic people until that bear is found," Marybeth said. "I'm guessing it'll be the one thing everybody is talking about tomorrow."

Marybeth was the best source of local intelligence Joe knew of, since the library where she worked was the epicenter of the small town. She was able to gauge the mood and opinion of the locals better than anyone.

"It was only a matter of time before this happened," Nate said to Liv. "I've been telling you that."

Liv dismissed him with a wave of her hand. "Not now, honey," she said.

Joe knew Nate well enough to guess what his friend had

been saying. Nate had a special relationship with predators and carnivores in the wild that came from his years as a master falconer as well as a special operations warrior. He had radical theories about game management and man's role in nature. Most of the theories concluded that humans weren't as smart and all-knowing as they thought they were, that most biological scientists were quacks, that every good human intention in altering the balance of nature resulted in disaster and unintended consequences, and that if ninety percent of civilization was decimated by angry wild animals it'd be a good start.

"Excuse me," Joe said to Nate and Liv after wolfing down a few bites of lasagna. "I think I need to talk to Sheridan."

"I'm going with you," Marybeth said.

Liv nodded her understanding.

"I'll get you a drink," Nate said. "It sounds like you need one."

"Yup," Joe said.

"THE THING IS," Sheridan said, "I just feel so *guilty*."

She sat at the foot of the bed in the guest room. Joe sat on one side of her and Marybeth on the other.

"Why would you feel guilty?" Joe asked.

Sheridan shared a glance with her mother.

"You can tell him," Marybeth said.

"I didn't want to say no to him," Sheridan said while dabbing away tears on her face with the heels of her hands. "Now I won't have to."

Joe looked at her, puzzled.

"Nobody understands this because Clay Junior was . . . Clay Junior," Sheridan said. "All the guys wanted to be like him and all the girls wanted to be with him. And for reasons I'll never understand, he chose me. But I'm not ready, not with Clay Junior, anyway."

Marybeth said to Joe, "I told her Clay said he had an engagement ring with him."

"Ah, yes," Joe said.

"I knew he was going to ask me," Sheridan said. "Probably tonight. He said he wanted to take me to dinner and that he had an important thing he wanted to discuss. I knew what it was going to be, and I just dreaded it. *I dreaded it.* I told him I was coming over here tonight and he said he'd come by and we could go out later. Now none of that will ever happen and I feel just horrible. I feel horrible about what I was going to do to him, and horrible because I'm a little relieved that I won't have to tell him no. But this—this is so horrible I can't even wrap my mind around it."

Joe wasn't sure how to respond. He hadn't wanted his oldest daughter to marry Clay Junior unless she was as wild about him as he apparently was about her. But it had all seemed so inevitable for the past year. It had all seemed like a fait accompli. Sheridan's sisters thought she was nuts not to reciprocate Clay Junior's feelings, and Marybeth seemed okay with having him as a son-in-law. Now all of that was off the table.

"Please don't tell his dad what I just told you," Sheridan said to Joe. "It would really upset him."

"I won't."

"What's so awful about this, along with everything else, is that everyone will look at me like some kind of tragic victim," Sheridan said. "The sad fiancée." Then, after a moment, she said, "I don't know why I'm telling you two all of this. We should be talking about Clay Junior, not me. We should be mourning him instead of me yammering on about my feelings. I feel so . . . pathetic."

"We're glad you can talk to us," Marybeth said, pulling Sheridan into her. "Please don't feel guilty. You have nothing to feel guilty about."

Sheridan let out a sob that broke Joe's heart. "He died thinking there was a future for us," she said. "He had no idea there wasn't."

Marybeth gave Joe a wan smile and rubbed Sheridan's back. He could go. He *should* go.

"I'm just so sorry this happened," he said as he left the room.

NATE SLID A tumbler of bourbon and water on ice across the table toward Joe like an Old West bartender and Joe grabbed it. "Thank you," he said.

Liv was in the living room wrapping Kestrel in a blanket so she could sleep for a while on the couch. Liv mimed *Shhhhh* to the two of them.

Nate kept his voice near a whisper when he asked, "Is Sheridan going to be okay?"

Joe shrugged. "This is hard on her."

"She's tough," Nate said. Then: "I was going to send her out of town with some birds for a job in Colorado. Do you think she's up for that?"

"I think so," Joe whispered back. "In fact, a change of scenery might help her get over this. But you should ask her if she's okay with it."

Nate agreed. "We've got more work than we can handle right now. Liv can barely keep her head above water."

"What about Geronimo?" Joe asked. "Isn't he working to expand the company? Hire more falconers?"

"Eventually," Nate said.

Geronimo Jones had become a partner in Yarak, Inc. in the past year and had taken on the challenge of growing the company to include additional locations and more master falconers. His idea of financing the expansion via cryptocurrency mining had hit a snag when the market tumbled the previous winter. Although the crypto mines he'd built hadn't gone completely bust, they were barely breaking even.

"Geronimo is home being a new dad," Nate said to Joe. "It's more than he bargained for. I know the feeling."

"So do I," Joe said.

"He's got some other ideas he wants to run by me, but for now we're just doing our best to keep the business running. That's one of the reasons Liv and I want Sheridan to take on a bigger role."

"I think she can handle it," Joe said.

"I know she can," Nate said. "I've taught her everything I know. She's an excellent master falconer now, and she's better with people than I am."

"Imagine *that*," Joe said with a grin. Liv giggled at that as she approached them from the living room.

"Kestrel's out for the count," she announced as she joined them.

Nate poured himself a second bourbon and asked Joe, "This Predator Attack Team—do they always get their target?"

"So far," Joe said. "They've been very lucky and very lethal at the same time."

He said he'd read the recent incident reports from the bear attacks that fall and the year before.

"Some of the bears were collared previously and they were easy to find," Joe said. "But it depends on the bear. Predatory bears tend to stick around, but in surprise or defensive encounters the bears will likely run away. I don't think there's any doubt this was a predatory bear."

"What if the bear doesn't want to get caught?" Nate asked.

"I don't know," Joe said.

CHAPTER FIVE

Rawlins

LATER, WHILE DALLAS Cates and Bobbi Johnson were naked in a motel room on the west side of Rawlins, Johnson drained her plastic cup of Jim Beam and 7Up and stared at his bare arms and the redness of the skin on the undersides of his forearms and the back of his left hand. She was sore and she wanted to distract him.

"You got new ink?" she asked.

He nodded.

"Let's see," she said.

He smiled and held up his right arm and bent it so that his fist was near his right ear. The new tattoo was large and scabbed over and she wasn't sure what it was. It looked like a big dark half-moon with jagged edges to the inside.

"I don't get it," she said.

He raised his left arm and did the same pose so that the two undersides of his arms joined at the elbows.

The scabbed image was the right and left sides of a bear's face. The bear's jaws were open and the teeth on each side were huge.

"*Rowwrrr*," he roared.

She extended her little finger from her grip on the glass to point at the six empty boxes that had been recently tattooed on the back of Cates's left hand.

"What's that mean?"

"That's my special list," he said. "Each box means something to me." Then: "Hey, give me that pen from the desk."

She rolled over and found it and handed it to him. Cates carefully sketched out a seventh empty square underneath the other six.

"I added another one today," he said. "His name is Winner."

"Who are the first ones? What is the list *for*?"

"I'll tell you later. Now roll over."

She rolled over.

Johnson knew from experience that rodeo cowboys were always ready for another ride. And for that matter, they'd stay on for about eight seconds.

Johnson had a plan, one she'd proposed to Cates while he was in prison, and Cates had acquiesced. They needed to get out of Wyoming, the both of them, she'd said. She would never be able to shake her history, no matter where she went in the state.

That was the problem with Wyoming, she'd said. Everybody knew everybody. One degree of separation still existed in a state with less than a million people in it. If she got a job as a waitress in Jackson, say, somebody would recognize her as *that* Bobbi Johnson from Gillette, the one who had worked in a local diner and deliberately urinated in the soups of four members of the city council because they'd opposed a petition to legalize weed.

She'd been caught when a fellow employee ratted her out, and her name and photo had made all the news outlets in the state and had been picked up by the *New York Post* and the UK *Daily Mail*.

While in the Campbell County jail, Johnson had discovered meth. She'd followed the case of champion rodeo cowboy Dallas Cates from her cell, and she'd begun writing him letters.

The rest was history.

Dallas had an even tougher row to hoe, she'd said. His name was infamous everywhere in the state because of the saga of his family.

There was only one place the two of them could go, she said: California. The state was tolerant of people like them, she claimed, because it no longer had rules and many of the cities were no longer even civilized. The social welfare system would reward them until they could get on their feet, establish themselves, and start fresh. Maybe Dallas could get a job in the movie business, she said. *She* certainly found him charismatic and attractive, and all those rodeo buckle bunnies who used to follow him around on the circuit did as well.

They'd pick up Bobbi's sister, Carmin, along the way and take her and her two fatherless babies with them, she said. Carmin needed a new start, too.

"Yeah, sure," Cates had said. California it would be. He'd competed there many times at rodeos up and down the coast and the weather *was* good.

"YOU ASKED ME about my list," Cates said as he held up his hand and displayed the tattooed series of boxes. They were in the process of recharging, which meant drinking Jim Beam and eating M&M's and pork rinds.

"These are the people who ruined everything for me. They took away everything I'd ever accomplished, they killed my dreams and my future, and they destroyed my family," he said.

Johnson listened intently with her head on his bare chest, her eyes glued to his face.

"They were the only reason I was able to go on day after day in that place. This list was pure motivation to rise to the top and run my pod. Because I knew someday I was going to get out and go after them one by one for what they did to me and my family.

"My dad was first," he said. "They broke his neck and left him to die in a sewer pit. They crippled my mom and turned her into a quadriplegic. I couldn't even go to her funeral when she died last year. She died alone in the women's prison and I don't even know where she's buried. And they were responsible for killing my two brothers, Bull and Timber."

"My God," Johnson said. "That's terrible."

"There was a time when folks coming to the Cates place used to pass by a sign that said DULL KNIFE OUTFITTERS, C&C SEWER AND SEPTIC TANK SERVICE, BIRTHPLACE OF PRCA WORLD CHAMPION COWBOY DALLAS CATES."

As he said it, he used the thumbs and forefingers of his two hands to frame the memory of the sign.

"We were a close family," he continued. "My momma was so damned proud of me that she had that sign made. That was before everything went to shit."

"That's her face on your shoulder," Johnson said.

"Yes, God bless her."

Cates was silent for several minutes as he stared at the flickering images on the television that was bolted to the wall. Then he said, "I made a promise when they sent me away, a promise to my momma and to myself. I swore I'd go after the people who went after us."

"Who are they?" Johnson whispered, stroking his hand and the empty boxes.

"You wouldn't know 'em," Cates said. "Let's just say they all contributed to me being here right now and my family being in the ground."

Then he shifted to look at her fully and said, "The sheriff, the prosecutor, the judge, a crazy falconer and his wife, and a game warden."

Then he gestured at the pen-drawn box: "And now a CO who disrespected me inside for five years and stole my championship buckle. I'll deal with him first. The others won't see me coming."

Johnson cooed and burrowed into him. "You're making me hot," she purred.

"I like that," he responded.

"You like me, don't you?" she asked.

"You know I do."

He also liked the fact that she had a valid driver's license, some cash, and a truck. His license had expired while he was in prison.

AN HOUR LATER, Cates lay naked on top of the bed drinking whiskey straight from the bottle while Johnson snored next to him. Her pale white skin danced with flashing colors from the crappy TV. Cates nudged her so she'd turn from her back to her side to stop her snoring. It worked.

The Wyoming news out of Casper was on, and he watched it dumbly. The sound was turned down, so he could barely hear what the blow-dried twenty-something newscasters read off their teleprompters. He was fine with that.

Then Cates saw a chyron that got his attention: ANOTHER GRIZZLY BEAR ATTACK IN NORTHERN WYOMING?

Even more than the chyron itself, the image gripped him. A man wearing a red uniform shirt and a battered cowboy hat was reluctantly answering questions from a local reporter. The man had a pronghorn antelope shoulder patch on his uniform and a thin gold nameplate above his shirt pocket.

He said something about an "alleged human and bear encounter" and calling in the "Predator Attack Team." In the background of the shot, Cates recognized the very familiar outline of the Bighorn Mountains.

The newscast quickly cut away from the man to a graphic made up of bullet points of four previous bear attacks that year. One of them had been near Jackson, one had been near Dubois, and the last two near Cody, Wyoming.

This was the first in Twelve Sleep County, which was one hundred and eighty-five miles from the east gate of Yellowstone Park, where grizzly bears were "supposed" to stay.

Cates sat up in bed, his head swirling. A killer grizzly bear in the Bighorns?

He hadn't even tried to read the name tag of the man in the news story, because he knew him. He hated him. The game warden had a spot waiting for him on the back of Cates's hand. Joe Pickett.

Cates thumped Johnson on the shoulder with the back of his hand hard enough to wake her.

"What, goddamnit?" she asked.

"Get your bare ass up and get dressed," Cates said. "We've got a change in plans."

"What in the hell are you talking about? What about California?"

"We'll end up there eventually," he said. "But first there's a couple of guys I need to find. One of them wrote to me in prison and we kind of bonded, you might say."

"I don't know what you're talking about," Johnson said.

In response, Cates raised his hand and chinned toward the tattooed boxes.

"We both deserve justice, and we're going to get it," he said.

"Who is this person?"

"You don't know him," Cates said. "So his name doesn't matter right now." As he said it, Cates slit the plastic packaging on one of the prepaid burner phones Johnson had purchased for him at the Rawlins Walmart. He activated the device and typed in a number with his thumbs and sent a message.

"We'll see if he shows up or not," he said.

"Hold it," Johnson said with alarm. "Who are you inviting along? I thought it was just going to be *us*. And maybe Carmin."

"I've got things I gotta do," Cates said. "And I may need some help. First, I needed to contact this guy in Colorado who reached out to me. Second, I need to find my former cellmate. He's got . . . unique abilities. I've never met anyone like him. Of course, he's also goofier than shit. But I think I know where he lives and he owes me."

"What about Carmin?"

"Carmin will have to wait," Cates said. He pulled her close and glared into her eyes. "It's all coming together for me."

OCTOBER 16

Bears are not companions of men, but children of God.

—John Muir

CHAPTER SIX

Double Diamond Ranch

O N THE DAY after Clay Junior's body was found near the Twelve Sleep River, Joe accompanied the Predator Attack Team as they hunted the bear.

The team consisted of four members: regional Game and Fish Department supervisor Brody Cress; Dubois game warden Tom Hoaglin; Cody game warden Bill Brodbeck; and Jennie Gordon, the agency's large-carnivore specialist, based out of Lander. The team had arrived in a helicopter and Joe had met them at the Twelve Sleep County airport. He'd helped them load their equipment into two four-wheel-drive pickups. In addition to standard-issue clothing, weapons, communications equipment, and tactical clothing, armor, and other gear, they were armed with semiautomatic Smith & Wesson M&P rifles chambered in .308 Winchester and twenty-round magazines, and he'd offered to lead them to the scene on the Double D Ranch.

BRODY CRESS WAS an experienced LEO with twenty-two years of service and badge number one of fifty, the most senior warden still in the field. He was tall and lean with a weathered face and a distinctive handlebar mustache that made him look like an Old West gunfighter. Cress was the nominal commander of the team, and Joe sensed immediately that the man was liked and respected by the others. Cress had surprised him right away by greeting him with: "It's an honor and a privilege to work alongside you, Joe."

Tom Hoaglin wore badge number thirteen, meaning he was one badge senior to Joe. Like many wardens, Hoaglin had bounced around the state from district to district until landing in Dubois in northwest Wyoming. He was short, stout, and dark, with piercing eyes that belied an easy manner. Hoaglin was a deadeye marksman, a former sniper in Special Forces, and was responsible for the most grizzly bear and wolf kills on the team. He'd asked Joe when he might meet "this Nate Romanowski character," because he said he'd heard so much about him.

"One never knows," Joe replied. "He can be hard to track down."

"Does he still carry that Freedom Arms .454 Casull revolver?"

"Yup."

"That's a hand cannon. I heard about that shootout last spring."

"Yup."

"Fucking amazing," Hoaglin said.

"He's settling down," Joe said. "He's legit now. You should have seen him before he got married and had a little girl."

BILL BRODBECK WAS the youngest warden on the team, as well as the most fit and athletic. He was tall and broad-shouldered, and his high cheekbones and chin looked like they were carved out of white marble. He was a former bull rider at Montana State who had won a couple of rodeos. He proudly wore his Cody Stampede buckle with his uniform. He admitted to being tongue-tied when he first shook hands with Joe. "You're the reason I became a game warden in the first place," Brodbeck confessed. "I've been following your work for years."

"Now I feel old *and* embarrassed," Joe responded.

"Not as old as me," Cress cut in.

"No one is," Brodbeck said with a sly smile.

JENNIE GORDON HAD been raised on a ranch near Kaycee and gone on to achieve her PhD in fish, wildlife, and conservation biology at Colorado State University before becoming the pre-eminent expert and spokesman for the large-carnivore division.

She had a mane of unruly red hair bound into a ponytail and she exuded intelligence and calmness, as well as empathy for the predators she studied, hunted, and sometimes had to kill. It was well known within the agency that Gordon had to sign off on any actions that dealt with problem carnivores, from trapping and relocating them to euthanizing the dangerous ones. Like Joe, she had three children, but they were all boys. They were in elementary and middle school in Lander.

Unlike any of the other team members, Gordon had experienced a grizzly bear attack firsthand ten years before when a sow ripped through her tent in the Slough Creek drainage in Yellowstone Park and bit her leg, hip, and buttocks before going away as suddenly as it had appeared. To this day, Joe had heard, Gordon refused to talk about the incident in public, and if it weren't for her slight limp, no one would have guessed that it had happened.

"Promise me you'll introduce me to your oldest daughter," Gordon said to Joe. "I've always wanted to meet a master falconer. Raptors fascinate me, and the partnership between the falcon and the falconer can't be replicated with any other predator."

"I'm sure she'd like to meet you as well," Joe said.

"Great," Gordon said, looking at the mountains over Joe's shoulder. "Now take us to where the attack took place."

Joe was impressed by the calm professionalism of the team thus far, and he was struck by the contrast between them and the clown show in his own county law enforcement community since the sheriff had retired and skipped town.

JENNIE GORDON RODE with Joe in his pickup on the way to the ranch. Daisy made fast friends with her and rested her snout in her lap. Joe tried to call his dog off, but Gordon said she wouldn't hear of it. So while stroking Daisy, she peppered Joe with questions.

"I read the preliminary incident report," she said. "Are you sure it was only one bear?"

"I'm sure of nothing," Joe said. "Only what I saw when I got there."

"You said you saw tracks. Were they from one bear only?"

"I saw one good track in the mud. You probably saw the photo I sent along."

"I did, but it's hard to get much perspective. I hope the track is still there."

"Me too," Joe said. "I hope none of the locals stepped on it last night."

"Is it possible this fisherman provoked the bear in any way that you could tell?"

"Not from what I could see. Like I wrote in the report, it appeared that he was attacked while wading in the river. I could see drag marks from the water to where the body was found. Plus, his clothes were still wet. There was no evidence that he made it to the bank before he was attacked. So I guess what I'm saying is that I don't see a plausible scenario where he could have provoked a grizzly while standing in the river with a fly rod in his hand."

"And no blood from what you could find?" she asked.

"Not that I could see. And I haven't heard that the forensics tech found any, either."

Gordon nodded. "I agree with you that the attack likely took place in the river, based on the death scene. When a human is attacked by a grizzly in the field, there is usually a lot of blood on the ground. But if it happened in water . . . *Damn.*"

"Meaning what?" Joe asked, although he guessed the answer.

"Meaning we may not be able to re-create the attack as it happened. It means both blood and DNA might have been washed away in the current."

They turned off the highway onto an improved gravel road that took them beneath an arch for the Double D Ranch.

"From what you've told me," she said, "it looks like we only have one choice here. We've got to find that grizzly bear and kill it."

"That's what I figured," Joe said. "I don't like killing bears."

"None of us do," she said. "But one thing I've learned about grizzly behavior is that the vast majority of bears know that they're not supposed to attack a human. It's hardwired into them to avoid that kind of scenario, and they'll do anything they can to not have an interaction. But if a bear crosses that line and kills in a predatory nature, a behavioral switch can take place and it's likely they'll cross it again. So we have to kill them."

As he drove, Joe felt a chill wash over him, thinking about what that bear had done to Clay Junior, and what it might do to somebody else.

ON THAT FIRST day after the body was found, the Predator Attack Team had formed an armed perimeter around Clay Junior's remains while the body was exhumed by the county coroner's team on the bank of the river and taken away. They did so, the team explained to the coroner, in case the bear was still lurking.

The day was still and cool, with barely a breeze in the canyon. The sky was cloudless.

Gordon approached the body bag on the gurney and unzipped it. Joe stayed well away.

"He's got defensive wounds on his hands and arms," she said as she examined the victim. "So he fought. But from what I can see, there are a half-dozen wounds on him that could have ended with death. The cranial wounds alone would have done it."

Then she sealed up the bag and stepped away. She had asked that DNA samples be taken from the bite marks and sent separately to the Game and Fish Department forensics lab in Laramie to help identify the bear. She'd explained that it was possible the killer grizzly had been previously trapped, examined, or collared and could be found in the database of the interagency grizzly bear task force.

After the body was transported to town and the sheriff's department personnel and town cops had left, Joe asked Gordon how likely it was that she could actually identify the killer bear.

"It's possible," she said.

"How many grizzlies have been assigned numbers?"

"Over eleven hundred since the 1970s."

"That many?"

Gordon raised her eyebrows. "That many. Most people don't realize that at the present time we have over a thousand grizzly bears in this state, maybe even eleven or twelve hundred. We've identified maybe a third of them to date, and at any given time we only have sixty to ninety bears marked with radio collars. A lot more have tattoos or ear tags, but we can't keep track of them on a day-to-day basis.

"If we're really lucky," she said, "this bear was collared at some point and we can track it with radiotelemetry. Unfortunately, those collars only last a couple of years. But it's possible the bear is marked with a lip tattoo and we'll at least know where it came from and when it was trapped."

"That means two-thirds of the bears have never been captured or marked," Joe said.

"Yes," Gordon said. "And maybe more."

BEFORE PROCEEDING TO the river, Brody Cress had dug into his gear bag and handed Joe an armored vest.

"This is heavier than I'm used to," Joe said as he pulled it on.

"It's filled with ceramic plates. We all wear 'em."

"Seems like it would stand up to a cannon blast."

"We *hope* it will stand up to a grizzly bear bite," Cress said. "A griz bite is something like eleven hundred pounds per square inch. Compare that to a human with a hundred and sixty-two PSI."

Joe's eyes got wide and he recalled the large puncture holes he'd seen on Clay Junior's face and head.

"We've never had a bite on us," Cress said, "and I hope like hell we never find out if these vests work or not."

Cress went on to explain that the team would maneuver like a patrol squad in a war zone: tactical gear on, rifles out and ready, lapel mics and earpieces on to communicate.

He said, "I'll take point and Bill will bring up the rear. Tom and Joe will take the flanks and we'll move in unison in a diamond formation. Jennie will be our jewel in the center of the diamond."

At that, Gordon moaned and rolled her eyes.

"We've got to protect our expert at all costs," Cress said. "I'm only partly kidding."

Joe agreed.

"What kind of rifle are you carrying?"

Joe showed him his bolt-action .338 Winchester Magnum.

"That's fine for big game," Cress said as he placed it aside. "But you'll want more firepower. More rounds, anyway."

Cress then handed Joe a spare .308 rifle. Like the others Joe had seen with the team, it had a bipod attached to the front stock and a red-dot scope.

"Go ahead and chamber a round," Cress said. "You might not have the time when you need to."

Joe did as instructed and caught a glimpse of a bright silver cartridge in the receiver as he armed the weapon.

"If you see movement in the brush, call it out immediately. You can't believe how fast these bears can charge if they want to. It's like a freight train coming right at you, and the more people we have shooting, the better.

"Sometimes, they'll do a bluff charge," he said. "They'll come at you like a freight train and then pull up short. Don't wait to find out if it's a bluff in these circumstances. Jennie has given the okay to remove this target, and that's what we're here to do."

Cress raised his left hand and patted his underarm with his right. "Aim for just behind the front shoulder if you can. Hit it in the heart or lungs. A headshot can work with these rifles, but sometimes the round can't penetrate that thick skull. And don't stop pulling the trigger until the target is down and not moving at all."

Joe winced. Then he thought of Clay Junior.

"TELL ME," JOE asked Gordon and Cress as they made their way through the open gate for the river and the exhumed cache, "how unusual is it for an attack to happen on the water?"

"It's rare, but it's not unheard of," Cress said. "You can find a video on YouTube of a bear charging a boat on a river in Alaska. And we've had reports of grizzlies swimming after drift boats and rafts. In one instance, the fisherman in the boat grabbed an oar and started whacking the bear when it got too close. That happened just last summer."

"I've never heard of such a thing before," Joe said.

"We've learned to never say never when it comes to grizzly bears," Gordon added.

"What is the likelihood that it's still around?" Joe asked.

"Pretty good," Cress answered. "Most of the bears we've hunted stick close to their kill. They're very territorial that way."

THEY FOUND THE exhumed cache as well as the bear track that Joe had described. The cache was dismantled when the coroner removed Clay Junior's body, but the track was undisturbed. Gordon knelt down and measured it with a cell phone app.

"Not as large as a full-grown male," she said. "So our killer is either a large yearling male or more likely a sow."

"Can you guess how big it is?" Brodbeck asked her.

"Based on how deep the depression is, maybe three-fifty, three-eighty," she said.

The snare Joe had set was sprung but empty, its steel cable coiled like a rattlesnake near the tree line.

"You had her for a while in your snare," Hoaglin said to Joe. "You probably made her mad and she broke loose."

"I've used these snares for black bears before," Joe said. "But nothing this big."

He tried to imagine the power it would have taken to snap the cable. Joe wasn't sure that he could do it even by attaching the snare to the bumper of his truck and gunning the engine.

While Gordon took more photos of the cache, the track, and

the broken snare, Cress retrieved a telemetry device from his backpack and powered it up.

"There's no signal from a collar," he said after a minute of tuning the handheld device.

Then: "Let's go find her the old-fashioned way."

JOE KEPT HIS eyes open and his senses at full alert as they departed the cache site. Brodbeck was apparently the best tracker on the team because he led the way and the others fell in naturally behind him. They carefully moved down the left bank to where the river bent to the east.

After an hour, Brodbeck said, "Nope. No tracks along the riverbank at all. She didn't come down this way and she didn't leave this way."

"Then where is she?" Hoaglin asked.

Brodbeck pointed across the river toward the steep wooded slope. Joe followed his gesture. The intense fall colors made it hard to pick out individual objects through the foliage. Every dark boulder or sheet of rotting bark looked—for a second—like a bear.

"I think she ran off the same way she came down," Brodbeck said.

"This is where I can help," Joe said. "I'll go back to my truck and get waders for everybody."

"You've got *five* pairs of waders?" Cress asked, incredulous.

"I find them all the time where fisherman take them off and

forget them," Joe said with a shrug. "I've got a whole duffel bag full of them from over the years."

AFTER WORKING THEIR way across the river over slippery smooth river rocks, the team made its first discovery when Brodbeck found a trail coming down the slope. The topsoil on the trail was churned up, and small pines were flattened in the path. Rocks had been dislodged from the soil, and on two flat spots, grizzly tracks could be clearly seen. One track was coming down the mountain and the other was going up.

"What's this?" he asked, nudging a one-inch triangle-shaped piece of green fabric with the toe of his boot.

Joe bent down and studied it. "That's Gore-Tex material," he said. "From Clay Junior's waders. It must have stuck to the bear's teeth or claws and come off here."

"Which meant she climbed back up the mountain sometime last night after she broke free of the snare," Hoaglin said. "Which means we've got a unique situation: our bear didn't hang around."

"That's unusual?" Joe asked Gordon.

"We've never hunted a hit-and-run bear before," she said.

IT TOOK ANOTHER hour to climb the slope. They hiked on the left side of the bear path. Joe was out of breath by the time they reached the summit, and he reminded himself to take more breaks because he needed to be ready if they came face-to-face with the sow. He knew from experience how difficult it was to aim accurately when he was out of breath.

But there was no bear to be found on the top of the slope. Instead, a huge mountain meadow stretched out to the east until it was bordered by a wall of dense black timber that continued for miles. Beyond the timber, humpback peaks of the Bighorns stretched on for as far as they could see.

"We're going to have to request aerial assistance," Gordon said.

"Can we ask for a fixed-wing plane with an FLIR?" Joe asked.

FLIR was the acronym for forward-looking infrared, and Joe was familiar with the device because it was used by search and rescue teams to detect the thermal images of lost hunters in thick timber.

"An FLIR won't work for finding a grizzly," Gordon said. "The bear's hair is too thick to emit much heat, and it's easy to mistake a bear-sized boulder that retains heat from the sun from a grizzly. Believe me, there are a million bear-sized boulders on this mountain." Then, suddenly, she exclaimed, "*Oh no.*"

Joe turned to her, expecting to see her pointing at the target grizzly in the distance. Instead, she had wheeled completely around and was gesturing toward their vehicles parked across the river. At the altitude they'd climbed, they could see them clearly: three green Wyoming Game and Fish Department pickups.

A gleaming white new-model SUV was slowly making its way across the hay meadow toward their trucks.

"Oh shit," Cress said. "It's them."

"How'd they find us so fast?" Hoaglin asked.

"This has been all over the news," Brodbeck said.

"Who are they?" Joe asked. "Do you recognize the vehicle?"

Gordon turned and scowled. "Oh, we know them all too well. They're known as the Mama Bears. They've come to save the life of our killer."

"I wish we'd found her," Cress spat. "It's gonna be a shit show now."

CHAPTER SEVEN

Double Diamond Ranch

JOE PICKETT TRUDGED back down the mountain with Jennie Gordon and Bill Brodbeck to intercept the Mama Bears.

Brody Cress and Tom Hoaglin had stayed on the ridge to look for tracks and signs of the bear. Cress had already been on a satellite phone requesting flyovers by fixed-wing aircraft from the Game and Fish Department and the Wyoming Wing Civil Air Patrol.

Meanwhile, Hoaglin had climbed to the top of a large boulder and was sitting there, glassing the mountain meadows and openings in the timber for signs of the target. The two of them had agreed to stay put and in radio contact until Joe, Gordon, and Brodbeck could rejoin them.

Brodbeck had volunteered to return to the vehicles. Because the grizzly hadn't been found in the first few hours, it would be necessary to set up trail cameras and snares with heavier-gauge wire to try and trap it during the night. Because Brodbeck was the youngest and fittest and newest to the team, everyone seemed fine with letting him shoulder the gear and equipment back up the slope.

"So tell me about the Mama Bears," Joe said to Gordon as they worked their way down through the trees.

"Well, I'd say they're well-meaning activists," she said over her shoulder. "But we've got to try and persuade them to stay back and out of our way while we hunt for this grizzly. Of course, it's for their safety as well."

"The Mama Bears are a pain in our butts," Brodbeck added from behind Joe. "They consider us the enemy because we're out here trying to deal with these grizzlies—even when the bears are killers."

"What can the Mama Bears do?" Joe asked.

"What they've done before," Gordon said. "Try and save the bear from us evil, fanatical bear murderers. That's the way they see it, anyway."

"Where do they come from?" Joe asked.

"Jackson Hole."

"I'm shocked," Joe said.

Brodbeck chuckled.

Gordon said, "There are two of them. You've probably heard of that big 'Save Our Bears' fundraiser they do every year in Teton County. They bring in Hollywood celebrities and social media influencers and the national media covers it all. It makes a *lot* of money for their cause."

"Even though they don't need it," Brodbeck interjected. "I've heard these two ladies are married to multimillionaires."

"You have to be if you live in Jackson," Joe said. "My mother-in-law lives there."

Gordon said, "It's amazing what happens when the Mama Bears show up on the scene. Our traps get sprung, and logs get pushed out in the road so we can't drive where we need to go. People show up from all over the country to protest in front of our offices and block us from getting out. Signs go up saying we should be defunded. Posts appear on social media showing old photos of dead bears that were shot to death.

"We've never caught them in the act of messing up our snares or using air horns to chase the bears away," she said. "But it's not a coincidence that none of those things happen until the Mama Bears swoop in and start the outrage on social media."

"Why do they do it?" Joe asked.

Gordon shrugged. "Like I said, they're well-meaning, I think. But I'm a scientist and biologist, so that's not the way I think. There are just some people who identify with bears in what I'd consider a very unhealthy way. You've heard of anthropomorphism? You know, attributing human characteristics to nonhuman species?"

"Yup," Joe said, thinking that Marybeth and his daughters were somewhat guilty of it when it came to their horses and dogs. Of course, he probably was, too, when it came to Daisy . . .

"That's what the Mama Bears do," she said. "But to an extreme degree. They go out into Yellowstone to view bears and they think they understand them. They claim to know a few of the grizzlies personally, and even give them names."

"How are you going to make them go away?" Joe asked.

"I might need your help with that," she said to him.

"Glad to help."

He thought about how much of his job, and apparently Gordon's as well, was becoming less concerned with managing wildlife and more about dealing with people who fetishized animals. He blamed it partly on the disconnect between modern Americans and nature. Although it was beautiful and fascinating, Joe knew how rough it was out there in the wild. Brutal, bloody, and completely ruthless. The circle of life, he knew, was amoral at best.

As THEY CROSSED the river, Joe looked back over his shoulder at the slope they'd traversed. He could see the silhouette of Cress on top, still on his phone. Hoaglin was out of view.

When they approached the exhumed cache, Joe felt another chill run through him. The proximity of the scene triggered a reprise of the raw fear he'd felt when he found Clay Junior's body: real, bone-chilling fear. He unslung the .308 and carried it at his side as a cautionary measure.

"I'm going to get the gear gathered up," Brodbeck said to Joe and Gordon. "I'll leave the persuading to you two."

"Thank you," Joe said, not really meaning it.

———

LYNN FOWLER AND Jayce Calhoun stood with their hands on their hips as Joe and Gordon approached them. Both women were in their late fifties, Joe guessed. They were thin and fit and had expensive haircuts, and the skin on their faces looked stretched tight and wrinkle-free, which belied how much time they apparently spent outdoors tracking grizzly bears. Fowler had a mane of dark hair streaked with ginger, and Calhoun's long wild tresses of pure white made her blue eyes and plumped lips stand out like a child's drawing. Both wore matching anoraks with *Patagonia* embroidered on one breast and *Mama Bears* on the other.

Their new-model white Range Rover had County 22 plates, meaning Teton County.

"Jennie," Fowler said to Gordon, "you know why we're here. This just has to stop."

"Meet Joe Pickett," Gordon said. "He's the local game warden."

Joe nodded his hat brim to them, but neither responded in kind.

"We know this bear," Calhoun said. "We know her and we know her tragic circumstances. You cannot kill this beautiful creature. We forbid it."

Gordon leaned against the grille of her pickup, crossed her arms, and said, "Explain to me how you know the bear."

Calhoun and Fowler exchanged glances, and Fowler addressed Joe instead of Gordon. Apparently, he guessed, he must look like the softer touch.

"We call her Tisiphone," she said. She pronounced it "Tie-*sif*-o-nee." "After the Greek goddess of vengeance and retribution. This woman you're with," she said, pointing at Gordon, "calls her 'Number 413.'"

Gordon rolled her eyes but didn't interrupt Fowler, who continued. "Tisiphone is one of the most tragic stories you will ever hear, game warden. She is the embodiment of a mother whose entire world is destroyed by man. The incident was so horrible and violent that Tisiphone lost her mind, and she travels the earth exacting revenge against those who destroyed her family."

Joe squinted, trying to understand. He looked at Gordon for support, but Gordon looked away.

"Are you a father?" Calhoun asked Joe.

"Yup. Three daughters."

"*Three*," Calhoun said, once again exchanging looks with Fowler. "How interesting. How *connected* you'll be when you hear this story.

"Now imagine, Mr. Pickett, that you are on a hike with your three young daughters. Imagine that during that hike you cross a road, you leading and your three daughters following you one by one. Maybe you're holding hands."

She paused for effect, then said, "Now imagine that a careless driver just plowed into all three of your daughters at the same time, killing two instantly. Imagine turning around and seeing your third daughter still alive, but bleeding out in the road. How would you feel?"

"Not good," Joe said.

"This actually happened last August," Fowler took over for her colleague. "In Yellowstone Park, near the junction of West Thumb and the road to Old Faithful. A California man distracted by his phone slammed into three eight-month-old cubs following their mother and killed them all. *Killed them all*.

"You can imagine the manic rage Tisiphone felt. She went briefly insane for weeks afterward, roaring and crashing through trees in the forest."

Joe winced.

"That's what I would do," Fowler said, placing her hands on her heart and leaning forward. "I would howl at God and I would curse him. I would blame the species that did it. I would want vengeance. I am Tisiphone."

"*I* am Tisiphone," Calhoun echoed.

"Is that story true?" Joe asked Gordon.

"Yes, it is, partly," Gordon said. "A tourist hit and killed the three cubs of 413 last August. It was a tragedy."

"It was more than a tragedy," Fowler said while blowing a stray wisp of hair from her face. "It was triple infanticide. Of course Tisiphone has gone mad with grief and rage. What would your wife do, Mr. Pickett, if all three of your daughters were murdered in front of her eyes?"

Joe couldn't even imagine the scenario.

"Time out," Gordon said, putting her palms up as if to hold back the Mama Bears. "Just hold it. First, we have no evidence at all that the bear that caused our fatality is 413. Bear number 413 had a collar on her and we've picked up no signal here at all. Second, and with all due respect, Jayce and Lynn, what you're contending here flies against all the behavioral science we've studied on female grizzly bears. No mother of any species wants to lose her offspring, but we've got no instances where the mother went insane and sought revenge.

"I hate to say it, but bear cubs get killed all the time. It isn't rare and their mortality rate is high. In many instances, it's the male grizzly that kills them. Sows have two or three cubs per litter and sometimes even four. When a little one dies, the mama bear just kind of goes on with life. It's like raising puppies or kittens. The mother doesn't go into mourning when they're sold or given away to new owners. They don't go crazy and they don't seek vengeance."

"So *you* say," Fowler responded with anger. "You'd be happy if they were all dead."

"You know that's not true," Gordon said. "I'd rather our bears thrived—as long as they don't kill people."

Fowler and Calhoun began to talk over each other and direct their vehemence at Gordon, who remained very calm. Joe held his ground but said nothing.

In his peripheral vision, he saw Brodbeck shoulder a heavy pack from the bed of the other truck. There was so much weight in it that when he swung it on his back he stumbled a few steps before slipping his other arm through the strap to regain his balance. Joe didn't envy Brodbeck packing it all up the slope.

Despite the weight on his back, it was obvious that Brodbeck was eager to get going and not let himself be pulled into the dispute between the Mama Bears and Jennie Gordon. He slung his rifle over his shoulder and waved goodbye to Joe with a wry grin. Joe nodded back to him.

"Do either of you have any evidence this is 413?" Gordon asked when there was a break in the stream of accusations. "If so, I'd like to hear it."

"When we last saw her two weeks ago, she was headed east," Calhoun sniffed.

"East from Yellowstone?"

Calhoun indicated yes.

"Do you think she covered two hundred miles to get here?" Gordon asked. "Female grizzlies traditionally have smaller home ranges than males and rarely go out on excursions. Do you have any real reason to suspect that she decided to leave her stomping grounds and jet in a line to the east? All the way to the Big Horns, where she's never been before?"

"We don't know that she didn't do that," Fowler said. Then she pointed at Gordon and said, "Most of all, *you* don't know that."

"True," Gordon conceded. "I don't know it for a fact."

"It's Tisiphone," Calhoun said with certainty. "We know her. We know what kind of pain she's in."

"Are you saying this killing was justified?" Gordon asked them.

Neither woman spoke for a moment.

"Do either of you even know the circumstances of the attack?"

"We don't need to know," Fowler said. Calhoun nodded her head in agreement.

"Joe, could you please show them the photos you took of Mr. Hutmacher on your phone?"

So *that* was why Gordon asked him to come along, Joe thought.

"They're graphic," Joe warned the Mama Bears.

"No, I don't want to see them," Calhoun said, recoiling toward her SUV.

"Maybe you should," Gordon said. "That way you'd have a better idea of what a grizzly bear can do to a human being."

"That's sick," Fowler said, stepping back to join her friend. "That's disgusting."

"You claim to know so much about bears," Gordon said. "Maybe you should take a look at what one can do. Then maybe you'd understand why sometimes we have to euthanize the killer before the bear does it again.

"The victim was innocent," she continued. "As far as we know, he did absolutely nothing to provoke the attack. He was as innocent as 413 was when her litter was killed. He wasn't behind the wheel."

"We're not here to judge," Calhoun said. "We're here to save—"

From behind him and to the side, Joe heard a dry branch crack on the slope across the river. Then another. And then a distinctive muffled drumbeat of heavy footfalls increasing in volume.

He glanced from the figure of Brodbeck in the middle of the

river to the distant silhouette of Cress on top of the ridge. Neither man had produced the sound.

Both Joe and Gordon turned away from the Mama Bears in time to witness a massive tan and brown form emerge from the timber on the slope they'd climbed before. The grizzly was a little over a hundred yards away. Its wedge-shaped body hit the surface of the river with tremendous force. Joe saw a flash of teeth from an open mouth and heard a heavy splash when the grizzly hit the water. It was headed straight for Brodbeck.

Bill Brodbeck turned, but the weight on his back made his movements ungainly as he tried to face the oncoming bear and unsling his rifle at the same time.

"Shit," Gordon shouted. "It doubled back on us!"

Joe scrambled for his rifle, which he'd leaned against the grille of Gordon's pickup. He shouldered it quickly and thumbed the safety off. By the time he leaned the red-dot scope to his eye, the bear had closed the distance with Brodbeck and the two forms had merged into one. It happened so quickly that Brodbeck couldn't even pull the bear spray off his belt or get a shot off. There wasn't even a hint of a bluff charge.

Joe heard the collision on the surface of the river and it sounded like a three-hundred-and-fifty-pound linebacker hitting a defenseless receiver in a helmet-to-helmet takedown.

On top of the ridge, Cress hollered and waved his arms.

The action was furious and hard to follow through Joe's scope. His red dot flashed across the glistening hide of the grizzly to Brodbeck's flailing hands to the terrifying moment when the bear's jaws engulfed Brodbeck's head and shook him like a puppy playing with a sock. The man's arms flailed and his legs retracted into a fetal position.

Joe felt himself go steely. He had no clean shot at the bear without the possibility of hitting Brodbeck, who was still alive, but the mauling would continue for every half second he held off. Beside him, he heard Gordon curse again as she raised her own rifle. She obviously had the same problem.

He elevated the muzzle of the rifle above the fray and fired four rapid shots into the hillside, hoping the concussions would distract the grizzly. If the bear paused and separated from Brodbeck, he might get a shot.

Boom-boom-boom-boom. The shots echoed in cadence through the canyon.

But instead of letting go of its grip on Brodbeck's limp body, the grizzly furiously backpedaled through the river, dragging the man along with it. Joe could sense no independent movement from Brodbeck. Not until the bear was onshore again and nearly hidden under brush cover did it unclamp its jaws from the man and leave him there in a wet heap.

Both Joe and Gordon fired repeatedly into the dense wall of willows and buckbrush where they'd last seen the grizzly. The heavy shots drowned out the screaming of the Mama Bears, who urged them to stop.

REMARKABLY, BILL BRODBECK was still alive when Joe and Gordon reached him on the far bank of the river. He wasn't conscious, and Joe could see horrific puncture wounds from teeth in his scalp at the hairline. There were holes in his armored vest where it had been bitten through, and his head, face, and neck were covered in blood.

Gordon called for EMTs to come from Saddlestring as she shed her daypack and let it drop to the ground. Joe stood over Brodbeck's body with his rifle at the ready, while Gordon dropped to her knees and ripped into a first-aid kit to attend to him. Joe glanced down to see bubbles appear in the blood streaming from the man's mouth and nose.

Cress had left his position on top of the ridge and was crashing down through the timber toward the scene, followed by Hoaglin. Joe's eyes raked the hillside for signs of the bear. His breath was shallow and total fear filled him once again.

This time, he could smell the dank, musky odor of the bear lingering around Brodbeck's body. Pungent, viscous saliva from the bear's mouth oozed down the man's face and neck.

Joe glanced over his shoulder to see that the Mama Bears had left the scene and were tearing across the meadow in their SUV toward the road.

CRESS STOPPED ABOUT fifteen yards uphill and crouched for a moment, his fingers brushing the mat of loam and pine needles on the forest floor. When he raised his hand, Joe could see a smear of blood on his fingertips.

"One of you hit her," he said. "I thought I heard a hit from up on the ridge."

"We just started blasting," Joe said. "I don't think either one of us had a clear shot."

"Is Bill still with us?"

"Barely," Joe said. "He's breathing."

"Thank God for that. I've never seen anything like it before in my life," Cress said. "I'm still a little in shock."

"I think we all are."

"Did you call for help?"

"Jennie did."

"I hope like hell they get here in time."

Cress stood to full height and waited for Hoaglin to catch up to him. When Hoaglin did, the two men scoured the ground for more signs. Hoaglin pointed out a depression in the loam and said, "She went up the hill again toward the south this time."

Joe followed their gaze up the timbered slope, downriver from the attack. About three hundred yards away and halfway up the canyon, he saw the top of a spindly aspen vanish from view as it was smashed down by force.

"Did you see that?" he asked.

"Affirmative," Hoaglin said, pointing out to Cress where the tree had been felled. "She's moving fast and she doesn't care what she smashes along the way."

"Let's go get her and finish it," Cress said to Hoaglin. "Let's hope she's mortally wounded and will bleed out." He showed his fingers to Hoaglin.

"Not a lot of blood," Hoaglin said. Then to Joe: "Do you know where you hit her?"

"Nope."

"Joe," Cress said, "I'm going to ask you to stay here with Jennie and Bill until the EMTs show up. I don't want to chance it that the grizzly circles on us again and comes back to cache Brodbeck's body. Are you okay with that?"

Joe nodded. Although Gordon had shown she was fully capable of defending herself, she was presently engaged in patching up Brodbeck's wounds and stopping him from losing too much blood. He just couldn't leave her there on her own.

"If that bear comes back, do what you did last time," Cress said. "Keep shooting until your barrel melts down."

Joe patted the deep pockets of his jacket to confirm that he had a fresh twenty-round magazine within easy reach. He did.

"Got it," Joe said. "Now go end this nightmare."

BRODBECK WAS BARELY alive, but fading, after he was carried across the river to the Twelve Sleep County emergency medical van a half hour later. The response time had been impressive given the distance to the ranch, but to Joe it had felt like an eternity.

He looked for Gordon and found her sitting with her back to a tree trunk, her rifle across her thighs. She looked shell-shocked, and Joe felt the same.

"I can't see how he makes it," she said. "He lost a ton of blood and some of those bite wounds looked deep. I can't believe what happened. That bear came down the mountain by a different route and just attacked him. She hunted him down right in front of us."

"Yup."

"Bears don't do this, Joe," she said, almost plaintively.

"Let's hope one of us made a solid hit on her," Joe said. "And that Cress and Hoaglin can track her down."

JOE WAS GRATEFUL when, an hour later, one of the fixed-wing aircraft Cress had requested appeared over the mountains and descended to search the timber in tight concentric circles. The pilot made radio contact with Gordon and confirmed they were searching for a lone grizzly bear.

They'd heard nothing from either Cress or Hoaglin over the radio since they'd left.

"You don't think that bear is crazy enough to go after them both, do you?" Gordon asked aloud. Joe was startled to hear in Gordon's voice what he was thinking to himself.

CRESS AND HOAGLIN didn't find the grizzly, and they returned to the scene of the attack looking worn-out and frustrated. So was the pilot of the plane and his spotter. They'd radioed to say that they'd failed to get a visual on the bear and that they were forced to return to the Jackson airport before they ran out of fuel and sunlight.

"She's gone," Cress reported to Gordon. "We got on her track for a while, but she outran us."

"The blood trail dried up," Hoaglin sighed. "She must not be hit that bad."

"Which means we need to find her tomorrow," Gordon said. "And now we know we're looking for a wounded bear who shows absolutely no fear of humans, and who wants to kill us before we kill her."

"Not exactly the most optimal situation," Cress deadpanned.

CHAPTER EIGHT

Hanna

THREE HOURS LATER, and two hundred and thirty miles away, as the dusk sun lit up the western flanks of sagebrush-covered but treeless hills, Dallas Cates pointed at an exit sign for Walcott Junction and said, "Turn here."

They were on Interstate 80 driving east from Rawlins. The right lane of the highway was a stream of big rigs. They reminded Dallas of train cars that were inexorably linked together, but with no engine and no caboose. The hundreds of trucks all struggled up hills together and shot down the other side. It was the same scenario on the westbound lanes.

"Why here?" Bobbi Johnson asked. "Aren't we headed the wrong direction?"

"No, ma'am," he said.

"Okay, well, I need gas anyway," she said. "I'm down to an eighth of a tank."

"There's a Shell station," he said. "Pull in there."

"I'm a little low on cash, Dallas. You'll need to help me out here."

He bit his lip. Johnson had all kinds of elaborate plans about picking up her sister and driving to California to start a new life, but she didn't think very hard on the here and now. *Of course* she was a little low on cash. Of course she hadn't brought a firearm with her when she picked him up. And *of course* she didn't have a problem taking the desolate interstate highway across southern Wyoming with barely an eighth of a tank of gas.

"I'll cover the gas," he said.

"Where are we going, anyway?" she asked as she pulled up next to a bank of pumps.

"You'll see," he said as he climbed out.

His CREDIT CARD had expired while he was in the penitentiary, so in order to fill the tank he needed to go inside the lonely station and pay cash in advance. That was best anyway, he thought, because he didn't want to leave a paper trail of his whereabouts. On the way in he noticed a hand-painted sign that read ARMED GUARD AFTER DARK.

Inside, it was claustrophobic and the racks were filled with candy, snacks, and automobile fluids. Yacht rock played from a tinny speaker—"Sailing" by Christopher Cross, a song Cates hated and that he wished had gone away during his time in prison. The man behind the counter was rotund with a mullet and shifty eyes. He wore a shoulder holster with the grip of a semiauto pistol in clear view. He glared at Cates in an unhealthy way, Cates thought.

"I'll give you a hundred dollars and come back for the change after I fill the tank," Cates said.

"That'll work," the attendant said. He had an airy, high-pitched voice. He was a strange one, Cates thought. The kind of guy who worked at a gas station thirty miles from the nearest town and probably slept in the single-wide trailer out back.

Eighteen hundred dollars seemed like a lot of money inside prison, but it wouldn't last very long at this rate, he thought. Not at a hundred bucks a tank. He peeled off a bill from inside his roll and placed it on the counter.

"I know you," the attendant said. "You're Dallas Cates, ain't ya?"

That was why he was looking at him so strangely.

"Who?"

"Dallas Cates. World champ rodeo cowboy."

"Never met the man."

"Damn, you sure look like him. Last I heard, he was in Rawlins."

"Maybe he's still there," Cates said, turning his back on the attendant.

He sent Johnson inside to get his change—all of seven dollars' worth.

———

"I LOVE IT," Cates said as he looked at the landscape after they'd left the Shell station. "I just fucking love it."

"It looks like a whole lot of nothing to me," Johnson said as she drove.

They were on a two-lane highway headed northeast. The interstate hummed with trucks behind them, but there was no traffic on U.S. 30.

It was stark country with rolling sagebrush hills, large herds of pronghorn antelope, snow fences, huge electrical transmission lines, and no trees. Elk Mountain loomed to the south and was half-shrouded with low-hanging clouds illuminated by the setting sun.

Rattlesnake country, Cates thought. There was row after row of granite outcroppings stretching north to south in the terrain. They looked like the exposed spines of massive dinosaurs.

Cates's burner phone chimed and he drew it from his pocket and read the new text message.

"Why are you smiling?" she asked him.

"I got good news," he said. "Remember that guy I told you about who I bonded with while in prison? The guy I actually haven't even met?"

"Yes. What about him?"

"He's on his way," Cates said. "He just needs me to text him where to meet."

"This is all fucking weird and mysterious," she said. "Why meet up with a guy you don't even know?"

"I told you already," Cates said. "We have a common purpose, and now I have a plan that came to me last night. Plus, he's loaded, and at this rate we're gonna run out of cash soon."

"I don't think I like where this is going," she said.

Cates ignored her. "You don't know how good it feels to be in open country again," he said. "It's hard to describe."

"We're in the middle of nowhere," she said. "It's kind of creepy."

He grinned.

"Now tell me where we're going, Dallas Cates," she said firmly.

"Have you ever been to Hanna?" he asked, gesturing ahead.

"I ain't even heard of it," she responded.

"Then it will be a new adventure," he said.

"I'm game."

"I knew you would be."

THEY TOOK THE exit for Highway 72 and passed by a green sign that read:

Hanna
Population 683
Elevation 6,818

State Highway 72 descended into a swale pockmarked with scattered houses and other structures. Railroad tracks neatly split the town in two. A tall line of pine trees bordered the left side of the road and acted as a "living snow fence," protecting the road by affecting wind speed and direction and causing snow to drift short of the blacktop.

They drove by the high school on their right, which was a brick building marked by a billboard with a painted figure of a heavily muscled man wearing a hard hat and swinging a pickax. HOME OF THE MINERS, the sign read.

"They used to mine coal here," Cates said as Johnson drove over the train tracks on a long overpass. "It looks like a mining town, the way the houses are built into the hills and they're all over the place. But you know what happened to the coal industry. A few people stuck it out, I guess."

"And that matters to me how?" she asked.

"Just giving you some background," he said. "I used to rodeo with a guy from here named Cody Schantz. He told me all about it."

As the sun set, it was obvious that only about a fifth of the homes they could see had interior lights on. A complex of apartment buildings up on the highest hill was totally dark.

"Lots of empty houses," she said. "It feels real lonesome. Does your friend still live here?"

Cates shook his head. "He died in a car crash trying to get to the Pendleton Round-Up." Then: "Nearly everybody I know is dead. Friends, family, everyone."

Johnson's eyes got moist and she wiped at them with the back of her hand. "You've got *me*," she said.

"And I'm thankful for that," he said. "Up there—that bar up on the hill. The lights are on. Let's go there."

IN THE GRAVEL parking lot on the side of Skinny's Beer Garden, parked right in front of a faded painted mural of a tropical island scene, Cates asked Bobbi Johnson to go inside and get them a fresh bottle of Jim Beam and a six-pack of beer. He handed her two twenties.

"Don't you want to go inside?" she asked.

"No."

"Why the hell not? I don't want to go in this place by myself."

As she said it, she gestured toward the four muddy oil-field and utility trucks parked haphazardly in the lot.

He said, "You know what happened back there in that gas station, right? That guy recognized me. This is a little redneck town full of rodeo fans. I stopped by here with my buddy Cody once on the way to Steamboat. I've got to be low-key."

"Why?" Johnson said. "What do you plan to do here?"

WHILE JOHNSON WAS in Skinny's, Cates leaned against the passenger window and surveyed the town below. It didn't take long before he spied what he was looking for. His rodeo buddy had described it as being almost directly below the overpass looking out at the train tracks.

The interior lights of the cab came on when Johnson returned and climbed back in. She seemed flustered as she plopped the bourbon and beer on the bench seat between them.

"You can only imagine the attention a woman alone gets in

that place," she said. "One guy wanted to dance with me and started feeding quarters into the jukebox."

Cates smiled. "But you disappointed him."

"Dude, I was out of there before the first song played."

CATES DIRECTED JOHNSON to drive around the entrance to the overpass toward the tracks, through two blocks of clapboard houses that were dark and boarded up. Except for the ribbons of train tracks that reflected the moon out front, there was nothing in the field in front of the museum.

They took Front Street and slowly cruised by a neatly appointed white structure with three brick chimneys and brown trim around the doors and windows.

A sign out front read:

HANNA MUSEUM
SUMMER HOURS:
FRIDAY THROUGH SUNDAY 1–5 PM
WINTER HOURS: FRIDAY 1–5 PM

"There it is," Cates said.

"A *museum*?" Johnson asked, exasperated. "We came all this way to go to a *museum*?"

"Yes."

"It's very clearly closed."

"Drive around back and park," he said. "We don't want to be seen from the street."

"There's no traffic," she said. "Not a single car."

"Please, Bobbi," he said in a quiet tone that others had described to him as menacing. As usual, it worked.

"YOU STAY HERE," Cates said to Johnson after they'd parked. The overpass stretched over them and he'd asked her to position the truck so that it couldn't be seen from above.

Johnson was clearly flummoxed. "If we were gonna rob someplace, why not that bar back there? Why not a damn ATM or something? I saw one on the way in. Why a museum?"

"It's not for money," he said, stepping out of the truck. Before closing the door, he leaned back inside. "Stay right here and keep your eye out. Turn the truck off so there's no lights. And if anybody comes, let me know."

"How long are you going to be?" she asked. "I'm getting hungry."

"Ten, twenty minutes, I'd guess."

"Hurry," she said. "I don't want to freeze in here."

He closed the door without responding.

THE WINDOWS ON the back of the museum were shoulder-high, with old wooden frames and wavery glass. They were locked, but he could clearly see on top of the nearest window the inside metal latch that held it in place. It was obvious that the facility didn't have a security system of any kind, at least not in the back of the building. There were no embedded wires in the glass or exterior cameras. Not in a town of six hundred and eighty-three people.

Cates found a rusted railroad spike in the tawny grass on the side of the building and carried it back. He used the spike to break through one of the panes of the window most deeply in shadow, then reached in through the hole and unlocked the hardware and slid it up.

There was no gust of warm air from inside, he noted. They probably kept the heating system off when the museum wasn't open, which was most of the time, it seemed. Before making his move, Cates looked around. Johnson sat behind the wheel in the dark cab, studying his every movement. He was grateful she wasn't staring at her phone, reading Facebook. There were no cars on the road in front of the museum or on the side.

Satisfied they were alone, he deftly launched himself up and through the open window and he was inside.

THE MUSEUM WAS mostly dark, but what he could see was lit by the red glow of several emergency exit signs mounted over the front and side doors. They threw a pink light through the interior and created deep shadows. He didn't want to turn the lights on and he cursed himself for not buying a cheap flashlight at the Shell station.

Cates waited for his eyes to adjust to the gloom. What he could see had been described to him by his buddy Cody. It was primarily a railroad museum, with dioramas of Union Pacific model train sets, old mining tools and equipment, and a corner filled with memorabilia from when Hanna was founded in 1889 to service both the mines and the Union Pacific. The displays were neat and orderly and no doubt interesting.

But that wasn't what Cates was looking for.

Around a glass display case filled with local jade and other minerals, he saw it: Zeus the Grizzly Bear. The mount towered nearly eight feet tall, the top of its head brushing the ceiling.

Cody had told him the story that he'd heard from his mother, who at the time had been the volunteer director of the museum. Her name was Peggy Schantz. In the 1900s, the five-hundred-pound male had wandered down from Elk Mountain into the outskirts of Hanna and killed several cattle and a mule. A local killed Zeus, and a collection was raised among the new townspeople to have the bear mounted for posterity. Eventually, it wound up in the museum.

The grizzly's coat was thick and dusty, but its massive claws and gleaming teeth glowed in the pink light. The creature had been positioned to look like it was roaring and about to lunge at the viewer. It was huge and menacing, even while frozen in time. Cates felt a chill shiver up his back, since Zeus was the inspiration for getting the grizzly tattoo on his arms in the first place.

It took less than a minute to locate a large crosscut saw that was hanging on the wall of the museum. It was in a display describing how tie hacks cut and shaped wooden ties for the railroad out of lodgepole pines that had been floated up the

North Platte River from the south. As he pulled the saw from the wall, one of the teeth tripped a light switch and suddenly the interior of the museum was bathed in light.

Temporarily blinded and his heart beating fast, Cates located the switch and doused the museum back into gloom.

"Damn it," he whispered.

THE GRIZZLY BEAR mount crashed hard to the floor when Cates pushed it over, the carcass narrowly missing two glass display cases. It landed between them and produced a cloud of decades-old dust from the thick fur.

He used the saw to cut off the huge front paws and he stacked them beneath the open window. They were the size of pizza pans.

It wasn't quick work. While modern taxidermists used Styrofoam to replicate the body shape and mass of the animals, Cates learned that beneath the hide of this creature there was a heavy plaster mold. It was difficult to cut through and soon the interior of the museum was coated with a fine layer of white dust. He was grateful that he'd spent so many hours pumping iron in the prison gym to build up his muscles.

There were only about two and a half inches of the neck left to saw through when red and blue wigwag lights lit up the front windows.

"*Dallas, there's a cop out front*," Johnson hissed from somewhere. He looked up to see that she was at the open window, her hands pressed against the sides of her face in alarm. "He came out of nowhere," she said.

"Now you tell me?" he said. "Were you staring at your damn phone when he drove up?"

"Come on, come on," she implored. Then: "What in the hell are you doing?"

"*Shhhhh*," Cates said, holding a finger to his lips.

She vanished from the open window, but he could hear her grumbling and cursing to herself just out of sight.

He stood up from where he'd been bending over the mount and working with the saw. The lights outside continued to pulse and spin, but the vehicle they came from was obviously stationary. He tried not to make a sound.

Maybe the cop would just move along.

Then there was a knock on the front entrance door, and an older male voice: "Hey, this is Marshal Bertignolli. Is anybody in there?"

Cates thought, Hanna has a marshal? *A marshal?*

"Peggy, are you in here tonight? Somebody called and said they thought they saw the lights flash and that maybe someone was in here."

Peggy Schantz. Cody's mother.

Cates was still. He looked over at the two bear paws under the window, then at the nearly decapitated head at his feet. Another minute, and he'd have it off. The head was huge, and likely heavy, he thought.

There was a jangle of keys on the other side of the door, and for a moment Cates froze. Dive out the window without the paws and head, or confront the visitor?

THE FRONT DOOR cracked open and the beam of a flashlight lit up the dusty floor inside.

"What the hell?" the man said, pushing his way in behind the flashlight. As he reached out with his right hand for the light switch, Cates stepped out from behind the door and pressed the tip of a rusty railroad spike into the base of the marshal's neck.

"Don't move or I'll blow your head off," he said. "And keep that light off."

The marshal, or whatever he was, stiffened. Cates could see in the undulating pulses from the vehicle's light bar that the man wore a battered cowboy hat and a canvas coat with a patch on the sleeve that identified him as **HANNA MARSHAL**. He was armed with a weapon in a belt holster, but the safety strap was still fixed.

Cates pulled the marshal inside and closed the front door behind them with the heel of his boot. As he did, he reached down with his free hand and drew the marshal's gun from its holster. A Glock 48 Slimline nine with a ten-round magazine. A solid piece.

"Let me go and we can work this out," the marshal said. "I don't know what you think you're doing here, but there isn't anything of value in here. Just don't tell Peggy I said that."

He was in his late sixties or early seventies, Cates thought. Tall but soft, no muscle tone, a weak chin, and a classic cop mustache. An unimposing man who happened to have a badge and a gun.

"I mean, there's no cash," the marshal said, his voice rising with anxiety. "This place runs strictly on donations, and I'm afraid to say there just aren't many."

Cates replaced the railroad spike with the Glock and he used the muzzle to push the marshal forward against a glass display case. As he did so, the marshal nearly tripped over the almost-severed head of the grizzly bear.

"What in the hell are you doing in here to old Zeus?" the marshal asked. His eyes slid from the bear to the glass, and Cates found himself looking into the man's eyes in the reflection.

"Hey," the marshal said. "I think I might know you."

"You don't."

"I met you through Cody a few years back. You're Dallas Cates."

"I'm not."

"Look—"

Cates grabbed the marshal by his opposite shoulder and spun him around until they were face-to-face, nose to nose, eye to eye. "I'm not going back to jail," Cates said.

The marshal started to speak, when Cates shoved the muzzle under his chin and fired. The exit wound blew his hat off his head and painted the glass of the display case red.

Cates stepped back while the marshal slid down the glass case to the floor, where he sat with his head flopped to the side and his legs sprawled out.

"Dallas? Are you all right?" Johnson yelled from the window.

"Fine," Cates said.

"I thought I heard a shot."

"You did. Now start up the truck. I'll be right out."

BEFORE TOSSING THE bear's head and paws out the open window, Cates returned to the marshal's body and stood over it. He thought about staging a suicide, leaving the gun in the marshal's hand. Cops killed themselves all the time with their own weapons, and it wasn't out of the question that a small-town marshal, who probably got paid next to nothing with no further job prospects due to his age, might be the victim of depression.

But Dallas Cates wanted to keep the gun. He needed it.

Plus, his DNA was probably all over the museum. He hadn't worn gloves, and his fingerprints were on the saw and his footprints were everywhere in the fine plaster dust on the floor. That idiot Shell station attendant could place him in the vicinity the night of the murder.

So, after locating several gallons of isopropyl alcohol in the storeroom and splashing it across the floor, Cates tucked the Glock into his belt and climbed out the window. He loaded the bear parts into the back of Johnson's truck bed. That grizzly head was as heavy as he thought it would be.

Then he returned to the building and tossed a lit match through the open window. Not until the fire caught with a breathy *whoosh* did he jump into the truck and tell Johnson to get the hell out of Hanna, Wyoming, now population six hundred and eighty-two.

OCTOBER 17

He is like a man
In the body of a violent beast.
Its muscles are his own . . .

—Wallace Stevens, "Poetry Is a Destructive Force," 1942

CHAPTER NINE

Jeffrey City

LEE OGBURN-RUSSELL LIVED in Jeffrey City in the home he'd grown up in, for better or worse. Dallas Cates wanted to find him.

The wind howled across U.S. Highway 287 as Cates and Bobbi Johnson approached the town from the southeast. Tumbleweeds the size of medicine balls rolled across the asphalt and a massive dust devil descended from Green Mountain to the south, its tail tethered to the ground and its funnel top splayed out like an opened fan. Waves of wind buffeted Johnson's pickup from the side and rocked it while they drove. To the north were two central Wyoming landmarks: Devil's Gate and Independence Rock, both on the Oregon Trail. Devil's Gate was a severe slash down the middle of a granite mountain where the Sweetwater River flowed. Independence Rock was a lone turtle shell–like rock formation covered with initials and carvings made by pioneers headed west a century and a half ago. Both faded out of view as the pickup got closer to the town.

"Slow down or we'll miss it," Cates said to Johnson. "There ain't much there anymore."

"Why do we keep going to places like this?" Johnson whined. "Can't we go to someplace with people in it? Someplace to eat and shop? And maybe someplace a lady can take a shower?"

"I'll tell you why," Cates said. "Because a guy like Lee can't live among actual human beings." Then: "You'll see."

JEFFREY CITY WAS a post-nuclear-age ghost town that was remarkable for its isolation, even in Wyoming. It was sixty-eight miles from Rawlins, ninety-seven miles from Casper, and fifty-eight miles from Lander. Once a uranium mining town of nearly forty-five hundred residents in the late 1970s, the population had dwindled to fewer than thirty since the mines shut down. No one lived in the vandalized two-story apartment buildings or abandoned trailer homes, and despite the street grids and signs that had been laid out with Germanic precision, the only life on the streets were roaming pronghorn antelope, jackrabbits, and coyotes. Paint had long ago been blasted off the exteriors of the empty single-family homes by grit-filled wind and horizontal snowstorms.

A battered roadside motel claimed on a hand-painted sign

that it was open, and beer signs were lit in the windows of a bar with two muddy pickups parked outside.

"There," Cates said, gesturing toward a metal square attached to the side of a long-closed service station. It read LOR AMUSEMENTS, 0.7 MILE.

Under the sign was a steel arrow pointing south down Rattlesnake Street.

"LOR Amusements," Cates said. "LOR stands for Lee Ogburn-Russell."

"What's amusing about him?" Johnson asked.

"I've got to think about how to answer that," Cates said. "'Amusing' probably isn't the word I'd use. Maybe 'eccentric' or 'on the spectrum,' but not necessarily *amusing*. He can fix anything mechanical and he can make anything you ask for, though. I've never met anyone like him."

"And why are we here to find him?" Johnson asked.

"He owes me," Cates said. "He owes me his life."

WHEN OGBURN-RUSSELL HAD been assigned to Dallas Cates's cell, he was cowed and recovering from a severe beating at the hands of several La Familia members who'd caught him in the yard. The gang members claimed he'd smirked at them in the lunch line, where he was a server. When he showed up, Ogburn-Russell wore a patch over his right eye and his face was a road map of recently removed stitches. Cates had no regard for the man and told him so.

It wasn't until three weeks later that Cates discovered his cellmate's value. That was when he saw his new cellmate kill a mouse with a device he had fashioned from parts pilfered inside the prison. The little zip gun–like weapon, which had been constructed using a length of metal conduit, a spring removed from his mattress, a trigger fashioned from a ballpoint pen, and a handle melted down from a plastic container, had fired a steel pellet seven feet across the cell and nailed the rodent in the head, killing it instantly.

The zip gun was followed by other inventions that Ogburn-Russell shared with Cates: a garrote made of thin wire with handles, ceramic shanks that were so sharp they could shave hair off the back of his hand, an eye-gouger fashioned from a stolen metal cooking spoon, and an ice pick made from hundreds of metal shavings molded together by the heat of a homemade welding torch.

Cates had gotten the names of the three La Familia attackers from Ogburn-Russell and he'd put each of them in the infirmary using the new weapons, one at a time. After that, La Familia put out the word that Ogburn-Russell was under Cates's—and the WOODS'—protection.

Ogburn-Russell had told Cates that he was in prison for attempted murder and reckless endangerment charges in his hometown of Jeffrey City. He said that after the uranium mines were shut down, unemployed residents became unhinged. A group of them targeted his father because he had worked as a manager in the uranium mine. That was unfair, LOR said, because his dad had been laid off as well.

Several of the criminals vandalized the property where he lived with his dad at the time. Once, his father was forced off the road by drunken ex-miners. Then pieces of his artwork were smashed up and stolen, and his father was pummeled when he caught the criminals in the act.

The local cops did nothing to stop the harassment, Ogburn-Russell said, because several of them were in on it. So he took matters into his own hands.

After weeks of planning and tinkering in his shop, Ogburn-Russell booby-trapped locations where he knew the vandals frequented. Three men were severely injured on the same night. One had his legs blown off when he stepped on a pressure-plate explosive, another was impaled through his clavicle by a steel rod shot out of a length of pipe mounted to his fence, and the third had his hands crushed when he reached into a hinged steel box to retrieve a piece of pie on his front porch.

Ogburn-Russell was quickly caught, arrested, and sentenced in the Fremont County courthouse. The judge said he wouldn't go easy on him because of the smirk on his face during sentencing.

Offering protection to LOR wasn't easy for Cates. The man had a way of annoying everyone around him. Ogburn-Russell's face was set in a kind of permanent superior sneer that made Cates want to slap him.

On the day LOR was released, Cates said he'd find him someday and get payback for keeping the man alive and unharmed.

That day had come.

———

ON THE DRIVE north, Cates had scanned the stations on the AM radio while Johnson drove. He finally found KTWO out of Casper. On the hour, the station had a newsbreak between country songs and local commercials.

Carbon County Sheriff's Office investigators were on the scene of a fire that had occurred the night before in Hanna. The building that had burned was the historic local museum. It was a total loss. In addition to the fire, county officials were also searching for Marvin Bertignolli, the Hanna marshal, who was suspected to be the charred body found within the museum. The implication of the news report, Cates thought, was that the two items were linked in some way.

"That poor guy," Cates said. "I forgot what he said his name was."

"What poor guy?" Johnson asked.

"Never mind."

LOR AMUSEMENTS WOULD have stood out anyplace, and it certainly did in the empty exoskeleton of a town that was Jeffrey City. Located on one square city block with no other structures of any kind surrounding it, LOR bristled with eccentric metal sculptures, figures, wrecks, and ruins surrounded by a six-foot-high chain-link fence. A small faded-white home stuck out in the middle of the scrap-metal garden. Next to the home was an attached shop with corrugated metal siding.

The closed front gate of the lot had a sign on it that read:

LOR AMUSEMENTS
SINCE 1989
ENTER AT YOUR PERIL

"Park here," Cates said to Johnson.

JOHNSON SHUT THE engine off and took in the twisted metal figures inside the lot. "I'll stay. This place is creepy."

"So is the owner," Cates said. "Now come on."

The gate was not locked, and Cates slid it open to enter. He marveled at the sign as he did so. Every individual segment of every letter was constructed of disparate materials to form the words: cut tubing, steel tools, lengths of bone. He guessed that it had taken months or maybe years to gather the bits and assemble it. Cates rolled his eyes and whistled.

Inside, it was even more crowded with objects than it had appeared. Looming above them was a knight on horseback grasping a lance made out of a long shaft with a drill bit on the end. A creature built to look like Bigfoot peered over its shoulder at them as it appeared to lurk away. A twelve-foot-high human skeleton stood above everything, its arms outstretched and its head tilted to the side as if it were crucified. Every work had been assembled from scrap metal and other scrounged items. Bigfoot was constructed almost entirely from rusty tire rims and chrome fenders. Every bone of the skeleton looked anatomically correct.

Beneath them along the path to the house were turtles made of hubcaps and rabbits twisted from long lengths of barbed wire.

"Who would buy this stuff?" Johnson asked.

Cates shrugged. "People who are as weird as Lee is, I guess."

The wind changed tone as it blew through the lot and through the hollow metal artworks, making the place hum in an eerie way.

"I'm getting freaked out," Johnson said, gripping Cates's arm. "Maybe we should go back to the truck."

As she said it, Cates inadvertently stepped on a concealed pressure plate with his boot and a grotesque goblin's face shot out from a suspended metal box that was hung at eye level. The face shot through the air on a telescoping steel rod, its jaws snapping.

Cates reacted instinctively by stepping back and turning his head away. As the goblin shot by his ear, he grabbed it and held it fast. When the goblin tried to retract back into the box, Cates twisted its head off with a sharp snapping sound.

Johnson screamed and jumped back, then covered her open mouth with her hands.

A figure appeared at the doorway of the shop. He wore a welder's apron, gloves, and a full white welding helmet decorated with stickers from the *Star Wars* universe. A lit acetylene torch hissed in his right hand.

"Ain't nobody ever caught that goblin in midair," he said, his voice muffled by his face shield. "But if anyone could do it, it would be Dallas Cates. I always said you had the quick reactions of a damned cat."

Cates examined the head of the goblin in his hands, turning it over to see the exposed copper wires and pneumatic tubing that extended from it. Then he tossed it toward the man and it rolled until it bumped into his boots.

"Sorry I busted it, Lee," Cates said. "How long did it take you to build it?"

Lee Ogburn-Russell shut off the torch and raised his face shield. His face, like his frame, was gnomish and soft and his eyes seemed both perpetually amused and disdainful. It was a face, Dallas had once heard a fellow inmate say, that just begged to be punched.

"It took me a few days," Ogburn-Russell said. "Once I got the thrust mechanism figured out. I experimented with hydraulics, then I tried a gunpowder charge like they use for airbags, you know? Finally, I figured out that the best and fastest way to shoot that goblin head out was compressed air. I should have known that from the beginning."

Then Ogburn-Russell turned his attention from Cates to Johnson. "Who's the fine-looking split-tail you brought along?"

Cates turned his head and grinned at Johnson. "He's always had a way of charming the ladies, as you can see."

"*He's a pig,*" she mouthed.

"He is," Cates agreed.

"Why are you here, Dallas?" Ogburn-Russell asked. "I didn't know you were out."

"I've got a project for you," Cates said. "A really important one that you can't fuck up."

Ogburn-Russell winced. "What's the project?"

"I'll tell you about it after you invite us in," Cates said. "You owe me."

"I haven't forgotten. I knew this day would come."

Ogburn-Russell lowered the torch and placed his helmet on a bench outside the shop. He gestured to them to follow him into his house.

"I've got some beer inside," he said. "You can pull up a chair and tell me all about it. You," he said to Johnson, "can sit on my face and wriggle around."

"I *hate* this asshole," Johnson said through clenched teeth.

"I wish I could say you'll come to like him," Cates said to her, "but that would be a lie."

As he followed Ogburn-Russell, Cates said, "Lee, you need to cool it with comments in regard to Bobbi here."

"Then tell her to stop provoking me," LOR said with a smirk that vanished as soon as he saw Cates's dead-eye glare.

"You're serious?" Ogburn-Russell asked.

Cates didn't indicate otherwise.

"Thank you," Johnson whispered to Cates as they entered the cluttered home.

"So what is it you're looking for?" LOR asked Cates. He sat in a stained cloth-covered recliner across from Cates and Johnson, who were seated side by side in a mushy couch. The walls were covered with bizarre metal artwork and the house had a peculiar burnt-hair odor. Ogburn-Russell had given them cans of Pabst Blue Ribbon, and the three of them had toasted.

"Something special," Cates answered. "That goblin out there times a thousand. I need a device that can clamp down at a short distance with eleven hundred pounds per square inch."

"That's powerful, all right," LOR said. "That could kill a man." He seemed to like the idea.

Cates noticed that Johnson recoiled at the exchange. She looked from LOR to him, trying to understand what was going on.

"I've got to run to our truck," Cates said to Ogburn-Russell, handing his beer to Johnson and standing up. "I've got some materials I want you to work with."

"This is getting interesting," LOR said. To Johnson, he said, "He's challenging me. I love a challenge."

WHEN CATES WAS gone, Johnson narrowed her eyes at Ogburn-Russell. "Stop staring at me, you creep."

Ogburn-Russell drained his beer and chinned toward the huge flat-screen television mounted on the wall. He grasped a remote control from a chairside table and aimed it.

"Do you like porn?" he asked.

"Fuck off."

"Is that a yes or a no?" He crumpled his empty beer can in his fist and leered at her before he went into the kitchen for another.

That was when Johnson noticed that Dallas had left his burner phone face down on the arm of the couch. She quickly slid over on the cushions and grabbed it. Johnson knew from observing him use the device that Dallas hadn't programmed in an access code.

She felt guilty about looking, but her curiosity outweighed that concern. Besides, she thought, if Dallas was going to invite someone else to their party, she deserved to know who it was.

There was only one text thread on the screen, and she quickly scrolled through it.

I've been released, Cates had initially texted. Are you still on for the project we discussed?

Absolutely, came the reply.

I'm putting a plan into place. It'll take a few days to get set up. Want to meet?

The recipient replied with a thumbs-up emoji.

From the day before: I'll text you the address when I can.

Another thumbs-up.

Then, from a few minutes before: LOR Amusements, Jeffrey City, WY.

On my way.

Before placing the phone back where it had been, Johnson glanced at the name of the recipient.

"Doing a little spying on good old Dallas, I see," Ogburn-Russell said as he settled back down in his chair. Johnson reacted with alarm. She hadn't heard him reenter the living room.

"Please," she said, trying to project calm. "Please don't say anything to him."

"What will you do if I keep it between us?" he asked.

"What do you want?" she asked. She regretted her words as soon as they were out of her mouth.

Lee Ogburn-Russell pointed down at his crotch and grinned. "Not now," he said. "But at the time of my choosing."

She sighed and moved back to her original place on the couch. Cates kicked at the front door and grunted, "Someone let me in. This bear's head is heavier than hell."

Ogburn-Russell scrambled out of his chair to grab the doorknob.

While he did, Johnson recalled the name on Cates's phone and asked herself: *Who the fuck is Axel Soledad?*

OCTOBER 24

The mountains have always been here, and in them, the bears.

—Rick Bass

CHAPTER TEN

Saddlestring

A WEEK LATER, JOE and Marybeth sat together at a table in the Ramshorn Restaurant and Lounge, waiting for the arrival of Judge Hewitt, who had asked them to join him for lunch. In Saddlestring, there were two choices for a midday meal: the Burg-O-Pardner, which specialized in fried foods like chicken-fried steak and Rocky Mountain oysters, and the Ramshorn, which was a step up in atmosphere and fresh food, but was chronically unable to keep staff. Apparently, the judge now preferred the Ramshorn ever since he'd sentenced a Burg-O-Pardner short-order cook for dealing narcotics.

"So what does he want to talk to us about?" Marybeth asked Joe. She was wearing a smart dark suit and a white blouse with her hair up, and had on her reading glasses so she could scan the menu. She looked to Joe to be very much the sexy librarian, and he told her so.

"Please," she said, pretending to be annoyed at him. "I wanted to look good for our board meeting this afternoon."

"You succeeded," he said.

Marybeth looked *him* over and smiled. Joe was in uniform and he'd spent the morning on patrol in the breaklands west of town, checking deer and antelope hunters for their licenses and conservation stamps. His boots were coated with dried mud and there was a smear of blood from a hanging mule deer carcass on the thigh of his jeans.

"I didn't dress up," he said.

"I see that. Is there any word on how Bill Brodbeck is doing?"

"He's still in critical condition, but stable, from what I understand. They flew him to a hospital in Denver for more surgery."

"Poor guy," she said. Then: "Oh, I meant to tell you that I got a text from Sheridan. She's on her way to that job in Colorado with no problems."

"Walden, right? Has she met her contact yet?" Joe asked.

"I don't think so, although she said she's hoping to find a place to stay that will allow her to bring her falcons into her room. She seems to be okay, considering all that she has on her plate."

THE PREDATOR ATTACK Team, plus a new game warden from Powell, who'd been sent to fill out the squad in Brodbeck's absence, had dispersed earlier in the week when the rogue grizzly could not be located either by air or on the ground. Although two of the culvert traps had been tripped, the creatures inside turned out to be local black bears and they were immediately released. A mountain lion had been caught in one of the snares and it, too, was freed. There had been no images of the grizzly bear on the trail cameras the team had set up on the slopes around the river.

Fortunately, there had been no more bear attacks in the Twelve Sleep Valley, but the unresolved nature of the hunt had darkened the mood of the team, including Joe. Jennie Gordon had spoken for all of them when she said she hoped the bear had been mortally wounded and had died somewhere in the Bighorns and wouldn't kill or maim any more human beings. But, she said, it was unsettling not to know for sure. Joe felt the same way.

The plan was for the Predator Attack Team to return and comb the area a second time to try and get a resolution one way or another. Joe had been asked by Jennie Gordon to reunite with them.

The aftermath of the two attacks had cast a pall over the area. Hunters in the breaklands and the mountains had asked Joe for details about the attacks, and several said they found themselves jumping at every sound in the woods. Men wore large-caliber sidearms and bear spray holsters at all times, and several long-established elk hunting guide operations had already broken up their camps and moved out when their out-of-state clients canceled at the last minute.

Three days before, a hunter from Michigan had killed an Angus steer in a ranch pasture, thinking it was a bear. He'd turned himself in and was negotiating with the rancher to cover the loss.

In another instance, a hiker from New Jersey bought a canister of bear spray from a local shop, but he didn't know how to use it and applied it to his skin as if it were sunscreen before setting off on the trail. The capsicum-rich formula burned his skin and temporarily blinded him and he wound up in the Twelve Sleep County Hospital.

The psychologist at the Saddlestring Middle School was quoted in the *Roundup* saying that a number of students refused to go outside for gym class because they were terrified of being mauled. Joe had rolled his eyes at that one.

But he'd felt the pall himself. He was looking over his shoulder more than ever, and was hyper-attuned to the snaps of twigs in the brush, as well as Daisy's early warning woofs. Even Marybeth, who fed her horses hay every morning and evening, no longer ventured from the house to the barn without a canister of bear spray clipped to her belt.

JUDGE HEWITT SHOWED up five minutes late in his usual concentrated fury, pushing through the front doors. He made his way straight to their table. Small, dark, and twitchy, Hewitt ordered "the usual" from a waitress en route without breaking stride. He'd left his robe in his chambers, although Joe assumed the man was armed, since he always was.

"Greetings, greetings," he said as he pumped Joe's and Marybeth's hands.

"You look very nice today," he said to Marybeth. "I like an attractive woman who wants to look her best."

Marybeth smiled woodenly at that, and Joe stifled a smirk. Political correctness was not something Judge Hewitt subscribed to.

"Sorry I'm late," he said. "Sometimes attorneys don't know when to shut up. Have you ordered?"

"Not yet," Joe answered.

"Colleen," Hewitt called to the waitress he'd brushed by.

"Coming," she responded.

Marybeth ordered a Cobb salad and Joe a cheeseburger and fries.

"Thanks for meeting with me," Hewitt said, placing his hands palms down on the table and fixing both of them with his intense stare. "Joe, did you find the grizzly bear?"

"Nope," Joe said. He caught the judge up on what had, and hadn't, happened in the past week.

"I take bear spray and my weapon with me every morning on my walk now," the judge said, shaking his head. "If that bear shows up, I'm going to blast him with the spray and finish him off with my .44."

Joe believed him. Judge Hewitt was a world-class big-game trophy hunter who started every morning with a vigorous three-mile walk around the golf course at the exclusive Eagle Mountain Club located on the outskirts of town. He'd once shot and killed a coyote fifty yards away who was sharing his path.

Inside the judge's palatial home was a seven-foot full-mount brown bear that he'd killed in Alaska, among other big-game trophies.

"Okay," Hewitt said. "Our time together is short, so I'll get down to brass tacks. As you know, the election is two weeks away."

Joe and Marybeth nodded. Both local and statewide elections would soon take place and the political atmosphere was charged. On the statewide level, Governor Colter Allen had announced months before that he wasn't going to run for re-election. The reason he gave publicly was to "spend more time with his family," but the actual impetus for his decision was to avoid being exposed for corruption and malfeasance while in office. His denouement had occurred in front of Joe in the state jet as it was parked at the Twelve Sleep County Municipal Airport months before. The real reason for Allen stepping aside wasn't public knowledge. Regardless, most of the voters of the state were pleased to see him go.

Governor Spencer Rulon, who had served two terms prior to Allen, had been drafted to run again and had no serious opposition. Joe welcomed the return of Rulon, with whom he'd had a special, if sometimes baffling, relationship.

"Governor Rulon has asked me to be his AG," Hewitt said. "He wants me to take on the feds in a blizzard of lawsuits. He wants me to bury them in litigation."

"Attorney general?" Marybeth said. "Congratulations."

"Are you going to do it?" Joe asked.

"Yes, but it'll be hell," Hewitt said morosely. "Living in

Cheyenne and dealing with the D.C. Blob every day. It should shorten my life span by a decade or so."

"But you'll be good at it," Joe said.

"Yeah, I will," Hewitt agreed. "Because I hate those federal agencies and bureaucrats with the white-hot heat of a thousand suns. Maybe the first thing I'll do is sue to get the number of grizzly bears down to a manageable population so they aren't running around like maniacs killing our innocent people."

"Good luck with that," Joe said.

"Another thing," Judge Hewitt said as his rare steak sandwich arrived, "I'd like you both to support Jackson Bishop for our new sheriff."

"Your son-in-law?" Joe said.

"That's him. What about it?" Hewitt said while sawing at the steak. "Isn't it a good thing to know personally about the good character of a candidate for sheriff?"

"Sure," Joe said.

"Look, I know you've had a bad run with our local sheriffs. We've had too many chuckleheads around here. Jackson is different. He's competent and experienced."

"Good to hear," Joe said. "A competent sheriff would be a welcome change around here. We haven't had a good one since Mike Reed."

Currently, Bishop was an undersheriff in Park County and married to Hewitt's only daughter. His opponent was Ruthanne Hubbard, who had been the county dispatcher for over twenty years. Hubbard had conducted a not-very-secret affair with the previous sheriff, Scott Tibbs, which had led to Mrs.

Tibbs relocating to California and the sudden retirement of Tibbs himself.

Joe had briefly met Bishop at the Burg-O-Pardner as the man was campaigning door-to-door. Bishop was tall and fit with dark hair, a full mustache, and pale gray eyes that darted over Joe's shoulder to see who else had entered the diner. Joe's instant impression of Bishop was that of a good politician, glib and smooth.

He'd introduced himself by complimenting Joe and saying, "I hear you've had a mixed working relationship with the sheriff's department."

"You could say that," Joe replied.

"Well, I want you to know that I value the job and responsibilities of game wardens. I think you're an important part of the law enforcement community and I would consider you a fellow LEO. I pledge to cooperate with you if you'll make the same pledge to cooperate with me."

"It sounds like you've already got the job," Joe said.

Bishop winked and said, "I have friends in high places."

"JUDGE," MARYBETH SAID to Jackson Bishop's friend in high places while her Cobb salad was placed in front of her, "why are you asking for our support? Joe is the game warden and I'm the library's director. We aren't political."

"No, but you're both honest and straightforward people," Hewitt said. "Folks around here know you can be trusted. And if you come out in support of Jackson, that will mean something in this county."

"I need to stay out of this," Joe said. "It's not Game and Fish business to get involved in local elections. Especially when I need to work closely with whoever wins."

Hewitt waved Joe's statement away with the back of his hand. "This state has barely over a half million people. Everybody knows everybody, and there aren't any of us without conflicts of interest. Hell, Ruthanne was diddling Sheriff Tibbs, and now she's running for his job. You don't think that isn't a conflict? I know you like to operate under the radar, Joe, but sometimes you have to step up."

Joe didn't respond.

"I work for the county," Marybeth said to Hewitt. "The sheriff's department is a part of county government. It wouldn't be ethical for me to weigh in on the election one way or the other."

Judge Hewitt sat back in a huff and glared at them both.

"Just don't oppose him, then," he said. "I'm sure you can do *that*, at least."

"I have no reason to oppose him," Joe said. "That's easy."

"Same here," Marybeth said. "I neither support nor oppose him."

"So it's a small victory, then," Hewitt declared, as if tacking on an amendment to a criminal sentence in his courtroom.

With that, he pushed his empty plate away and stood up.

"I've got to get back to court," he said. "I need to put a fentanyl dealer away. And you know why I need to throw the book at him and send him to Rawlins for the rest of his natural life?"

"No," Joe said.

"Because I can't publicly execute him where he sits," Hewitt said. As he spoke, he patted the bulge under his left arm, where, no doubt, his handgun was holstered.

AFTER JUDGE HEWITT had blown out of the restaurant, Marybeth turned to Joe. "Well, that was weird."

"The AG part or the sheriff part?" Joe asked.

"Both, I guess."

"I agree," Joe said. "I don't know why he thought we had that much influence around here. But I am curious to learn more about Jackson Bishop. I might call the Park County game warden and see what he thinks of him."

"I'll do a little digging myself," Marybeth said. "I know some people in county government in Cody."

As JOE STOOD up from the table and clamped on his hat, he felt his cell phone vibrate in his breast pocket. He took it out.

"It's Jennie," he said to Marybeth. Then: "Hello, Jennie."

The pause was unnaturally long, which to Joe signaled bad news.

"Oh no," Joe said. "Was there another attack?"

"Yes. And like the previous one, this one doesn't make any sense, either."

"Where?" Joe asked.

"Yesterday. North of Rawlins."

"*Rawlins?*" Joe said. "That's two hundred and fifty miles south of here."

"I know."

"That's not bear country," Joe said. As he spoke, he noticed that Marybeth had paused to listen in. There was concern on her face as well.

"Don't I know it," Jennie said. "As far as I know, we've never had an incident this far south."

"Is it our bear?"

"I don't know that, either," she said. "But the MO sounds similar and the photos they've sent me look very familiar. A man walks out of his rural house to go to work in the morning and the bear hits him before he can get into his truck. Tears the guy to shreds and kills him. His head was crushed and it appears to be an incidence of overkill."

"Were there other wounds? Defensive wounds?"

"Yes," she said. "There were deep claw marks on his forearms where it looks like he tried to fight off the attack. His belly was slashed as well."

"That's horrible," Joe said. "Who is the victim?"

He could hear her flipping through her notes, then she said, "Ryan Winner. *Sergeant* Ryan Winner. Big guy in his late forties. He was a CO at the men's prison down there."

OCTOBER 25

The Puritan hated bear-baiting, not because it gave pain to the bear, but because it gave pleasure to the spectators.

—Thomas Babington, Lord Macauley,
The History of England

CHAPTER ELEVEN

Walden, Colorado

THREE HUNDRED AND forty miles south of Saddlestring, Sheridan Pickett learned quickly from the woman behind the counter at the gas station as well as the motel owner that residents of Walden and Jackson County referred to themselves as "North Parkers" and that they were *not* to be confused with the woke elites (many of them new residents) from Denver, Boulder, Aspen, or even nearby Steamboat Springs.

This was tough country—high, wild, and lonesome—and just barely over the Wyoming border. The town of Walden itself had barely six hundred people, and it was the only incorporated municipality in the county. North Parkers lived at over eight thousand feet in elevation and were rimmed to the west by the Park and Sierra Madre ranges, south by the Rabbit Ears Range and the Never Summer Mountains, and east by the Medicine Bow Mountains. The tops of those mountains were already white with snow.

In late October, the location reminded Sheridan strongly of where she'd come from, with its single main street consisting of saloons, shops, eclectic restaurants, and muddy four-wheel-drive pickups parked diagonally against the curb. The busiest enterprise in town seemed to be the wild-game processing facility, with elk hunters lined up along the street with dead animals, antlers bristling from the beds of their trucks. The lone grocery store was located so far out of town that it didn't seem connected to it. A tall and magnificent granite courthouse stood just off the main drag, indicating that at one time somebody had very high hopes for the future of Walden.

She could clearly see that old courthouse when she opened the curtains of her window at the Alpine Motel and fed pieces of road-killed jackrabbit to the five hooded falcons she'd transported to Colorado in her SUV. Two prairie falcons, two red-tailed hawks, and a sleek female peregrine made up her flight of birds.

The raptors were all hooded with leather masks and they stood up straight while grasping the backs of motel chairs with their talons. She'd spread newspaper on the linoleum beneath them for their white squirts of excrement.

THE OWNER OF the Alpine Motel, who had introduced himself as DeWayne Kolb, had white muttonchops and reading glasses

poised on the end of his bulbous nose. He wore baggy jeans and
a faded red union suit top. He'd been obviously fascinated by
both Sheridan and her cargo when she entered the tiny lobby to
check in.

"Hello," she'd said. "Your sign says you allow pets."

"Well, it depends on the pets," he answered. "You've got to
be careful these days. A friend of mine told me he had to fly
across the country sitting next to a lady with her emotional support ferret."

A talker, Sheridan thought.

"I have five birds of prey," she said.

"Birds of prey? Like eagles or something?"

Sheridan detailed the species of the raptors and introduced
herself as a master falconer from Wyoming. She said the birds
were well-behaved and wouldn't do any damage to the motel
room.

"You don't look old enough to be a master *anything*," Kolb
said with a smile.

"That's where you'd be mistaken," she said.

"I didn't mean to offend you," he said. "Truly. I've never met
a master falconer before."

"Well, now you have," Sheridan said. "So can I rent a room
here?"

"How many nights will you need it?" he asked. "I've got a
group of hunters coming in next week that will take all of my
rooms."

"Maybe four nights," she said, handing over her new Yarak,
Inc. credit card. "I'll let you know if that changes."

He ran it through his machine. "I'll charge you for four nights, then. If it turns out to be fewer, I'll back the charges out.

"It would be a pleasure hosting a master falconer in my humble motel," Kolb said, sliding a registration card across the counter. "It's pretty much just elk hunters here this time of year. I'm afraid they come in at all hours and leave early in the morning. They can get kind of rowdy, so I hope they won't disturb you."

"I'm used to being around elk hunters," she said as she filled out the form and handed it back to him. Sheridan felt no need to explain that she had spent her formative years surrounded by hunters, fishermen, and landowners of all stripes. They'd shown up at her house at any time of day.

"Wyoming," he said while reading the card. "Lots of folks around here wish we could become a county in Wyoming instead of Colorado. There's a serious movement to convince Wyoming to annex us and get the libtards in Denver to set us free."

"I see," she said. She'd learned from her father to steer clear of local political movements.

"About the only thing we North Parkers have in common with those people are our green license plates and the income tax we have to pay," he said. "Colorado isn't the place I grew up in anymore. We've been flooded with people from other states, and it's disgusting. I went to a Broncos game last year against the Steelers, and half of the stadium was wearing black and gold and waving those stupid Terrible Towels. And the worst part was they were new residents.

"That's probably more information than you wanted on day one among the North Parkers," he said.

She smiled to herself. He was correct.

"Can I ask what you're doing here? With all those falcons?"

"I'm in the bird abatement business," Sheridan said. "We get hired to help get rid of problem species."

"Interesting," Kolb said. "Your falcons chase away bad birds?"

"Something like that."

"Who are you working for around here, if I may ask?"

"A man named Leon Bottom."

Kolb's eyes got wide upon hearing the name. He asked slyly, "Have you ever met him?"

"No. Why?" In fact, it was Liv who had set up the job.

Kolb shook his head. "I'm not one to gossip, but I think you'll find him kind of . . . unusual."

Sheridan tried to discern what he meant by that, but Kolb deliberately looked away. She'd already pegged the motel owner to be a local gossip, despite his disavowal. If Walden was anything like Saddlestring, half of the town would know about the twenty-something female master falconer staying there by sundown.

"A place like this tends to attract all kinds of different characters," he said.

"That," she said, "isn't unusual to me."

As she opened the door from the lobby to go get her falcons and gear, Kolb said, "If you need anything while you're here, I want you to know that even if the lobby is closed up, I'm here twenty-four seven. All you have to do is pick up the room phone and dial zero."

She turned. "Is there something I should be worried about?"

"Nothing like that," Kolb said quickly. "It's just that the town is a little rambunctious this time of year. Lots of out-of-state hunters drinking whiskey and carrying guns and whooping it up. They might get a little frisky seeing a young woman on her own who looks like you, if you catch my drift. Plus, my brother is the chief of police."

After a long pause and wondering if she should be grateful or offended, Sheridan thanked him for the room.

SHERIDAN TOOK A moment on the way to her Acadia to send a text to her mother and Liv saying that she'd made it and found a room and she would touch base with the client as soon as she could.

Moments later, her phone vibrated with an incoming call. Sheridan guessed that it would be her mother, but it was Liv Romanowski.

"So you made it," Liv said.

"I did."

Sheridan could hear Kestrel jabbering in the background and visualized the toddler being cradled on Liv's hip while she made the call.

"I'll let our clients know you're on-site," Liv said.

"Thank you."

There was a beat before Liv said, "Sheridan, I know this is a really tough time for you. I hope you're doing okay."

Sheridan smiled. The sentiment affected her more than she would have anticipated. "I'm doing okay," she said.

"I know what it's like to be a young woman alone in a strange place. It's important to keep your guard up and that you be alert. This job isn't all-important, and I know how smart you are. So if you feel uncomfortable at any time, for any reason, I want you to come straight back here."

"What about . . ."

"Nate?" Liv said, finishing Sheridan's thought. "Don't worry about Nate. I can handle him."

"Is there something I ought to know that I don't?" Sheridan asked. "About our client?"

"Nothing I haven't told you. I'd never send you on a job if it felt wrong to me. But I've never met this man and he's located in a pretty remote area, from what I understand. So all I'm saying is to be professional and polite, but also on alert."

"I get that," Sheridan said. "Thank you."

"No worries," Liv said.

"Kiss Kestrel for me."

"I'll do that right now," Liv said. Sheridan could hear the kiss over the phone.

SHERIDAN HAD LEFT Twelve Sleep County on the day after Clay Junior's memorial service, which had been held in a tiny cemetery on the hillside that had been there since the founding of the Double Diamond Ranch in the 1880s. She'd found the affair equal parts sad, uncomfortable, and bewildering. People she'd never met—most of whom were Clay Junior's relatives or family friends—had been cautious around her.

What did one say to an almost-fiancée? And how did that almost-fiancée respond when she knew in her heart that the inevitable wedding was never to be?

For the most part, Sheridan had kept her head down and stayed close to her mother and dad. Her emotions that day—and since—had been all over the map. Clay's shocking demise had opened a lane for her to proceed in life without him, and she felt horribly guilty for thinking that. Clay's father held her and cried and said that as far as he was concerned she would always be a part of the family, as if that had ever really been her goal in life. After all, she was perfectly happy being a part of *her* family.

As the peregrine crunched the hollow leg bones of the road-killed rabbit, Sheridan admitted to herself how grateful she was to be away from Saddlestring, Clay Junior's memory, and all of that. She needed a break from it and she welcomed an out-of-state bird abatement assignment.

Before she left, Liv had presented her with the Yarak, Inc. credit card to use for gas, lodging, and other expenses. It was the first time she'd ever had a company card, and she'd vowed not to abuse it.

And she wondered what DeWayne Kolb had meant when he said her client was "unusual."

—————

THE NEVER SUMMER Ranch owned by Leon Bottom was located eight miles west of Walden on a rutted gravel road that wound through swampy bottomland and eight-foot walls of willows. Sheridan drove to it while glancing down at the navigation feature on the screen of her phone in her lap. Through breaks in the willows, she noted both modern multimillion-dollar second homes of newcomers in the meadows above the bottomland and ramshackle homesteads littered with rusted-out pickups and farm machinery that no doubt belonged to hardscrabble old-timers. Mountains framed the valley on three sides.

Again she thought, *Just like home.*

As she bounced over the rough road and her SUV pitched from side to side, she spoke soothing nonsense to the hooded peregrine, the only falcon she had brought with her in case she needed to provide a demonstration. Although most peregrines she'd flown had dispositions that were as steely as an assassin, this one was young and a little agitated by the rough road.

"It'll be fine, sweetie," she cooed to the bird. "It'll all be just fine . . ."

Sheridan passed under an ancient archway that leaned to the left. Although some of the elk antler tines that made up the lettering were missing, she read:

NEV_R _UM_ER _ANCH

———

THE RANCH HEADQUARTERS itself was a collection of aged stone and log buildings scattered across a sagebrush bench framed by timbered foothills. Abandoned vehicles and a rusty Sno-Cat bordered the two-track road on the way to the main house, which was a three-story gabled structure that was higher than it was wide, despite the vast acreage all around it to spread out.

Sheridan had seen similar homes high in the mountains before. They were constructed so that if the snow got so deep on the surface, the residents could conceivably access and exit the house through the second—or third—levels. She'd also seen old outhouses constructed with the same thought in mind.

The only hints at modernity at the Never Summer were the two vehicles parked at odd angles in the ranch yard and the multiple small television and internet satellite dishes mounted to the top side of the headquarters building.

She parked between a four-wheel-drive pickup and an older-model Honda Civic and turned off her engine. The peregrine instantly settled down once they'd stopped. Sheridan cautiously opened the door and stepped out.

Immediately, she sensed that something was seriously amiss. Then she realized what it was: the quiet.

A slight breeze rattled the leaves of cottonwoods bordering the ranch outbuildings, and a red-tailed hawk screeched from miles away.

HER BOOTS CRUNCHED on the gravel as she approached the solid front door of the house. She climbed wooden steps to a veranda and knocked on the door. Nothing.

After a full minute, she made a fist and banged on it. A beat later, she could hear someone inside call out, "I'm coming. Just hold your horses." It was a harsh older female voice.

Sheridan stepped back and tucked her hair behind her ears. The door cracked open about three inches and a single light blue rheumy eye looked out.

"What do you want?"

The woman was shorter than Sheridan by half a foot, with cat-eye glasses and tight gray curls in her hair. Her mouth was pursed into a look of disapproval, highlighted by the web of wrinkles that framed her lips. The small hand that gripped the side of the door to keep it open looked to Sheridan like a talon.

"Hi there," Sheridan said, mustering a smile. "I'm here to see Leon Bottom."

"I asked you what you wanted," the woman said. Not friendly.

"I'm with Yarak, Inc. We're a bird abatement business out of Saddlestring, Wyoming. Mr. Bottom contacted our office about some problem birds here on the ranch. The arrangements were made for me to come here and look it all over and try to fix the problem."

The old woman's eyes narrowed suspiciously. Sheridan felt a little flustered because she had assumed she'd be welcomed instead of questioned.

"Where did you say you were from?" the woman asked.

"Saddlestring, Wyoming."

"And what did you say your name was?"

"Yarak, Inc."

"No, *your* name."

"Well, I didn't say. But I'm Sheridan." She held out her hand.

The old woman didn't reach out to take it. Her watery eyes were unblinking, and they slowly painted their way from Sheridan's face to her boots. Then out to Sheridan's Acadia and license plate, then back to Sheridan's face again.

Sheridan felt a strange chill run through her. She couldn't help but think there was something oddly *familiar* about this woman she knew she'd never met before. Sheridan was good with recalling faces and names. There was something about this woman's eyes and her mannerisms that set off a set of internal alarm bells. Had she encountered her somewhere before? Did she recognize this old woman from a dream, perhaps?

The woman spoke and Sheridan didn't hear what she said. "Sorry, what was that?"

"I said, what is your last name?" the lady asked.

Suddenly, Sheridan decided that the woman must doubt that she was who she said she was or who she was with. Like DeWayne back at the motel, the old woman was having trouble believing that someone so young and female could be a serious person. Sheridan had gotten somewhat used to it when she heard it from men, but it was extra annoying when it came from a woman.

She quickly dug out one of the business cards Liv had had printed recently and handed it through the opening in the door.

"My name is Sheridan Pickett," she said. "And as you can read, I'm a master falconer. Just like I said."

At that, the woman simply glared at her with what looked like terror. Her old pursed mouth opened for a second before snapping shut.

Then the old woman stepped back without another word and pushed the door closed tight.

Sheridan was flummoxed. What had just happened?

Behind her, a man called out, "Greetings! Welcome to the Never Summer Ranch!"

LEON BOTTOM WAS unusual, all right. He was short in stature with an exceptionally long face mounted on a pencil-like neck. His proportions were such that a photo of him would make him appear six foot six instead of five foot five. He was dressed in all black: black jeans, pointy black cowboy boots, a black silk scarf knotted around his neck buckaroo-style, and a black snap-button cowboy shirt decorated with swirls of white embroidery. On his head he wore a black cowboy hat with the brims folded up tight against the side of the crown that appeared much too small for him.

He looked to Sheridan like someone had drawn a cartoon based on the description "drugstore cowboy."

"You must be our falconer," he said, showing her a mouthful of straight but yellow teeth. "I'm so glad you made it."

She introduced herself again and handed the man one of her cards.

"I suppose you'd like to see the barn," he said. "The one filled with a million pooping starlings."

"Yes," she said. "I'd like to see it."

"Follow me."

Sheridan did. As they walked shoulder to shoulder toward the massive old barn, she said, "Do you mind if I ask you a question?"

"Shoot."

"When I arrived I expected a pack of dogs to come greet me," she said. "I've never been on a ranch before in my life where there weren't any dogs."

"That's very perceptive," Bottom said. "I'm sure you're right. I brought my dog with me out here, a little terrier named Juno. He would have rushed out to greet you except a wolf ate him three weeks ago. Did you know we have wolves here in North Park?"

"Yes," she said. Voters in Colorado had agreed that wolves should be reintroduced to the state several years before. She wondered what DeWayne Kolb had to say about that.

"So I'm not getting any more dogs," Bottom said.

As they passed by Sheridan's car, Bottom peered inside and saw the peregrine and asked, "You can do all this with only one falcon?"

"I left the others in town," she said. "I'll bring out as many as I need."

"Where are you staying?" he asked.

"The Alpine."

Bottom grimaced at the name. "That man doesn't like me. Plus, he's a gossip. I'd suggest you steer clear of him."

Sheridan nodded, more to acknowledge her client's advice than to abide by it.

"And I see you met Katy," Bottom said as they neared the barn.

"If Katy is the woman who slammed the door on me, then yes, I met her." Then: "I'm sorry. Is she your mother?"

Bottom chuckled. "No, she's not my mother, but she's been with the family for over forty years. Katy Cotton. Can you believe she's seventy-six years old? And yes, she can get a little cantankerous, especially with strangers."

Sheridan bit her lip, not wanting to say more. Especially about the odd feeling of familiarity she couldn't shake.

"I've owned this ranch for three years, but this is the first time I've spent much time on it," Bottom said, sweeping his arm around to indicate the whole of it. "It's one thing to visit for a couple of weeks in the summer, and a whole other thing to actually live here. This ranch is aptly named."

"Where did you come from?" Sheridan asked.

"Michigan," Bottom said. He spit out the word. "My whole

family is from Michigan, multiple generations of us. But when our governor locked us down because of COVID and decided we couldn't buy garden supplies—*garden supplies*—I knew I'd had enough. I looked to find a place in Idaho, Montana, Wyoming, or Colorado where I could feel free again, and I bought the first place my broker showed me: the Never Summer Ranch. Before that, I'd never even heard of Walden or Jackson County."

"Interesting," Sheridan said. And familiar, she thought. "What did you do back in Michigan?"

He smiled and said, "My family owns a multilevel marketing company. Have you ever heard of Bottom Balm?"

"I think I have."

"Or maybe Bottom Shampoo, Bottom Soap, or Bottom Sunscreen? That's us. No one ever forgets that name, is what we always told our sales associates."

"I kind of thought it was a joke," Sheridan said.

"It was," Bottom said. "But it worked. And when my parents decided to retire, Bottom, Inc. went to us kids—my brother, my sister, and me. It got real ugly fast, and they weren't unhappy to see me move west.

"I always wanted to be a cowboy," Bottom said, "but it's even better to be a rancher, you know?"

"I understand. So how does Katy fit in?"

"Katy raised me, my brother, and my sister. She was more a mom to us than our actual mother. She cooks, cleans, and looks after everything. She jumped at the chance to come with me. She had no real family ties in Michigan after her husband died five years ago, and she told me she had roots out here and wanted to get back.

"So," Bottom said, "lucky me."

"She doesn't seem to be enjoying it," Sheridan said.

Bottom laughed and said, "Maybe you just met her on a bad day."

SHERIDAN HAD NEVER seen so many starlings in one structure in her life, she told Bottom. It was truly unusual to find so many problem birds packed together like that in every crevice and on every rafter. There were thousands of them, and the cacophony of noise was numbing. The floor of the barn was white with bird excrement, and the entire building smelled of it.

Sheridan had to shout to be heard. "You probably know that European starlings are an invasive species in North America."

"I didn't know that," Bottom shouted back. "I just know they're obnoxious."

"Individually, I really like them," Sheridan confessed. "They're beautiful birds and they're really smart. But the trouble starts when they mass up by the hundreds, which is the situation you've got here.

"Not only that, but they displace native birds and they can carry diseases," she said. "They can contaminate water and livestock feed, and their excrement is full of bacteria and parasites. They are *not* good birds to have around in this kind of number."

"Do you think you can chase them away?" Bottom asked her.

"I'm sure of it," she said. "But I'll need all my falcons to do it."

They stepped outside the barn so they could talk normally.

Bottom said, "I've tried everything I can think of to get rid of them. I tried to smoke them out, scare them with fireworks. I've shot a hundred of them with a pellet gun. Nothing seems to work. And then I heard about your bird abatement company."

She said, "I'm glad you did. Starlings are either too stupid or too arrogant to be scared away. But there's one thing they're terrified of."

Sheridan explained that the imprint of a falcon in flight was hardwired into the tiny brains of the species from the moment they hatched. They knew instinctually that falcons could, and would, kill them with ease. Whether in the wild or from the glove of an experienced falconer, starlings knew that their only defense was to flee.

She said, "Once I put my birds up, those starlings might all leave at once in a big black cloud. Or it may take a couple of days."

"That would be wonderful," Bottom said. Then, hugging himself, he said, "I knew it would work. I'm so *brilliant*."

Which was what a man used to great wealth might say, she thought. He didn't praise the plumber for unclogging his toilet or the electrician for getting his lights to work again. Instead, he praised himself for calling the plumber or electrician.

She also thought that Liv back at Yarak, Inc. HQ knew what she was doing by sending Sheridan south instead of Nate. Nate might have twisted Bottom's ears off and fed them to his birds by now.

"YOU KNOW YOU can stay with us here on the ranch," he offered as they walked from the barn toward Sheridan's SUV. "We have four empty bedrooms in the house and I can deduct the rent from your fee. There's no need to waste your money with Kolb in town."

She thanked him for the offer and didn't say that there was no way she wanted to share a house with Katy, whoever she was. Or Leon Bottom, for that matter.

"I'll be back tomorrow with the full flight," she told him.

"This I want to see," he said enthusiastically. While he said it he actually rubbed his hands together in anticipation. "A black cloud of starlings flying off to Nebraska, or some such place. This I really want to see."

Then: "I'm glad you said it might take a couple of days to get rid of them all. I have an appointment with my banker in Fort Collins tomorrow that I can't miss, but I'll be back tomorrow evening and around the second day."

Sheridan knew that Fort Collins was a hundred miles to the east over the top of the mountains on Poudre Canyon Road. She was used to people driving distances like that for daily business transactions.

"I can't trust the local bankers," he said, as if she'd asked him for his reasoning on why he used an out-of-town bank. "When I get back, I hope you don't mind if I watch?"

"I don't mind," she said. "But give me lots of space. The falcons get jittery if there are people around they don't know."

"I'll be sneaky," Bottom said, crossing his heart. "I swear it."

THERE WAS A note on Sheridan's windshield, pinned against the glass by the wiper blade. Scrawled in old-fashioned cursive was:

Go away and never come back.

Sheridan had no doubt who had written it.

CHAPTER TWELVE

Little Laramie Valley

IT WAS ON late afternoons like this, when the clouds were low and close and had closed a lid over the Snowy Range and the sun could not yet break through, that former Twelve Sleep County prosecutor Dulcie Schalk hurt the most. She didn't know if it was low-pressure, atmospheric feelers from a coming snowstorm, a change in the humidity, or a combination of those factors that made her bones and muscles ache and took her back to that incident four years before when her life had changed on the steps of the county courthouse.

Whatever it was that caused her so much discomfort, she did as she always did and fought her way through it. She refused to let the pain slow her down. She walked along the footpath that paralleled the meandering left bank of the Little Laramie River through the family ranch she'd grown up on. As she did, Dulcie grimaced and put one foot in front of the other. Buster, her two-year-old golden retriever, kept his nose down in the cheat-grass that rimmed the path, his tail wagging like a metronome.

She wished Buster was smarter, or at least more intuitive and alert. He was very affectionate, which was nice, but when he was outside with her he lived in his own special world where deer droppings were snack food and distant airplanes in the clouds sent him into barking fits. When she took a break to gather her strength to keep going, Buster would stop and look over his shoulder and implore her to pick up the pace.

"Don't worry about me," she said through gritted teeth. "Just keep a look out for skunks." Knowing by experience that if Buster encountered a skunk he would try to play with it until the creature unloaded on him.

ALTHOUGH SHE WASN'T one for introspection, Dulcie Schalk could never have conceived of the path her life had taken. And although it hadn't gone as planned, she wasn't bitter or regret-ful. But that wasn't to say that at times she wasn't furiously angry. She channeled that anger into her physical and mental recovery, and her doctors said she was well ahead of schedule. On days like this, though, she wasn't so sure.

Top of her class at the University of Wyoming law school, the youngest county attorney in the state, a ninety-five percent conviction rate in court, great friends including Marybeth Pickett, and a future so bright everybody could see it.

Then it happened. And everything changed.

———

THERE HAD BEEN six of them together that day. A high-powered meeting in the conference room of the courthouse to discuss the incursion of Sinaloa cartel *sicarios* into the Mountain West. Dulcie, Sheriff Mike Reed, FBI deputy director Sunnie Magazine, two special agents from D.C. in Jeremiah Sandburg and Don Pollock, and state FBI agent in charge Chuck Coon.

At a table usually used for hosting the birthday parties for county employees, a strategy was laid out for identifying and apprehending the violent newcomers who had left a trail of blood and bodies from New Mexico to Wyoming.

As the meeting broke up in the late afternoon, Coon had suggested they all walk down the block for a drink at the Stockman's Bar. Although Dulcie wasn't fond of fraternizing with too many members of law enforcement—things often got too *familiar*—she'd agreed to go with them to maintain the comity of the mission and the newly formed team.

Coon hung back at the door to chat with a man called Stovepipe, who handled the X-ray machine and provided half-hearted security for the building. The other five pushed through the heavy doors and started down the courthouse steps in no particular order.

That was when two *sicarios* sitting in a parked vehicle across the street powered down their windows and opened fire with a submachine gun and a semiautomatic shotgun. There was a maelstrom of bullets and pellets, none sharply aimed, but the blizzard of lead cut down the entire group before any of the agents could draw their own weapons to retaliate.

Dulcie clearly recalled the stuttering *rat-tat-tat* of the automatic weapon and the throaty *boom*s of the shotgun. Bullets pocked the granite steps all around her, and pellets filled the air with what sounded like angry bees. There was a wild dance of death and the hollow thump of rounds and pellets hitting bodies on each side of her, and those sounds would punctuate her nightmares for months afterward.

Sheriff Reed, FBI deputy director Sunnie Magazine, and Agent Don Pollock were killed instantly. Agent Jeremiah Sandburg took two rounds in his torso and a dozen pellets in his back. Dulcie was hit *five* times—in the shoulder, forearm, pelvis, thigh, and right ankle. Of the FBI contingent, only Sandburg survived. Somehow, Dulcie had, too.

IT HAD TAKEN three years of surgeries, physical therapy, counseling, and sheer effort to get back to where she was today. On some subjects, her entire outlook had changed. She'd made a habit of immediately turning off television shows where the actors were shot in one scene and had recovered by the next. Dulcie had no patience anymore for cartoonish violence in books, movies, or television, and she despised Hollywood writers who casually created scenarios where humans were chopped down like cordwood, with no afterthought to the toll of the gunplay.

She knew from experience that it wasn't like that at all. Bullets did tremendous damage to bones, cartilage, muscles, organs, and nervous systems. And that was just the physical part.

Getting over that kind of sudden and unanticipated carnage and seeing a good man like Sheriff Reed bleed out—*in his wheelchair*—would stay with her for the rest of her life, despite the mental scar tissue that was slowly, *slowly* forming over her memory.

THE CLOUDS WERE low and dark over the mountains. There were breaks in the shadow that had been thrown over Dulcie's career, shafts of sunlight that had broken through. She'd decided against running for office again in the immediate future, but she'd been approached by several good law firms about joining their ranks. One offer in particular, from a rising Laramie firm, seemed promising. She could still live at the ranch, and they were flexible when it came to her schedule.

"What do you think, Buster?" she asked. "Should I do it?" Then: "Don't worry. I promise we'll still have our daily walks."

As she said it, she knew it might be a lie. Dulcie Schalk was a hard charger. She'd always been. She knew if she immersed herself in the firm like she probably would that she'd be lucky to ever make it home by nightfall.

"That being the case," she said aloud, "we'll move our walks to the early morning."

Buster seemed to be okay with that.

Another ray of light was the prospect of romance—something she'd avoided while building her résumé. Brandon was good-natured and reliable and he made her laugh. He had a little girl from a previous marriage whom Dulcie adored. Tom was a hard charger like Dulcie, but was as dedicated to his church and volunteering for Meals on Wheels as he was to his accounting firm.

Both men seemed to be more serious about her than she was about them, even though she'd made it quite clear that she'd vowed to take things slowly with both. Her aim was to enjoy dates with them, get to know them well, be on the lookout for red flags and deal-killing behavior, and not operate on a time-table or with an agenda.

So far, so good.

THE WALK DULCIE took was two miles along the Little Laramie River. When she reached the bridge, she cut across the bull pasture and worked her way back toward the house along the inside of their fence line. On her walks, she'd encountered elk, moose, deer, antelope, beavers, otters, coyotes, foxes, rabbits, ducks, and geese. And occasionally trespassers, which was why she always carried her cell phone and a slim Ruger LCP Max .380 ACP pistol in her back pocket. Recently, she'd added a canister of bear spray because of the fatal grizzly attacks that had occurred in northern Wyoming and as close as Rawlins.

Shadows lengthened across the footpath as she made her way

back to the house. This was the time of day she loved the most: when the wind died down and the sun ballooned before ducking behind the Snowy Range.

As she passed the barbed-wire gate in the fence about a half mile from home, Dulcie noticed that the wire loop that held the gate to the post on the top was askew. It was latched, but not horizontally. Her dad, she knew, was a stickler for closing gates the same way every time. This wasn't like him.

Dulcie looked carefully at the two-track road that led from the gate into the thick willows in front of her. Was there a new tire track? She couldn't be sure. The dirt was hard and packed down, and there hadn't been any rain in weeks.

It was possible, she knew, that someone had accessed the ranch by the side border fence. It happened, especially during hunting season, which was now. If someone had come on their place during the day, they'd closed the gate behind them. Meaning they were still somewhere inside, or they'd left and tried to make it look like they'd never been there.

While hoping it was the latter, she reached back and patted the Ruger for assurance, then drew her cell phone and held it in her right hand before proceeding.

Since it was nearly six in the evening, she knew her seventy-five-year-old father, Vernon, would be settling into his recliner to watch Fox News. But if he received a call from Dulcie, he'd freeze his program, grab a Winchester or Ruger Ranch Rifle, and be there in minutes. He'd always looked out for his own, and especially so when it came to his only daughter.

———

THE WILLOWS WERE thick and tall on each side of the path and shrouded in shadow. Buster led the way and Dulcie followed. Then the dog stopped and backed up, growling.

This had happened before when a cow moose and her calf were hiding in the thick brush. They'd nearly scared Dulcie to death when the two animals busted out of the cover and loped away down the road.

"What is it, Buster?" she asked.

The fur on the back of Buster's neck was up and stiff.

"Either go forward or come back," she said. "We can go around the willows and get to the house the long way."

Apparently because he was ready to eat, Buster continued on the two-track. But his stride was wary. She wished she could trust his instincts more than she did.

Dulcie followed Buster into the willows as the path took a sharp left.

As she rounded the corner, it happened all too fast.

She got a glimpse of something big, boxy, and dense hidden in the high brush to her right.

When she turned to face it there was a sharp snapping sound and a tremendous *WHOOSH*, and the last thing she ever saw were open jaws with daggerlike teeth coming straight for her face.

OCTOBER 26

Wild, dark times are rumbling toward us, and the prophet who wishes to write a new apocalypse will have to invent entirely new beasts, and beasts so terrible that the ancient animal symbols of Saint John will seem like cooing doves and cupids in comparison.

—Heinrich Heine, *Lutezia; or Paris*, 1854

CHAPTER THIRTEEN

Bighorn National Forest

JOE SPENT THE morning doing game warden things, but his mind was elsewhere. He'd left before dawn with Daisy in the cab of his pickup and a sack lunch. For four hours, he checked hunters for proper licenses, had cups of coffee at elk camps with guides angry that their clients had canceled at the last minute, and tried to calm down nervous landowners. All anyone wanted to talk about was the grizzly bear attacks, and Joe didn't blame them.

There was no news from Jennie Gordon.

WHEN HE RECEIVED a call from dispatch that a hunter on the hotline had excitedly reported that he and his buddies had "killed the beast," Joe pulled over to the side of the Forest Service road and opened his notepad.

"Could you please repeat that?" he said.

The dispatcher had a tinny voice, and she said, "The RP claims that they encountered the target grizzly bear this morning and that they killed it and took the carcass back to their camp. They're going to remain there until you arrive and provide confirmation."

Joe's heart leapt. "What's their location?"

"Crazy Woman Campground."

"Let them know I'm about fifteen minutes away."

"Ten-four."

JOE SPED ON the well-maintained gravel road and shot by the sign identifying the campground. It wasn't difficult to identify the reporting party, not only because they were the only hunters camped there, but because of the way the three men were acting: fist-pumping, howling at the sky in joy, and slapping each other on their backs.

He parked next to a four-wheel-drive SUV with Illinois plates and told Daisy to stay put. The camp consisted of the vehicle, a battered camper trailer, an ATV, and the standard Forest Service picnic table and raised firepit. Two of the men turned to him, one with his arm around the other's shoulder. The third beamed and approached Joe as he climbed out of his pickup.

"We fucking got him," the man announced. "We got him this morning down by the creek."

The hunter had a pudgy frame and a full red beard. He was dressed in bloody camo and a blaze-orange stocking cap. The two men behind him were also in full camo clothing, one a dark-haired beanpole with thick black-framed glasses and the other a wiry bald man with a shoulder holster and a fixed-blade knife that hung from his belt to his knee.

"I'm game warden Joe Pickett. Are you the reporting party?"

"Name's Buck Lewis," the bearded man said, "and I'm the one who killed the beast and called your office." As he said it, he raised his chin and puffed out his chest.

"Show me," Joe said.

"This way," Lewis said, turning on his heel.

Joe waited until all three hunters grouped and strode toward a copse of lodgepole pine at the back of the campsite. He remained five paces behind them, a precaution he'd learned from years on the job. Stay far enough back and to the side so that he could keep a close eye on them and so they couldn't easily jump him.

"We've been up here elk hunting for four days," Lewis said over his shoulder as he walked. "Haven't hardly seen nothin' worth shooting at. It makes sense to me now—those elk are *smart*. They don't want to be in the same area as a killer bear on the loose.

"So we were hunting the creek," the man continued, "and I heard a crashing in the trees up ahead of me. I was jumpy— who wouldn't be?—when I saw him up around a bend. I didn't wait for him to charge and tear me a new one, so I shot him right here." As he said it, Lewis cupped himself with his right hand under his left armpit. "Got him in the lungs or heart. He roared and tried to run off, but I blasted him two more times and he went down. Scariest damned thing I ever experienced."

As they entered the stand of trees, Joe could see the outline of a heavy teardrop-shaped form hanging from a crossbeam. The hunters had obviously dragged it to their camp from the creek with the ATV he'd observed, then hoisted it by its back legs into the air with a chain.

"Is there some kind of reward or something?" Lewis asked.

Joe put his hands on his hips and sighed. He studied the bear and recalled once again how much a hanging bear carcass resembled that of a heavily muscled man. Blood dripped from the red-stained teeth into a dark puddle on the pine needles below.

"No reward, I'm afraid," Joe said through clenched teeth. "But I will be writing you a citation for killing a female black bear without a proper license."

"A *black* bear?" Lewis said, his shoulders slumping. "How in the hell am I supposed to know that?"

"He's a she," the tall skinny hunter said to his bald buddy. "What the hell did we do?"

"*We* didn't do anything," his buddy replied. "Buck gets all the credit."

"Well, shit," Buck said.

"Sorry to ruin your morning," Joe said as he drew his ticket book out of his back pocket. "But you need to know what you're shooting at. This bear is half the size of a mature grizzly, and there's no hump on her back."

"Well, shit," Buck said again.

An hour later, with the confiscated dead black bear in the bed of his pickup, Joe wound his way to the top of a rock promontory with a three-hundred-and-sixty-degree view of the foothills and Bighorn Mountains and parked. He felt a little sorry for Buck Lewis and his friends, as he always did when he cited someone for being ignorant instead of malicious. The three Illinois hunters had been cooperative if remorseful, and they'd helped him load the carcass into his vehicle. Lewis had asked about good places to eat in Saddlestring, since he didn't feel like hunting anymore.

"You've sort of ruined it for me," he told Joe.

"You ruined it for yourself," the bald hunter said.

"Yes, I did," Lewis lamented. "Shit."

Joe clamped a spotting scope to the open window of his truck and scoped the timber for a while before feeding Daisy dry dog food in her travel bowl on the brown grass surface and pouring her water out of a gallon jug he kept in the bed of his pickup.

It was a fine fall day, crisp and clear, full of sun and very little wind. The air was perfumed with pine, lowland sagebrush, and slightly decayed aspen leaves from where they'd fallen. Eleven miles in the distance he could see the wooded curves of the Twelve Sleep River. Beyond that, the town of Saddlestring twinkled in the sun and appeared in the valley like a handful of broken glass scattered on the prairie.

He'd filled his briefcase with material about grizzly bears, and as he ate his sandwich and apple, he read. Although he knew a lot about the traditional species in his district, grizzlies were a new thing. Joe thought if he were better acquainted with them, he might be able to get a handle on what was going on and what might happen next.

Jennie Gordon had provided Joe with a compendium of her studies and observations boiled down to bullet points.

Some items he read out loud to Daisy, who appeared to listen to him:

"'The *Ursus arctos horribilis* are omnivores that hibernate five to seven months each year and emerge in April or early May . . .'

"'Grizzlies are variable colors from blonde to nearly black and they have a pronounced muscular hump on their backs . . .'

"'Males weigh from four hundred to seven hundred and fifty pounds, females from two hundred and ninety to four hundred pounds. Males live up to twenty-two years, females up to twenty-six . . .'

"'On average,'" he read, "'females have two cubs per litter, but they can have as many as four. The mother cares for the cubs for two years . . .'

"'Grizzles can run up to thirty-five miles per hour . . .'

"'The bite force of a grizzly bear is one thousand, one hundred and sixty pounds per inch. That compares to a hippo at one thousand, eight hundred PSI, an alligator at two thousand, one hundred and twenty-five PSI, or a human at a measly one hundred and sixty-two PSI . . .'

"'Our best estimates are that there are at least one thousand, one hundred grizzly bears in the Greater Yellowstone Ecosystem and at least seven hundred in the State of Wyoming . . .'

"'Bear attacks on regular prey or livestock are unique in that they kill with bites along the spine. Human injuries are usually to the head and face, although there are often defensive wounds on the hands and arms as well if the person fights back.'

"'Grizzles become quickly "food-conditioned," meaning that once they enjoy the taste of human food they will actively continue to seek it out . . .'

"'The bears "know" they're not supposed to attack a human and they'll usually try to steer clear. But once they've attacked in a predatory fashion, their natural resistance to doing it again may decrease . . .'

"'We average over two hundred confirmed conflicts between grizzly bears and humans annually . . .'

"'Bears can smell scents for several miles . . .'

"'The home range of a grizzly bear can stretch as far as six hundred square miles, and some are known to roam even farther. Young males tend to be more adventurous . . .'

"'Mature grizzlies tend to have two- to four-inch claws and up to three-inch teeth . . .'"

Joe shook his head and repeated, "Three. Inch. Teeth."

Then he lowered the study to his lap and shivered.

AFTER DEPOSITING THE black bear in a specially designated county landfill, he drove down the promontory to continue his tour of elk camps on the western side of the forest, when the phone in his breast pocket vibrated with an incoming call. The screen read: Nate.

It was rare for Nate to call him, or for Nate to use his phone at all. For reasons Joe didn't quite understand, Nate was suspicious of cell phones and was convinced that a shadowy federal agency was always listening in. Because of that, Nate tended to be maddeningly vague at times.

"Hey there," Joe said.

There was a long pause. Nate was prone to them.

"Nate?" Joe finally asked.

"I'm up in the hills looking at a situation develop that you might want to check out."

"What kind of situation?"

"It's a distance away. But there's an older gentleman who appears to be staking out an outdoor toilet in a public campground," Nate said. "I think you know him."

"*What?* What are you talking about? Who is this guy?"

"You'll probably want to check this out for yourself," Nate said.

Joe sighed. "Okay, where are you?"

"Remember that cliff face by Staghorn Creek that Sheridan and I scouted last year looking for falcon nests?"

"Yup."

"I'm up on top of it. The situation I told you about is down below me in the campground. I'm watching it through binoculars."

"Got it," Joe said. "I'm probably twenty minutes away."

"Do you know the road to get up here?" Nate asked. "It's a

crappy old logging road the Forest Service tried to block off to the public. Well, I cleared it on the way up."

"Please don't tell me things like that," Joe said.

Nate chuckled and punched off.

NATE HAD, IN fact, pushed aside downed trees that had been placed across the old road and had cut through other logs with a chain saw. His friend had also flattened two ROAD CLOSED: NO ACCESS signs placed along the old two-track by the Forest Service. Joe rolled his eyes as he passed them.

He said to Daisy, "And Nate wonders why the feds are always after him."

JOE FOUND NATE's location on the rim of the cliff. His dented-up Jeep was parked between two large boulders and there was a pile of items heaped on the ground that Nate used for scouting falcon nests: climbing rope, harnesses, and other climbing gear. Joe still felt a chill from the year before when he'd witnessed Sheridan rappelling down the sheer cliff face like a spider setting mesh bow net traps near nests to capture live falcons.

Nate was sitting on the edge of the cliff with his feet dangling over the side and his broad back to Joe. He'd shed his jacket to the side and Joe could see that Nate was wearing his shoulder holster with his massive five-shot .454 Casull revolver strapped across his midsection.

"I'm not going to sit there beside you," Joe said to Nate as he approached warily.

Nate had no fear of heights and wasn't bothered by the fact that below his climbing boots there was a straight two-hundred-foot drop to the rocks of the Staghorn Creek.

Instead of responding, Nate handed his Zeiss binoculars over his shoulder to Joe, who took them.

"Down there," Nate said, pointing toward the gravel parking lot of the Forest Service campground about a half mile away. Campsites extended from it into the timber in every direction.

Joe took the glasses and carefully focused in. There were two vehicles in the parking area: a muddy newer-model F-350 ranch truck and a white Range Rover. The Range Rover was parked haphazardly by a brick outhouse, and both front doors were agape. The F-350 was about fifty yards away from the outhouse. Its driver's-side door was hanging open.

Joe recognized both vehicles. "Uh-oh," he said. "I'm glad you called me. The Range Rover belongs to the Mama Bears and the pickup looks like the ranch truck driven by Clay Hutmacher."

As Joe said it, Hutmacher appeared from behind the outhouse, where he'd previously been out of view. The rancher circled the facility and seemed to be shouting at it. He was too far away for Joe to hear any of the words.

Hutmacher had a lever-action rifle in his right hand, the weapon upturned with the barrel resting on his shoulder.

"Who are the Mama Bears?" Nate asked.

"Grizzly bear activists from Jackson. I met them last week."

Nate moaned and said, "Hell, if I'd have known that, I wouldn't have called you and just let Clay finish them off."

"Again, please don't tell me things like that."

"Are you going down there?"

"Yup."

"Take it easy on Clay," Nate said, leaning back on his hands and peering over his shoulder. "He's kind of a blowhard at times, but he's lost a son and he's probably a little out of his head."

"I'm well aware," Joe said. "I just hope he hasn't hurt or threatened anyone." Then: "Thanks for calling me. Let's pray this ends in a good way."

Nate agreed and Joe returned the binoculars. "I'll be watching," Nate said. "And if you get into any trouble down there, things will get Western real fast."

Joe squinted at the distance between the cliff and the campground. Clay Hutmacher looked like an ant from that distance. Could Nate actually make a kill shot from there?

"I've done it before," Nate said, as if he'd heard Joe's thought.

As Joe turned toward his pickup, Nate said, "Come by my house when this is all over, Joe. I'll pour you a bourbon. I have a theory about this bear you're chasing."

"Is it different from your last theory?"

"It's more nuanced."

Joe couldn't dismiss his friend. Nate often had insights into wild predators and prey that were unique to him and him alone. He'd also shown the ability to summon certain creatures at certain times that Joe couldn't explain using logic.

"I'll come by," Joe said.

Nate chinned toward the campground situation below and said, "Don't do anything stupid, Joe."

"HOLD ON," JOE said to Daisy as he shot down the slope. She braced herself by placing her front paws on the dashboard.

There was no way to drive directly to the Staghorn Creek campground except to backtrack and take the Forest Service road that skirted the mountain. Other older roads through the national forest had also been blocked by felled logs and dirt berms to deny easy access.

The old logging road was rougher going down than it had been coming up, and Joe cursed as he cut a turn in the timber too tightly and a pine branch smacked his passenger mirror and flattened it to the side of his pickup. He tapped on the brakes to regain control. Time, he thought, wasn't on his side.

Finally, he shot past the upended NO ACCESS signs and fishtailed onto the Forest Service road toward the campground.

"Take it easy, Clay," he whispered as he drove. "Take it easy . . ."

Bouncing in and out of ruts that had been created since the fall rains, Joe cleared a hill and plummeted down the other side. Ahead of him, through densely packed lodgepole pine trees, he caught glimpses of the white Range Rover, the F-350, and the blond-brick outhouse in the center of the clearing.

Clay Hutmacher stood facing the metal door of the women's toilet. He was bent forward at the waist and shouting. Hutmacher turned when he heard Joe's pickup enter the clearing and squinted at the unwanted encroachment. Joe registered both pain and anger in his face. He looked exhausted and desperate.

Joe parked behind a large wooden sign posted with campsite rules and regulations and swung out of his pickup. He envisioned the scenario that had likely developed in front of him:

The Mama Bears had been chased into the campsite, had exited their vehicle, and fled to the sanctity of the outdoor toilet with Hutmacher in pursuit. The women had scampered to the facility in such a hurry that they hadn't even closed the doors of the Range Rover. Hutmacher had likely found the toilet door locked when he tried to open it, and he'd circled the facility, yelling at them to come out.

Joe stepped cautiously around the campground sign with his hands up, palms showing. "Clay, what's going on here?"

"Joe, I don't need your help."

Hutmacher, who never appeared outside without his hat, was hatless. His hair was matted and wild and his eyes were rimmed with red. He held the Winchester down at his right side with the muzzle pointing toward the gravel between him and Joe.

Then Hutmacher swung the rifle toward the outhouse and pointed at it with the barrel. "They've been bushwhacking me," he said. His words slurred and Joe recognized that Clay had been drinking hard—probably for days. "They've been fucking around with me, torturing me until I finally snapped. Now it's their turn."

"Slow down," Joe said, approaching with caution. "Slow down and tell me what the problem is."

"These two rich ladies have no business here," Hutmacher

said. "I've been hunting the bear that killed my boy, since you folks can't seem to do it. Every night I set traps, and every morning I find them sprung. The sticks they use to trip them are still in the jaws. My trail cams are all disabled, and when I'm stalking that grizzly on the Double D, they shoot fireworks in the air to scare him off. Two nights ago, they let the air out of the tires on my truck so I couldn't get off the place when I wanted to.

"Not only that, but my phone won't stop ringing from assholes all over the country calling me to tell me to forgive the bear. Someone posted my profile and private number online! I don't even look at my phone or email anymore, because it's full of messages and emails from these fucking environmentalists telling me what to do.

"So I laid a trap for them last night," Hutmacher said, his eyes growing wild. "I set some snares down by the river and camped out all night in the trees to see what would happen. And what do you suppose happened?"

"You tell me," Joe said.

Hutmacher pumped the rifle toward the outhouse for emphasis and said, "I wake up and see these two old lunatics tiptoeing through the trees to trip the snares. One of them does it while the other one records it on her phone so they can show their social media followers what big heroes they are."

"They were trespassing on the Double D?" Joe asked.

"Damned right," Hutmacher said. "And I chased them all the way here. Now they're barricaded in this shitter and it's time to face the music. I want them to come out."

From inside the outhouse, either Lynn Fowler or Jayce Calhoun shouted, "We are *not* old lunatics. How dare you?" Then: "Game warden, is that you?"

"It's me," Joe said.

"He's crazy. It stinks in here. He said he'd throw us in the pit!"

"*Head first*," Clay added with a maniacal grin.

"Let's all calm down," Joe said. "Clay, please put the rifle down on the ground."

Hutmacher started to argue, but then dropped his head, apparently defeated. His eyes pleaded to Joe for understanding, and Joe nodded. Then Hutmacher lowered the rifle.

"That bear killed my boy," he said. "They just don't understand that, or they don't care. All they've done is torture me for days. There's something seriously wrong with them. They need to go back among their own kind in Jackson Hole. This is no place for them and their lunatic ideas."

Joe approached the ranch foreman and placed his hands on his shoulders and slowly turned him around. Hutmacher offered no resistance as Joe pulled the rancher's hands behind his back and placed handcuffs on his wrists. He didn't cinch the cuffs too tightly. Joe could smell whiskey on Hutmacher's breath since he was so close to him.

Joe said softly to Hutmacher, "It'll be okay. I'll get you someplace where you can sleep it off, Clay." Then to the outhouse, "You can come out now."

"Has he been arrested?"

"He's detained," Joe replied.

"Detained," Hutmacher echoed, more to himself than Joe. "*I'm* the one detained," he said with sadness. "It just ain't fair."

The bolt was thrown inside the women's restroom and the door opened an inch. Joe could see Lynn Fowler's eye appear in the crack.

"Are you sure he won't hurt us?" she asked.

"I'm sure."

The door opened the rest of the way and the Mama Bears appeared. They looked disheveled and shaky.

"It was horrible in there," Jayce Calhoun said, wiping her eyes. Then to Joe, "All we were doing was trying to give Tisiphone a fighting chance to survive, after all she's been through."

"*Enough* about Tisiphone," Joe barked. It startled both women. "We don't even know if that was the bear or where it went. This man lost his son and you've been harassing him on private land. It's a game to you, but it's not a game to him."

"You don't need to use that tone," Fowler sniffed.

"See what I'm dealing with?" Hutmacher asked.

To the Mama Bears, Joe said, "I'm going to get Clay in my pickup and take him into town. Then I'm going to come back here and cite you both for trespassing, vandalism, and harassment. We also have a law against interfering with the lawful pursuit of wildlife, which is what this grizzly is.

"Then," he said, "I suggest you both get in your Range Rover and go home. Your game is over, and believe me when I say that this is for your safety, too. You two aren't exactly the most popular folks in Twelve Sleep County right now."

The Mama Bears were speechless.

———

AFTER CALLING INTERIM sheriff Elaine Beveridge and alerting her that he'd be bringing Clay Hutmacher in to the county jail, Joe turned to his friend in the passenger seat to discuss the potential charges against him. Joe's job provided him with plenty of discretion, and he had no intention of throwing the book at Hutmacher.

In response, Hutmacher snored loudly, his head slumped forward with his chin on his chest. A string of saliva ran from his bottom lip to his belt buckle.

"Sleep it off," Joe said.

Right then, Marybeth called. He punched her up and his eyes got wide when she said, "Dulcie's dead. *Dulcie.* That grizzly bear got her, Joe."

CHAPTER FOURTEEN

Thermopolis

DALLAS CATES AND Axel Soledad lounged in the far corner of the deep end of the indoor hot springs mineral pool while wisps of slightly sulfur-smelling steam rose from the water. Gentle waves lapped at them, the disturbance emanating from the splashing of a young American Indian family in the shallow end. Cates could barely make them out through the steam, their forms rendered into shadowy outlines. A young mother and her four- or five-year-old twins. A boy and a girl. The girl was shrill and her cries cut right through the stillness of the late afternoon.

Thermopolis, or "Thermop," as Wyoming residents called it, had fewer than three thousand people. Its claim to fame was the large volume of geothermal water that came out of the ground and filled a number of public and private pool facilities. Hellie's Tepee Pools, where Cates and Soledad were located, was a large geodesic dome-like structure with diving boards and a curved plastic waterslide and very few visitors this time of day.

Thermopolis was only one hundred and thirty-eight miles southwest of Saddlestring over the top of the Bighorn Mountains. Legend had it that it took "twelve sleeps" for the Native American Indians to make the trek on foot and horseback, thus the eventual name of Twelve Sleep County.

The drive would be less than three hours in Bobbi Johnson's vehicle.

BECAUSE SOUND CARRIED across the water in the indoor facility, both men spoke in whispers.

"She doesn't like me, I don't think," Soledad said.

"Who, Bobbi?"

"Yeah, Bobbi."

"She doesn't like anyone," Cates said. "Especially not LOR."

"That's obvious. If those two got in a knife fight, I'd bet on her."

"Me too."

"I don't think she likes this whole deal," Soledad said, using his chin to sweep around the facility to include them all. "She doesn't like sharing you with me, and especially not LOR, for that matter."

"She'll get through it," Cates said. "She doesn't have anywhere else to go."

"That's harsh," Soledad chuckled.

"It is, but it's true."

"She won't talk, will she? Do you trust her to keep her mouth shut?"

Cates filled his cupped hands with warm water and raised them over his head to soak himself. As he smoothed down his hair, he said, "Bobbi knows what would happen if she turned on me. On us. Plus, she knows she's implicated. She'll keep her mouth shut."

"You know her better than I do," Soledad said.

Cates shrugged. "I don't know her all that well, but I know people like her. I just spent the last few years with them."

"Where did you find her?"

"She found me," Cates said with a snort. "She sent me a bunch of letters when I was in Rawlins. It kind of escalated from there."

"She likes bad boys, I guess."

"She doesn't like you, though," Cates said, and Soledad agreed.

Bobbi Johnson also apparently didn't like the mineral water. She sat in a lounge chair in a rented one-piece swimsuit, looking at her phone.

A few minutes before, Cates had seen LOR, in his bright orange rental suit and flip-flops, try to sit next to her. She'd told him to fuck off loud enough that the mother tried to cover the ears of her children and she held them tightly for a moment. Only when LOR sulked away to an indoor picnic table a hundred feet away did the mother usher her children out of the pool area.

Cates and Soledad looked up when they realized someone was hovering over them. It was the attendant, a ginger-haired teenager with problem acne wearing a Hellie's polo and red Converse tennis shoes. He was the one who had sold them tickets to enter, as well as rented swimsuits to them all, which Soledad had paid for in cash.

"This is just to let you guys know that we close the pool at five in the winter months."

"It's winter?" Cates asked.

"Technically, our winter season starts in October," the attendant said. "So in twenty-five minutes, it'll close."

"Gotcha," Cates replied.

But the attendant lingered.

"Something I can help you with?" Cates asked finally.

The attendant shoved his hands deep in his pockets. "You're Dallas Cates, aren't you?"

Cates and Soledad exchanged looks, then Cates said, "Dallas who?"

The attendant laughed like he was in on the joke. "I remember seeing you on TV. My dad is a great rodeo fan—he used to rope in college. We watch every minute of the national finals every year, and since you're from Wyoming . . ."

When Cates didn't respond, the attendant said, "Don't worry. We get celebrities here. It's no big thing. Last summer, Carrot Top was here. You know, the comedian? He was right here in the same pool you guys are in."

"Imagine that," Soledad said. "*Carrot Top*."

"Swear to God," the attendant said. "We also had the host

of a TV game show. Wink or Blink Something. I can't remember his last name." Then: "Wait until I tell my dad I met Dallas Cates."

After the attendant skipped away, Soledad asked, "Does this happen often to you?"

"More often than I'd hoped," Cates said.

AXEL SOLEDAD WAS a strange and enigmatic creature, Cates thought. Since Axel's arrival in Jeffrey City, Cates had been trying to figure him out. All he knew about the man was from messages they'd sent back and forth to each other while Cates was in prison.

Cates clearly remembered the first message he'd received out of the blue:

> My name is Axel. We are destined to be friends because
> I know we have common enemies.

Cates had waited days to reply. He had good reasons to be suspicious. The message could be from a crank, from a troll, or even from a CO trying to set him up. Inmates weren't allowed to communicate with anyone from the outside without approval, and he knew he should fully expect the conversation to be monitored or recorded. But Soledad's initial message had come through an illicit and obscure chat site on the prison library's computer, which was supposed to filter out that kind of interaction.

Finally, Cates had written back.

Tell me more about yourself. And who are these common
enemies?

THE CORRESPONDENCE WENT on for months. Cates found out
that the app was engineered to delete their communications a
few minutes after they'd been read by the other party, so there
was no thread and no digital record of the exchange. And it
appeared that the communication channel was one-on-one,
with no other participants involved. Soledad had explained that
he was the designer of the app, and that he'd built it solely to
talk to Cates.

Cates had become comfortable with Axel Soledad, whoever
he actually was. He'd tested him several times to find out if
Soledad was in contact with the COs by claiming he planned
to break out on a certain date and how he was going to do it.
When there was no reaction on that day by the officers, Cates
had confessed to Soledad what he'd done. Soledad had replied
that he'd have done the same thing in that situation, no hard
feelings.

OVER THE MONTHS of electronic communications, Soledad had
tried to get Cates to buy into his ideology. It was something
about taking down the deep state that had betrayed him while
he was in a special military unit overseas, serving what he later

found out was a pack of self-interested liars in Washington, *blah-blah-blah*.

To strike back, Soledad had begun a movement that manipulated parties already at each other's throats in already-broken American cities and encouraged violent riots and unrest. He did so by arming members of the homeless, destitute, oppressed, and forgotten and urging them to rise up against local governments.

It had all been going according to plan, until . . .

Blah-blah-blah, Cates thought.

He was bored by it all, and only read Soledad's long diatribes because it was something to do. None of that stuff interested him. What happened in cities had *never* interested him, especially since all the racial enmity could plainly be seen throughout the cell blocks of the prison. What *did* interest him, though, was the possibility of aligning with a brilliant mind with a common goal.

Which was why, Soledad had explained, he'd researched Dallas Cates and figured out a way to reach him.

DALLAS CATES HAD outlined *his* story because Soledad kept prompting him to do so. Even as he did it, Cates had the suspicion that Soledad already knew the details.

He'd started at the beginning, growing up as the youngest brother of three on the family property outside of Saddlestring that served as the headquarters for Dull Knife Outfitters and C&C Sewer and Septic Tank Service. His parents were Eldon and Brenda, third-generation blue-collar locals from the county. Later, a sign at the gate was added that the property was also the birthplace of PRCA World Champion Cowboy Dallas Cates.

The older Cates brothers, Bull and Timber, were bigger, duller, and more brutish than Dallas, who was a star athlete and the unabashed favorite of his mother, Brenda, who had also conceived of and hung the birthplace sign. His mother was his biggest cheerleader and fan, and she hadn't believed any of the sexual assault rumors about her youngest son, and especially not those involving the game warden's middle daughter, April.

When those allegations surfaced, the Cates family circled the wagons around Dallas, starting a cycle of incidents and mis-understandings that escalated far beyond anyone's expectations.

Even though it was later proven that Dallas hadn't assaulted April, that hadn't stopped his persecutors.

Timber and Bull were eventually killed, and Bull's wife, Cora Lee, was, too. Eldon had broken his neck when he was shoved into a deep hole, and Brenda became a quadriplegic. She was eventually sentenced to the Wyoming Women's Center in Lusk.

Dallas had been convicted of trumped-up charges at the height of his rodeo career, in the same year that he had won $243,187 in saddle bronc competitions and was destined once again to lead in the standings going into the NFR in Las Vegas.

While in prison, Cates had been denied permission to visit Brenda during her last days on earth, while at the same time the family property had gone into receivership for nonpayment of the mortgage and accrued property taxes that were well beyond what Dallas could accumulate in prison.

But his tormentors—the people who had banded together to destroy him and his family and seize their property—were still out there. Those self-righteous, smug bastards. Something Brenda had once told him would forever stick in his mind. She'd said, "It don't matter what you've done in your life. They will always think of us as white trash."

The judge. The local sheriff. The county prosecutor. The game warden. That falconer and his wife. Winner came along later, but he was of the same mindset.

Soledad had listened to it all, then he'd asked a question: "Do you understand what a Venn diagram is?"

Cates had confessed that he didn't.

"A Venn diagram is a representation that shows the logical relation between names, words, or symbols. You put all those items up on a board and then you draw circles around the ones that create a common set."

"Okay," Cates had written back.

"In the Venn diagram representing Dallas Cates and Axel Soledad and the people who screwed them over and ruined their lives, there is a set of names that overlap."

Soledad had then gone on to detail the specific set that contained the names Dulcie Schalk, Joe Pickett, and Nate Romanowski and his wife.

"Where we don't overlap is the sheriff in your case and a person named Geronimo Jones in mine," Soledad wrote.

"The sheriff is dead," Cates wrote. "But the others are still out there."

"And in my case," Soledad said, "Geronimo Jones is still very much alive. The last time I saw him was after he and Joe Pickett practically blew my legs off with shotguns and left me to bleed out in the dirt in downtown Portland. If it wasn't for an activist who happened by who believed in my mission and drove me to an underground clinic, I wouldn't be here today. But that really set me back, and it set back our cause."

"*Our* cause?" Cates had asked.

"There are a lot of guys with me. They're lying low now, waiting for me to activate them. Then we can finish what I started."

He explained that there were sleeper agents all across the country, but especially in the South, Mountain West, and Texas. They were people no one would suspect.

"I'm talking leading community members, more than a few politicians, and even some cops," Soledad said. "We're all pissed off and we're in position."

"Are you talking about this 'taking down Washington' thing again?" Cates asked.

"Yes. The political atmosphere isn't what it was a couple of years ago, but the rage is still there. As long as the spooks are running everything for their own best interests . . ."

And Cates heard, *blah-blah-blah.*

"So what you're saying," Cates had finally ventured, "is that we work together on eliminating the common names. Then you can restart your little war."

"Exactly."

"I don't hate our country enough, though," Cates said. "I kind of like it. I don't get involved with politics."

"You don't have to," Soledad assured him. "I'll take care of that. And I don't hate our country. I hate our leaders and the elites who don't have accountability. But when we're through with this, maybe you'll think highly enough of me to help me out with Mr. Jones."

"Maybe," Cates said. "But figuring out how to do it is another thing. I'm afraid they'll see me coming."

"I believe we'll come up with something," Soledad replied. "Something they'll never suspect until it's too late."

Cates had agreed with that.

"There's one thing you should know," Soledad said.

"What's that?"

"When I mentioned that I had people with me. They're in some surprising places."

"Are you saying you have someone on the inside?"

Soledad didn't reply. Cates wasn't sure whether to believe him or not.

CATES WAS A little surprised by Soledad's actual arrival in Jeffrey City. His physical appearance was divided into halves. His upper body was strong and fit and imposing. He had a shaved scalp and a five-day growth of dark beard, as well as a large bladelike nose and piercing dark eyes. Like Cates's, Soledad's arms were festooned with tattoos. Only, in Soledad's case, all of the art was devoted to falcons and falconry.

Soledad's lower half was that of an eighty- or ninety-year-old man. His legs were thin and spindly, and his boots often splayed out to the sides as he glided along using braces that strapped around his forearms and extended on tubular legs to the ground.

Later, Soledad showed Cates that one of the braces contained a hidden eighteen-inch stiletto, and the other a razor-sharp flexible steel garrote that could behead a man in seconds. He'd had them custom-made, he said.

"How long do you plan to keep LOR around?" Soledad asked Cates.

Soledad was propped up in the corner of the pool, his elbows splayed out on the lip of the painted concrete wall, while his legs were suspended uselessly below him in the murky water. His two aluminum braces were stacked on the deck within reach.

Cates shrugged. "Until we can get that machine right. He's the only one who understands how it all works, since he built it in the first place. I want it to operate like a Swiss watch."

Soledad reluctantly agreed.

"I didn't like it when we almost missed the first time with that CO," Cates said. "That could have been a fucking disaster. It hit high and to the right. Another couple of inches and we could have missed that guy altogether. We need a way of sighting in that shooting head better, like a red-dot sight or something. As it is, we're making a big guess when we pull the trigger."

"It worked with that lady lawyer," Soledad said.

"Yeah, but that was pure luck. I was guessing distance and impact. It helped that she leaned into the jaws at the last second.

"I think we need to buy some watermelons at the grocery store to practice on," Cates said. "Do you think they have watermelons here?"

"Probably not this time of year," Soledad said. "Not in Thermopolis, Wyoming."

"Cantaloupes might work," Cates said. "They're about the right size. I'd bet they have cantaloupes in that store."

"Maybe," Soledad agreed.

Then the lights blinked on and off twice.

"It must be closing time," Cates said.

"Let me go talk to the attendant," Soledad said. "Maybe I can get him to extend our time, given you're such a celebrity and all."

Cates watched as Soledad launched himself out of the pool using his impressive upper body strength, then gathered up his braces and glided toward the front office.

LOR made his way to the men's locker room to change, and Johnson made her way to the women's.

CATES WAS TOWELING off when Soledad rejoined him. The man could cover ground quite quickly with his braces, faster than if he walked.

"What'd he say?" Cates asked.

"He didn't say much," Soledad said while he removed the stiletto from his left crutch and cleaned the blood off the blade with a used towel. Then: "You might consider wearing some kind of disguise when we go buy the fruit. Too many people seem to know you in this state."

ON THE WAY out of the facility, Cates passed by the ticket booth and looked at his reflection in the window. Johnson and LOR had already gone out to the truck.

He *did* look good now that he had his belt buckle back, he thought. That Winner son of a bitch had hidden it in his underwear drawer and it had taken a while to find it.

The lights were shut off in the office, but he could see the soles of a pair of red Converse sneakers sticking out from beneath the counter.

"One good thing about these small towns," Soledad said, "there's not so many cameras. But even with that being the case, I suggest we skip town and go buy that fruit in Worland or Buffalo. Let's get out of town before someone starts looking for your rodeo fan."

Cates slowly turned around in the passageway next to the ticket booth to take in Axel Soledad, who was behind him. Soledad winked at him as he glided by on his braces. Now Cates understood much, much more about his new traveling companion. The man was strategic, pragmatic, and absolutely ruthless.

And that the two of them might, in fact, fulfill their common cause and wipe out that Venn diagram together.

CHAPTER FIFTEEN

Yarak, Inc.

JOE FOUND NATE in a shed next to the falcon mews on the Yarak, Inc. property, an assemblage of buildings located in the center of a vast sagebrush bowl several miles off the highway. Nate was dismembering dead jackrabbits with his hands to prepare for the nightly feeding. The small dark shed smelled of blood and the musty odor of exposed viscera. Nate had replaced his shoulder holster with an over-the-shoulder falconry bag that contained thick gloves, leather jesses, and whistles used in training.

"Is Clay sleeping it off somewhere?" Nate asked over his shoulder. Joe was flummoxed, as he always was, by his friend's intuitive ability to know who was approaching without actually looking up.

"County jail," Joe said. "They said they'd call me when he

finally wakes up. That poor guy is a mess." Then: "The Mama Bears are hightailing it back to Jackson with a couple of citations in their pockets. I suspect that they're not real pleased about that."

"They're lucky to be alive," Nate said. "I hung around the cliff until I was sure you had that situation handled."

"Thank you."

Joe cleared his throat and said, "Dulcie Schalk was attacked and killed on her family's ranch outside of Laramie. Marybeth is absolutely gutted by the news, of course. They were tight. But this might be our bear."

Nate went still for half a minute.

"Repeat that," he said, and Joe did, adding, "Jennie Gordon is on her way to the scene. We should know more when she gets there."

"Dulcie?" Nate asked.

Marybeth had once confided to Joe that she suspected Nate had feelings for the county prosecutor, although to her knowledge he'd never acted on them in any way. That was before he'd married Liv. Nate's reaction to the news, Joe thought, confirmed that his wife had been prescient once again.

"What happened?" Nate asked.

"We don't have all the details yet, but apparently she was on a walk on her ranch when she was attacked and killed. Her dad found her and said she had a handgun and a canister of bear spray on her that hadn't been deployed. It must have happened quickly."

"Did the dad actually see the bear?"

"No. He just saw the result."

"Damn."

"Yup."

"Help me feed my birds," Nate said. "Then we'll go inside. Like I told you earlier, I have some thoughts to run by you."

Joe dug a pair of thin black nitrile disposable gloves out of a box of them and pulled them on. "Lead the way," he said.

WHILE LIV WAS in the family room reading children's stories to Kestrel, Nate and Joe sat at the kitchen table. Nate had poured them each a quarter tumbler of Wyoming Whiskey on ice and placed the bottle on the surface next to a yellow legal pad.

"As I mentioned, I have some thoughts on the matter at hand," Nate said as he sat down. He flipped open the first blank page of the pad to reveal scrawled columns of dates, locations, and numbers that at first glance made no sense to Joe.

"Peregrine falcons are the apex predator of the skies," Nate said without preamble. "Some falconers might argue that it should be a goshawk or a golden eagle, but they're just wrong. Peregrines are the fastest and most efficient killers in existence. When they're in a state of *yarak*, when they are at their peak in conditioning and frame of mind, I'd say they're the most ruthless species on earth.

"By the same token," he added, "grizzly bears are the apex predator on the ground in our part of the planet. No other creature can go toe-to-toe with them. Instead of the state of *yarak*, grizzlies can experience hyperphagia, where they're more active and gluttonous leading up to hibernation. For a grizzly in hyperphagia, his entire focus is on feeding and much of his natural wariness gets pushed aside.

"Those two conditions might not be exactly the same, but it helps me get a better understanding of our grizzly if I think of them as similar. Two species, kings of their own domains, at the absolute top of their abilities."

Joe nodded, wondering where this was going. Wondering what was on the pad that Nate was covering with his forearm.

"I once saw a peregrine in full *yarak* take on an entire lek of sage grouse," Nate said. "Maybe eighteen to twenty birds. If you've never seen them do it, sage grouse protect themselves from falcons by flipping over on their backs and windmilling their big feet into the air. It's like a buzz saw. Their talons are razor-sharp and they can slice the hell out of much larger predators who try to eat them. I've seen them send foxes and coyotes packing with their tails between their legs and their muzzles cut to ribbons.

"But in this instance, as I watched, that lone peregrine took out a dozen of those sage grouse, one by one. The falcon went at them so hard and fast you could barely see what was happening. The scene was a bloody mess, and when it was all over, the peregrine sat on one of the dead sage grouse and ate it all, feathers and bones included. He left the others for posterity."

"Does this story have a point?" Joe asked.

"It does," Nate said. "If that peregrine just wanted to eat, it would have stopped attacking after it killed the first grouse. But it didn't just want to eat. It wanted to kill and to punish that group of sage grouse.

"I know you know this, Joe," he said, "but people think animals in nature only kill what they can eat, or in self-defense. But in some instances, like this peregrine, they kill for no good reason. Something in them compels them to do it. You said Clay Junior didn't provoke the bear in any way that you know, right?"

"Right," Joe said.

"And as far as we know, neither did the prison guard in Rawlins. I read about that and it sounds like an ambush. And I can't see Dulcie making a mistake that would provoke a grizzly bear. She's too smart for that and she grew up in the country."

"Okay . . ."

"I think our grizzly is operating under a similar condition to that peregrine I saw. Our bear is compelled to kill."

Joe sighed. "Nate, I get it. But I don't think this is news, and it really doesn't help us get any closer to getting that bear."

Nate glared at Joe. It was the glare he reserved for times when he thought that Joe was being obtuse and *not* getting it.

But instead of speaking, Nate quickly added a few more lines to the bottom of the pad. When he was through, he turned it around so Joe could finally read it.

Nate tapped his index finger on the first entry. "October 14, Clay Junior gets it in the middle of the Twelve Sleep River, right?"

"Yes."

He tapped the next line. "October 16, Brodbeck gets hit in

roughly the same place. The attack isn't more than a hundred yards from where the first one occurred. You guys chase it and shoot at it, but you can't find it. Correct?"

"Correct."

"So between October 14 and 16, that grizzly bear hung around here."

"It did."

"Then on October 23, seven days later, a CO from the prison gets hit outside of Rawlins."

"Yes."

"That's two hundred and fifty miles away from here, Joe. That means our bear bolted out of here and covered an average of thirty-six miles a day on a line. Our grizzly passed through ranches, towns, and across highways and rivers. He probably boogied right past hunters in the field, ranchers moving cattle, and schoolkids playing outside for recess. All to go straight to Rawlins and take out this poor guy."

Nate jabbed at the last entry. "Then, on October 25, two days after the last attack, he goes after Dulcie on her ranch, right?"

Joe sat up straight. His throat was suddenly dry and he sipped on the bourbon.

"Two days from Rawlins to outside Laramie," Nate said. "A hundred miles over the top of the Snowy Range that's not only steep and high, but probably covered with tourists, hunters, and hikers. But for whatever reason, he lets them all go. And he's increased his pace, because now he's covering *fifty* miles a day."

"What are you saying?" Joe asked.

Nate sat back in his chair. He looked around the kitchen

as if checking to see if anyone was lurking and trying to eavesdrop.

"Either this grizzly has superpowers way beyond a state of *yarak* or hyperphagia," he said, "or you've got two or maybe three different bears attacking humans hundreds of miles apart from each other. And they're doing it in places that are not known grizzly habitats."

Joe shook his head. It was incomprehensible.

"Or maybe you've got something else entirely going on," Nate said.

"But what?"

"I don't know, obviously. But something about this string of incidents doesn't set well with me. I know about predators—I've studied them all my life. Hell, I've been accused of being one," Nate said with a cold smile. "Predators have certain traits and patterns, even if we can't figure them out at first.

"Clay Junior was probably just in the wrong place at the wrong time. Brodbeck got hit because he was a threat to the bear, and the grizzly probably thought the man was encroaching on his new territory. There's a kind of logical explanation to that.

"But," Nate said, "to boogie two hundred and fifty miles to the next kill? Then a hundred more miles to get Dulcie? That's where the logic breaks down. No, those last two kills seem targeted."

"Targeted? Then what's the link between them?"

Nate raised his eyebrows. "Beats me, game warden. Maybe you and your Predator Attack Team need to start thinking outside the box."

———

WHEN LIV AND Kestrel joined Nate in the kitchen so they could start preparing dinner, Joe stepped away from the table and went outside to the covered porch, where he speed-dialed Jennie Gordon. She was out of breath when she answered her phone.

"Please tell me you've got some good news," she said as a greeting. "I really need some good news for a change."

"Not really," he said. "I sent the Mama Bears packing and Clay Hutmacher is in custody for chasing them down. Not that he's been charged with anything yet."

Gordon said she was with Brody Cress and Tom Hoaglin and that they were at the crime scene at the Schalk Ranch outside of Laramie, along with local law enforcement and an ambulance waiting to take Dulcie's body to the medical examiner in Laramie.

"It's a bad scene," she said. "Unfortunately, it's one we've experienced before."

Joe asked, "So you'd definitively say it was our grizzly bear?"

"It's too early to make that call with absolute certainty," Gordon said. "But from the MO and the wounds, I'd give it a ninety-nine-point-five percent chance that we're dealing with the same bear."

"Not a different bear?" Joe asked. "You're sure?"

Gordon paused a beat. When she replied, her tone was professionally defensive. "Like I said, we still have to do a lot of work with the body and the crime scene to declare it's the same bear. But at first glance, the attack is similar to the first three. It appears unprovoked, for one. Second, the fatal wounds are very similar: severe punctures in the facial and cranial area, deep claw marks on her arms, shoulders, and abdomen. Third, the body wasn't fed on at the scene or cached. Fourth, the bear moved on after the attack.

"Joe, why are you asking me these questions?"

Joe outlined Nate's thesis to her and Gordon listened patiently.

He said, "I agree with all your points. They make sense to me. But when you look at all the attacks from thirty thousand feet, the most dissimilar encounter is the first one: Clay Junior. He was hit in the river and his body was cached on the riverbank. Also, the grizzly hung around long enough to attack Bill Brodbeck two days later. It was in no hurry to cover hundreds of miles after the killing."

When he was through, she said, "Maybe our bear is learning and adapting. Maybe it realized that immediately after it attacks someone, a whole lot of people with guns show up on the scene."

"Maybe," Joe replied.

"But I do understand that a lot of this doesn't make sense. We've never had a bear behave this way before, so it's impossible to anticipate where it's going next and what it might do. But *targeting* the victims? How is that even conceivable?"

"I don't have the answer to that," Joe said. "Neither does Nate. Tell me: you said the fatal wounds are similar. I know there's no way to determine if the claw marks are similar because they're probably random and they happened during a frenzy. But are the bite marks on all four of our victims a match?"

"I'm judging the bite pattern based on my own field observations," she said, her voice dropping in register when she spoke. Joe assumed someone had come near her whom she didn't want to overhear her end of the conversation. "I've got photos, of course, but I haven't measured or analyzed the wounds and determined that they're an exact match. They look the same, I'd say. But I'm not a forensic pathologist, Joe, and no one on my team has that qualification. We're bear hunters, and a lot of what we do is based on experience and knowledge of the species. Are you suggesting that grizzly bears across this state have suddenly decided to collude? That's insane."

"It is insane when you put it that way," Joe conceded.

"Given that," she said, "I'm going to take some time tonight at the hotel to pull up all the crime scene photos I've got on my laptop. I'll get Brody and Tom to help me, and we'll look much closer at the bite patterns and measure them to see if they're consistent. We might even go to the medical examiner's office so we can take a close-up look at Schalk's wounds."

"It can't hurt," Joe said.

"But don't get your hopes up," she said. "'Bite mark' evidence has been pretty much debunked in court as junk science when it comes to humans. I don't know if it's any more reliable when it comes to bears."

"Ah."

"Nevertheless, I can reach out to some scientists I know to see if we can figure out something either way. And maybe we'll involve the state crime lab in Cheyenne. I hate the idea that bears are rising up on their own," she said. "It's important to knock that theory down before it starts to catch on. People are already getting panicky."

"You don't have to tell me about that," Joe said. "We've seen black bears and cattle killed up here recently."

She moaned. "Like I don't have anything else to do, with four victims and that bear still out on the loose."

"We'll find him," Joe said, knowing how hollow the words sounded even to himself. "We have to."

"But what if we don't?" she asked. "What if this bear just keeps killing people?"

JOE LOWERED THE phone after they'd disconnected. He'd had no answer to Gordon's last question.

"What'd she say?" Nate asked as he pushed through the screen door.

"She said it looks like the same bear, but she's going to dig deeper into the facts surrounding all the attacks. I'll keep you posted."

"Good," Nate said. Then: "Want to stay for dinner?"

"Thank you, but I need to get home. Marybeth will be back from work soon and I promised I'd grill."

"Give her my best," Nate said.

"Have you heard from Sheridan?" Joe asked.

"Liv's talking with her tonight, I guess. The job is a doozy, but she's pretty sure she can handle it. I am, too, because she's a good hand. But I guess the folks who hired us down there are a little . . . odd."

CHAPTER SIXTEEN

Never Summer Ranch

SHERIDAN WAS BOTH tired and dirty as she looped the weighted duck wing lure around her head through the air with her left hand to signal to the falcons to return for the early evening. The temperature on the Never Summer Ranch had dropped significantly once the sun began to descend, and she could see her breath as clouds of condensation as she worked the lure. It whistled as it circled.

The first falcon to come in was the peregrine, and it settled with surprising grace on her gloved right fist. The second raptor to come home was a prairie falcon. She secured both birds to dowel-rod perches in the back of her vehicle by their leather leg jesses. Before proceeding, she ran her hands over them to look for broken feathers or any other injuries. When that checked out, she gently touched their gullets with the tips of her fingers.

As she had suspected, the prairie falcon didn't need more food—it had blasted a few starlings out of the sky in the late afternoon and had fed on them. The peregrine hadn't eaten yet, although she'd seen the falcon hit and kill several of the target birds to send them spiraling down to the sagebrush like spent rockets—a warning signal not to come back.

The combination of a prairie falcon and a peregrine had worked very well to strike terror into the hundreds of starlings and send them packing to other locations. Once she'd put the birds into the sky in the late morning, she'd waited until they maintained a long oblong aerial route above the ranch, riding on thermal currents.

Soon, she could hear the shrill cries of the invasive birds increase in volume and pure panic inside the barn. The falcons had been spotted, and the din had become almost unbearable.

Then, in what looked like a black cloud, the starlings had broken out and poured from the openings in the barn to flee to the south, with the falcons accompanying them from above and at times shooting through the cloud like fighter planes. The prairie falcon had followed one of its kills to the ground.

A SECOND WAVE of starlings had emerged about fifteen minutes later, as if they'd grouped up and decided to wait to flee until the falcons were otherwise engaged. This grouping poured out nearly at ground level and flew east. It didn't take long for the falcons to double back and provide taloned accompaniment. Sheridan had watched the remaining starlings streaking toward the mountains until they were out of sight. In the last hour before calling her birds back, Sheridan had entered the building. It was eerily quiet inside the barn and she couldn't locate a single living bird still about. What was left, though, was disconcerting. The rafters were caked with white excrement, as was the barn floor. It smelled inside of avian panic.

Tiny errant feathers still shimmered in beams of light through windows and cracks in the walls. Hundreds of corpses of dead starlings lay in different stages of decay on the floor and shelving from the long occupation. Starlings didn't clean up after their own.

She was grateful that her job was complete after the bird abatement was over. She wanted nothing to do with cleaning up the building and making it suitable for any kind of use again. Years of bird shit and tiny rotting carcasses made the building reek ripe and rotten.

Sheridan was also pleased with how well her first lone assignment had gone. Nate had shown her how well peregrines and prairie falcons could team up to work together on the same mission. Some falcons turned on each other to claim the airspace, but these two had cooperated. There had been no need to release her remaining birds.

Nate attributed it to the fact that prairie falcons, while the only large falcon species native to North America, were distantly related to peregrines and shared similar attributes. Prairies were slightly smaller, but more perfectly adapted to a harsh arid western environment. What they shared with peregrines was their aggressiveness, their coloring, their grace while in flight, and their eager embrace of terror tactics when it came to going after prey.

Both birds had done their jobs, returned to her at the end of the day, and done so tired but unharmed. She still had fresh falcons in reserve if needed.

Sheridan was keen to return to her motel, have a nice meal somewhere in Walden, and report to Liv how well things had gone. The only thing that nagged at her throughout the day had been her repeated sightings of the old woman lurking about inside the ranch home.

Katy Cotton kept a very close eye on Sheridan's comings and goings. In fact, every time Sheridan glanced toward the house, she found Cotton in one of the windows on either the first or second floor, pushing aside the curtain to glare at her.

Once, Sheridan had waved. The old woman hadn't waved back. She'd simply stepped away and let the curtains meet.

SHE WAS CLOSING the tailgate on her SUV when Leon Bottom drove his pickup into the ranch yard and strode over to her with a smile on his face and a six-pack of Coors in his hand.

"How'd it go today?" he asked. He was wearing the same all-black cowboy outfit as he had the day before, with the addition of a white silk kerchief around his thin neck. Maybe to make it look thicker, she thought.

"It went very well," she announced. "There are officially no starlings left in your barn."

Bottom did a faux reaction as if he'd been pushed back in

the chest, then resumed his approach. "Man, that's the best news I've heard all month. I wish I could have been here to see it, but I had to meet with my banker in Fort Collins."

"I remember."

HE PULLED TWO yellow cans out of the container and handed one to Sheridan. He said, "I was almost hoping you would need to work again tomorrow. I really wanted to see those falcons of yours chase the starlings off."

"Oh, I'll be back tomorrow morning to make sure none of them came back during the night," she said, opening the can. "Sometimes a few of them return because they don't know where else to go. Also, there might be a few birds out there who don't know what happened today and think of the barn as their home. We can chase them all off tomorrow. Thanks for the beer."

"My pleasure," Bottom said, taking a long pull of his and exclaiming, "Damn, that's good. I should have asked you first if you wanted a beer. You might not even drink."

"I'm from Wyoming," she said. And it *was* good.

"So that's it," he said. "You come, you chase all the problem birds away, you give me a bill, and you leave."

"That's it. If they come back, you can call us again. But to be honest, it's unusual for starlings to come back within their lifetimes. Birds like starlings get hardwired fast to avoid places that have threatened them."

"Where did all the birds go?" Bottom asked.

"The bulk of them went west, and the rest to the south."

"So they'll be someone else's problem," Bottom said with apparent glee. "I hope a bunch of them end up in Walden to plague my enemies."

Sheridan didn't respond to that.

"Still, this is all fascinating," Bottom said.

"That barn will need a real cleaning," she said.

"I'll hire some illegals to do it," he said with a shrug. "I've seen a few of them hanging around the post office in town. There's no paperwork and I can pay them in cash. That's what's nice about my situation."

She looked away and drank the rest of the can faster than she normally would. Sheridan was tired of the conversation, and of Leon Bottom.

"Thank you for the beer," she said again.

"I'll see you tomorrow morning, then."

"Yes."

"For breakfast," he added. "I insist. Please come out for breakfast first. Then we can see if there are any more birds you need to scare away."

"I might pass on that breakfast," she said.

He was suddenly hurt. "Now, why would you do that?"

Sheridan chinned toward the house and he got it.

"Katy?" he said.

"She watched me all day, and not in a friendly way."

"Well, she may not be friendly at first," Bottom said. "I think she's just protective of me—of the ranch. She doesn't like to see me get cheated by the locals, and she's sure they're all up to no good. She probably considers you one of them."

"Whatever," Sheridan said. Then she dug in her jeans pocket and handed over the note that had been left on her windshield the night before.

Bottom read it and said, "Jeez, did you have a bad experience with her somewhere? Did you cut her off on the road or something?"

"I've never seen her in my life." Sheridan left out the part that there was something oddly familiar about the woman.

"She's not usually this nasty," Bottom said. "Did I tell you she's originally from Wyoming? Maybe that's what it is. Maybe you ran into her up there."

Sheridan said, "My dad is a game warden. Maybe he arrested her or something."

Bottom laughed as he pulled out another beer for her. Sheridan declined to accept it.

"I don't know much about her life in Wyoming," he said. "All I know is she was originally from there, and her first husband was, too. When that fell apart, she met Ben Cotton and they moved to Michigan and she's spent the rest of her life serving my family."

"So you don't know anything about her first husband? Like his name? Or where she's from?" Sheridan asked. She thought if she heard the name and town, she might be able to establish a connection. As her dad as always told her, Wyoming was the last remaining state with "one degree of separation," meaning that if you didn't know someone else outright you knew someone who knew that person. The place was still that parochial.

"No," Bottom said. "She never talks about her first husband. I don't know if she had any kids with him or anything. Katy is very tight-lipped about her past. I wouldn't even know about her first husband except that she told my mother something about him once—that he was a disaster and she had to get out for her own good. That's all I know."

Sheridan made a note to herself to ask her parents if they'd ever heard of the woman. But that could wait. It wasn't urgent.

As she turned to reach for the door handle of her SUV, Bottom sidestepped in front of her and again held up the second can. "Another one for the road?"

"No, thank you."

"Or," he said, pressing toward her, "you could just stay here and help me finish this sixer. I also picked up a few edibles in Fort Collins. They're legal here, you know."

"Back off," Sheridan said firmly.

The rancher responded as if he'd touched an electric fence. "I didn't mean to offend you," he said. "It just gets real lonely out here."

As he said it, Sheridan got the impression that Leon Bottom was often successful with some women, even though he was no prize in any way. He had money, and he had a big dose of self-delusion.

"I'm out of here," she said, shouldering around him. "I have birds to take care of."

"Come out for breakfast and we'll settle up," he said, as if waving away the previous exchange. "Katy is a hell of a cook and breakfast has always been my favorite meal."

Sheridan agreed to do it, although as she drove away from the Never Summer Ranch, she saw Katy Cotton framed in the kitchen window shooting twin laser beams at her from her tiny, squinted eyes.

CHAPTER SEVENTEEN

Saddlestring

DULL KNIFE OUTFITTERS, C&C SEWER AND SEPTIC TANK SERVICE,
BIRTHPLACE OF PRCA WORLD CHAMPION COWBOY DALLAS CATES

S ON OF A *bitch*," Dallas Cates said, spitting out the words.
"Someone took our sign down."

"What sign?" Bobbi Johnson asked sleepily from the back-seat. She'd dozed off once it got dark and was slumped against Axel Soledad's shoulder. Cates saw her scramble back into her place once she realized what she'd done. Cates admired her discomfort in the rearview mirror.

The interior of the pickup reeked of broken fruit, the odor emanating from the device in the bed of the vehicle. They should have cleaned it thoroughly after leaving Powell, Cates thought.

"What's the sign say now?" Johnson asked.

"Now it says BLUE SKY LLAMAS," Cates said from behind the wheel. "What the fuck is that all about?"

"I hate llamas," Lee Ogburn-Russell said from the passenger seat. "They look stupid and they spit at you."

"*Everybody* hates fucking llamas," Cates said, his mood suddenly black.

The compound in which he'd grown up was largely concealed by the dark, but Cates still knew every inch of it. The main two-story house; the four-stall garage, where his father, Eldon, had parked his service pump truck; the guesthouse, where his brother Bull and Bull's wife, Cora Lee, had lived; the original log cabin homestead house that had once been filled with saddles and other outfitting gear; the corral where Dallas had learned to ride wild bucking horses; the deep hole on the edge of the property where his mother, Brenda, had imprisoned Liv Romanowski before she was Liv Romanowski.

All that could be seen of it now, as Cates steered under the arch and his headlights painted the sagebrush on the side of the dirt road, were some yellow lights at the main house and a single blue pole light in front of the garage.

"So this is where you grew up?" Johnson said to Cates.

"It is."

"Who lives here now?"

"No idea. It went into foreclosure after they killed and crippled my mom and dad, and somebody must have bought it."

"Llama ranchers," Soledad said from the backseat. His tone

was more provocative than Cates appreciated at the moment. "Llama ranchers bought it."

Cates was miffed by the idea that strangers, *llama ranchers*, now lived in his family house. It was just one more humiliation on top of a mountain of them.

Cates felt a bolt of anger, like a lightning strike, arc through his chest. It was the same feeling he used to have when he dropped down into the chute onto his saddle and grasped the rope and settled in for the ride. That anger, directed then not only at the bucking horse but his competitors, had been his rocket fuel.

"When I get to the house," he said, "I want all of you to stay here inside. I don't want to spook the people living in my house any more than I need to. I'll let you know when the coast is clear."

"Let us know if you need any help," Soledad said, leaning forward and patting Cates on the shoulder.

"I won't, I suspect," Cates replied.

HE PARKED IN front of the house and got out and waited for the interior pickup lights to douse. Cates didn't want the occupants inside the house to see how many people were in the vehicle. When the inside of the truck went dark, he turned toward the structure. He could see by the glow of the interior lights that the wooden porch had been painted white and that the old rocking chairs Eldon and Brenda used to sit in on warm summer evenings had been replaced by a Peloton bike. Cates was disgusted.

He assumed the people inside the house must have seen him coming. The sight lines from the compound to the road were treeless and vast. It was a long driveway from the arch, and his headlights were the only thing out there. No one had *ever* sneaked up on the Cates family, especially at night. Brenda kept a shotgun near the front door if anyone ever tried.

But the porch light didn't click on as Cates approached the front door, and nobody looked out the windows at him.

He strode up the porch steps and rapped twice on the door.

There were tentative footfalls inside and then the porch light went on. Cates took two steps back so he could be seen clearly and appear nonthreatening. Then he manufactured a smile on his face and waited.

The door opened about eight inches and a woman looked out. She was thin, angular, and birdlike. Late thirties or early forties, wearing yoga pants and an oversized T-shirt. Her legs were like sticks and she wore flats that hugged her feet. She had short blond hair, a pair of readers pushed up on her head, and a multitude of plastic and leather bracelets on her thin wrist supporting a multitude of causes, he guessed. Beads of perspiration dotted at her hairline and she was flushed and mildly out of breath.

Obviously, she'd been working out. That was why she hadn't seen them drive up.

She looked at him with suspicion. "Are you lost?"

"I hope not," Cates said, maintaining his grin. "I'm out here looking for property and I understand that this place is for sale."

"For sale?" she said. Then: "No. It's not for sale. I don't know where you heard that."

"Are you sure?" he asked.

From inside the house, a male voice called out, "Britney? Is there somebody at the door?"

She turned her head. "Yes, Rob, but I'm taking care of it." Cates thought her voice had a certain edge to it.

"Is that your husband?" Cates asked.

"My partner," Britney nodded. She said, "Maybe you saw a listing from a year ago that hasn't been updated. The realtors around here aren't exactly on the ball, we've learned. No, we bought this place eleven months ago and even though there's a lot of work to do to get it up to our standards, we have no intention of selling it. We're raising llamas here."

Although the phrase "to get it up to our standards" grated at Cates, he ignored it. He said, "Yeah, I was confused by that sign out on the arch. In the listing, it shows this place as belonging to an outfitter, a septic service, and a world champion rodeo cowboy."

"We got rid of that, of course," she said with an eye roll. "I mean, how redneck can you get, right?"

"I guess so," Cates said. He put his hands on his hips and looked around. "Man, this is *exactly* the kind of place I want to buy. Lots of elbow room, no crime, low taxes."

She said, "Going to the grocery store is kind of a trek. And getting used to the people around here is . . . challenging."

"Where did you come from, if I may ask?"

"We're from the Bay Area."

Of course you are, Cates thought. "I bet your kids love it," he said.

"We don't have any children," Britney said. "Our llamas are my babies."

Of course they are, he thought.

"We're so lucky Rob can work remotely," she said. "This way I can spend more time with my babies."

Cates said, "I'm sorry to have bothered you so late at night. I'll get with that realtor and tell her to update her listings. There has to be another place like this around here, right?"

Rob called out once again. "Is everything okay, Brit?"

"It's fine," she snapped. Cates got the impression that Britney wasn't thrilled that her partner was fine to let her deal with the situation at their door by herself.

"Anyway," Britney said to Cates, "I'm afraid you might not find what you're looking for. My understanding is that housing around here has been pretty much snapped up by people like us."

"From the Bay Area, you mean?"

"From California," she said. "Not all of us have moved to Texas and Tennessee, you know."

Cates mock-chuckled at that. "Believe me, I get it. That's why I'm looking to relocate to Hicksville."

"I wish there were more of us here," she said. "This state could use some new blood, if you know what I mean."

"Oh yes," he said. "Well, again, sorry to have bothered you

and sorry for the misunderstanding. I hope you have a good night."

"You too," she said, stepping back to ease the door shut. Cates guessed that in seconds Britney would turn on Rob and rip him a new one for sitting out her odd encounter.

Cates shot his foot out and placed it between the door and the jamb. He said, "Do you mind if I take a look inside? I'd love to see what the interior looks like."

A look of alarm struck her face when she glanced down and saw his boot cross the threshold. As she said, "I don't know if I'm comfortable . . ." he rushed the door and slammed it open with a shove from both hands. It hit her hard and Britney flew back into a heap on the floor. Cates followed.

When she recovered and started to sit up, he pulled the Hanna cop's Glock nine-millimeter from the back of his waistband and brought it down on the top of her head, shattering her readers. Britney slumped over to the side and lay motionless and he quickly scrambled over her.

A bearded man sat in the adjacent living room in a recliner with an iPad on his lap and glasses perched on the tip of his thin nose. This was where Cates used to sit on the family couch and watch cartoons. Rob stared up at Cates with terrified eyes, his hands gripping the arms of his chair as if preparing to launch himself out of it. Cates hit him crisply in the temple with the Glock. Rob flinched and cowered, holding up his hands to ward off future blows. His iPad slid down his legs and clattered on the floor.

"I bet this feels just like where you came from," Cates said to him. "Home invasions are actually pretty rare in these parts."

"Please, just take what you want," Rob said.

"That's what I'm doing, idiot."

"There's some high-grade weed in our bedroom."

"Stop talking, idiot."

WITH THE STILL-UNCONSCIOUS Britney and bleeding Rob bound and sitting back-to-back against the wall in the living room, Cates said to Rob, "I was happy to see that you didn't move the duct tape from the utility closet."

"I told you," Rob said, his voice choking with emotion, "just take what you need and leave us alone."

Cates said, "Some partner you are, Rob. You haven't even checked on Britney."

She sat slumped with her chin on her chest, a knot on the top of her head and a bloody gash in her scalp where the broken lenses had cut through the skin. But she was breathing.

"What do you want?" Rob asked.

"I want you two squatters to shut the fuck up," Cates said as he stripped a six-inch length of tape from the roll and approached Rob.

"*Squatters?*"

"This is my house," Cates said, bending down and roughly applying the tape to Rob's mouth. "Llamas?" he said as he did so. "Fucking *llamas?*"

CATES WENT OUT to the pickup. "It's handled," he said as he opened the passenger door. "Lee, go park the truck in that garage over there. We don't want anyone to see it in the daytime."

He could see the couple's white SUV inside the open garage and an open space next to it.

"Are those people okay?" Johnson asked with a nervous giggle. "I saw that skeleton lady go flying."

"They're just fine," Cates said.

"Welcome to command central," Soledad added from the backseat.

OCTOBER 27

Bears, with their great size and strength, remind us of how weak and ineffectual we are as organisms: a bear, even a small one, could abolish a human fairly easily.

—Charles Fergus

CHAPTER EIGHTEEN

Eagle Mountain Club

"TWO HUNDRED TWENTY PSI and climbing fast," Lee Ogburn-Russell called through the sliding window in the back of the pickup at four-thirty the next morning. "The air compressor seems to be working like a charm."

"Gotcha," Cates said from behind the wheel.

"Can you please turn the heat up in here?" Johnson asked. "It's fucking freezing." She was in the backseat. Soledad rode shotgun.

Cates said, "Sure," but did nothing. He liked the sharpness of the cold morning on his face, which was why he kept his window open. It made him hyperaware and alert.

Cates doused his headlights as he crept the vehicle over a suspension bridge that spanned the Twelve Sleep River four miles downstream from the Eagle Mountain Club. The old planks on the bridge made a *rat-tat-tat* as his tires rolled over them. Cates could see the white undulating reflection of the moon and stars on the black surface of the river as he passed over it.

On the other side of the bridge, he turned left onto a grassy two-track that paralleled the river to the north. Spring floods had washed out parts of the road, and he flashed on his lights at a couple of turns to make sure he didn't drive over a gouge-out into the water. As soon as he was confident of the pathway ahead, he turned his headlights back off and navigated by natural light. It was pure luck that the moon was full and bright enough to illuminate the silvery branches of the ancient cottonwood trees and cast shadows across the road.

"Five hundred PSI," LOR announced from the back through the window.

THE EAGLE MOUNTAIN Club was the very exclusive gated country club and golf course outside of Saddlestring. Cates knew it well because he and his high school buddies used to sneak onto the property and steal all the flags from the holes the night before summer tournaments, which enraged the members. There was a real clear "town vs. gown" atmosphere in those days, when ultra-wealthy Eagle Mountain members arrived on their jets and held their noses as they passed through Saddlestring by limousine from the airport en route to the club. At the time, there was very little interaction between the members and the locals, and few if any local members. Locals were hired to clean rooms, landscape the grounds, and pick up garbage. The club even brought in their own waitstaff from other clubs for the summer.

But once the Eagle Mountain closed in late September, it was a ghost village until the following May. There were dozens of magnificent homes that sat empty for the entire winter and the greens of the course were covered by tarps. Elk, mule deer, and moose wintered on the property. Fewer than six homes were occupied during those months.

Which played right into Cates's plan.

WHAT *HADN'T* PLAYED into his plan was what had happened an hour ago, before they left the Cates compound.

Johnson was in the backseat of the pickup, bitching about having to get up so early. LOR was in the back of the truck beneath the covered bed, starting up the electronic air compressor. The pump hummed and rattled at times like a pressure cooker on a stove as it began the process of filling the two floor-to-ceiling gas cylinders that had been repurposed from LOR's welding use. It took quite a while to fill the two eighty-cubic-foot tanks.

"Getting up this early really sucks," Johnson moaned as Soledad slid into the passenger seat next to Cates. Soledad laughed in response.

Cates had started the engine so that the air pump wouldn't

draw down the battery any more than it had. As he reached for the gearshift, Soledad leaned over and placed his hand on Cates's arm.

"Hold on a second," he said. "I'll be right back. I forgot something."

Cates watched Soledad propel himself across the yard toward the front door.

After a half a minute, Cates got out. He wanted to tell LOR in back to open the slider between the rear window and the covered topper over the bed so they could communicate. He could see LOR systematically checking pneumatic hoses and gauges on the device by flashlight.

Then, from inside the house, there were two sharp sounds followed by two more.

Snap-snap. Then: *Snap-snap.*

Cates paused. The sounds were familiar to him.

A moment later, Soledad appeared at the front door smoothing the hem of his jacket in the front and back as if he'd just tucked something into his waistband.

Soledad looked up and saw Cates observing him. They kept eye contact from the porch back to the pickup, but Cates said nothing.

"Had to be done," Soledad said.

"Twenty-two?" Cates asked.

"Double-taps."

Cates looked over to see if Johnson or LOR had noted the gunshots or the exchange he'd had with Soledad. LOR was still scrambling around the equipment in the back like a monkey, his flashlight gripped in his mouth. Johnson huddled in the far corner of the backseat with a blanket she'd borrowed from her bed over her head. Neither showed any cognition of what had just happened.

He guessed that the rattling hum of the air pump might have drowned out the *snap* sounds from inside.

"I wish you'd talk to me about these things," Cates said in a low rumble.

"Like I said, it had to be done. You know that, too."

"Six hundred twenty-eight PSI," LOR announced as Cates entered the club grounds by the obscure river road that was used by local cowboys to move cattle on the pastures near the river. The road was virtually unknown to members of the club and most of the staff. It was the route Cates and his buddies had used to steal all the flags. Some of which, he guessed, still adorned basement wet bars in town.

There were three ways to access the gated property, Cates knew. The main gate had a guardhouse as well as closed-circuit cameras. In the offseason, members could enter by key code, but every entrance and exit by vehicle or foot was recorded. It was the same situation at the service entrance on the other side of the golf course.

But the river road had no gates, no cameras, and no security system.

WHEN CATES DROVE out of the tangled riverside brush and downed trees onto the manicured Eagle Mountain grounds, everything opened up and he could see clearly. The clubhouse was huge, dark, and boxy at the top of the hill and was flanked by empty cottages and visitor lodging. Showy homes lined the outside of the fairways surrounding the course, and old-growth pine trees stood like sentinels to break up the contours of the long fairways.

He took a paved narrow golf cart path and ascended a long slope on the left flank of the clubhouse facilities until he could see the back side of the lighted front gate.

Cates pulled over to the side of the road and turned to address Bobbi Johnson.

"This is where you get out," he said. "Stay hidden in the bushes on the side of the road and call me if anyone comes through the gate. Remember: don't let yourself get seen by anyone."

"I remember my instructions," she said sullenly. "But I wish you'd give me back my real phone."

"We'll talk about that later," Cates said.

During the night at his old house, Soledad had convinced Cates over glasses of pinot noir apparently brought there by the llama people that Johnson couldn't be trusted with her phone.

"We don't know who she's texting or what she's saying," Soledad had whispered.

"I think it's her sister," Cates had responded.

"She's a security risk."

He was right, Cates had concluded. So while she was sleeping, they'd replaced her iPhone with a burner from Walmart. She was told to communicate with them only with that, and she hadn't received the news well.

"You'll get your old phone back when we're through," Soledad had assured her. Cates was impressed by what a convincing liar he was.

"But it's so cold," Johnson said as she climbed out of her own truck.

"It'll warm up," Cates said. "Now, like we talked about, call me with a vehicle description if anyone comes into the club."

"*Yeah-yeah-yeah,*" Johnson grumbled as she walked away. She chose a good hiding spot in a bed of chin-high junipers, where she could clearly see the front gate but couldn't be seen by the entrants.

As Cates backed the truck away, Johnson gestured at him with her middle finger.

"What a charmer," Soledad noted.

CATES DROVE TO a dense copse of pine trees and high juniper bushes on the side of the eighth fairway that bordered the cart path. Before plunging straight into it, he clicked on his headlights so he could navigate the pickup between two stout tree trunks. He drove into the copse far enough that the back end of the vehicle couldn't be seen from the path itself.

"Eight hundred eighteen PSI," LOR reported from the topper.

Cates turned to Soledad. "Keep it running until we reach max air pressure."

"Will do," Soledad said.

"I'll set up the camera," Cates said. "Keep a good eye on the truck camera as well. You should have two good angles."

"Got it."

"Axel," Cates said, narrowing his eyes. "No more surprises."

"You got it, partner," Soledad said with a hard grin.

AT THE REAR of the truck, Cates activated a battery-powered miniature video camera and placed it on the bumper pointing to the south along the path. After it was set, he checked in with Soledad, who had moved from the passenger seat to behind the wheel.

"How does it look?" Cates asked.

Soledad drew out his phone and punched up the app that received the live stream. "It looks good," he said. "It's dark, but I can see all the way down the hill to the houses."

"Good." Cates was both impressed and a little intimidated by all the new technology that was available for pennies at places like Walmart. A lot had happened during the years he'd been incarcerated when it came to new gadgets.

"Are we sure he'll be coming from that direction?" Soledad asked.

"I think so," Cates said. "His house is to the south up there on that bluff. What about the north?"

Soledad shifted his gaze from his phone to the video screen mounted in the dashboard. "I can't see a thing."

"Put the truck's transmission into reverse, but don't go anywhere," Cates said.

Soledad did so and the screen lit up with a view from the backup camera. "Perfect," he said. "I can see anyone coming down the path from the north."

Cates tapped on the sheet metal of the door to indicate his approval, then he pushed along the length of the pickup to the back again. The brush and branches clawed at him as he did so, and one branch tried to take his hat off. When he got to the tailgate, he twisted the handle of the hatchback window and let the pneumatic gas springs raise it up. The inside was crammed with equipment. LOR, who was on his side in the bed of the truck checking the fittings in a snarl of thick rubber hoses, looked up and the beam from the flashlight in his mouth hit Cates in the eyes and made him recoil.

"Sorry," LOR said.

"Does everything look okay?"

"It does. I found an air leak a minute ago on one of the hose fittings that goes to the device, but I tightened it up and all is good."

"What's our pressure?" Cates asked. He wasn't at a good angle at the back of the truck to see the gauge that was mounted on the bed wall between the air tanks. LOR contorted himself so he could see it behind him.

"Right at twelve hundred PSI."

"Great," Cates said. "Keep an eye on it and watch the gauge. We can't let it go over two thousand, and nineteen hundred would be perfect."

LOR grunted and grumbled. He hated it when anyone told him how his own device should be armed and deployed. Cates knew that, but he didn't care.

"Now move aside so I can get in there and get to the controls," Cates said as he stepped on the bumper and began to climb into the back.

On his way to the metal bucket-chair seat that had been liberated from an old tractor left in a field outside of Jeffrey City, Cates shouldered past the complicated device. He was again struck by the Rube Goldberg–style engineering LOR employed when designing mechanical devices.

There were tangles of electrical wire and thick coils of pneumatic hoses looped in the bed of the pickup as well as zip-tied to the interior walls. Inside, it smelled of rubber, machine oil, and Lee Ogburn-Russell's flatulence.

The device, which Cates had dubbed "Zeus II," took up most of the back and stretched from the tractor seat on one end to the massive shooting head aimed out the open back window on the other. Cates shimmied along the side of it toward the seat, which was mounted on the inside of the front wall. As he

passed the gaping wide-open steel jaws attached to the telescopic scissor jib, he reached over and touched the tips of the
original Zeus's teeth, which had been fastened to the jaws with
stainless steel screws. The teeth were yellowed but extremely
sharp. Cates cleaned out the rind of a cantaloupe wedged between two of the long incisors before proceeding.

"I told you to clean the teeth," Cates said to LOR, who
grunted an uninterested response.

"Seriously," Cates said as he swung up into the seat. "What
if the wounds are contaminated by fruit? That wouldn't look
very good."

"Not my problem," LOR said. "My problem is to make sure
this thing works perfectly. You can brush its teeth. Or better
yet, make Bobbi do it."

Cates settled into the seat and grasped the joystick with his
right hand. LOR had looted an old video game setup and repurposed the controller.

With his left hand, he reached back and closed his fingers
around the grip of a wooden thirty-four-inch Louisville Slugger
baseball bat propped in the inside corner of the bed. The barrel
of the bat bristled with wicked curved bear claws embedded in
the wood with the points out. It was a vicious-looking weapon,
and the sharp claws ripped through fabric and flesh like a scythe.

Then he sat back, feeling fully prepared.

The air compressor hummed, and Cates used the light from
his burner phone to check the numbers. They were at seventeen
hundred PSI in the tanks. "Move aside," he said to LOR. "Let's
get ready."

ZEUS II WAS a marvel, Cates thought. Complicated, ugly, and temperamental, yes. But still a marvel that only someone like LOR could build. It had exceeded Cates's expectations.

Hidden behind the smoked windows of the cab-over so no one outside could see it from the outside, Zeus II weighed over eight hundred pounds and consisted of scrap metal and industrial wire and tubing originally designed for heavy diesel landmoving equipment. The scissored jib arm, which could shoot out to exactly fifteen feet in a straight line, came from an old wheeled device that had been used by the mining company to retrieve heavy fallen tools and parts from deep inside crevices and shafts.

At the end of the jib was the shooting head, a wide-open set of steel jaws cut and refashioned from the rims of an abandoned heavy-duty utility truck. The rims had been cut in half and polished by LOR and shaped to become the two oblong, toothfilled, U-shaped jaws.

Zeus II was powered by an explosive release of compressed air pressure from the two welding tanks within the cab. When it was deployed, it created enough velocity to rock the truck on its springs. At the push of the red button on the top of the joystick, the head would blast out and, at the apex of the extension, the steel jaws would clamp down with twelve hundred pounds per square inch of pressure. With the remaining air in the tanks, Cates could jerk the joystick and shake the victim like a rag doll.

They'd addressed the problem of aiming because the point

of impact had to be *exactly* fifteen feet. Any closer, and the open jaws would simply be a high-powered battering ram. It would bludgeon the target but not clamp down. And if the target was farther away than fifteen feet, the jaws would snap down on air with a terrifying hollow *clack*ing noise.

That was why they'd experimented on melons in Powell. LOR had come up with the idea of using a small laser pen beam aimed at the void in back of the truck and a golf range finder to measure the beam when it struck something solid. When an object, whether a person's head or a cantaloupe on a stick was at *exactly* fifteen feet away, the jaws of Zeus II could be unleashed.

They'd been lucky before that the shooting head had hit its target. But firing it in the dark was much different than during daylight hours.

The Louisville Slugger, when swung with power, created slashes and rips that looked as authentic as hell, he thought. There was no reason to improve or modify that particular tool.

Cates looked over his shoulder at the gauge and announced, "Two thousand PSI. Axel, you can turn the truck off now. I'll kill the air compressor. Just keep the power on inside so you can view the rearview camera."

"Roger that," Soledad said from inside the cab through the open slider. Cates appreciated the man's military manner. He planned to ask Soledad more about his history when they had the time.

Then Cates connected with Bobbi Johnson on *his* new burner phone.

"Anything going on, Bobbi?"

"Nothing. I'm colder than hell."

"It shouldn't be too long now."

"When this is over, you need to thaw me out," she said. "I have some ideas how to do that."

"You're on speaker right now, Bobbi. Everyone can hear you."

As if to illustrate his point, LOR leered at him from beside Zeus II and waggled his eyebrows suggestively.

"Text me if anything happens," Cates said to her. "I'll do the same."

He lowered the phone to his lap, screen down so there would be no glow that could be seen from the outside. The eastern sky had begun to fuse with vanilla light. It was a matter of time before the stars to the east blinked out and the sharp outline of the Bighorns formed from the gloom.

With the engine and air compressor off, it was completely silent inside the pickup. Magpies from the brush near the distant river were already starting to call out.

"Get ready," Cates said again to everyone.

JUDGE HEWITT EMERGED from his home on the thirteenth fairway the only way he knew how: in a hurry. He'd been up well before dawn and had reviewed his overnight emails, perused the *Wall Street Journal*, and checked out the latest posts on his favorite trophy big-game-hunting sites. Then he drained his coffee cup and pulled on a base layer of merino wool long underwear before stepping into Kuiu camo trousers. He then topped off his walking ensemble with a light Kuiu shell and stocking cap.

As he strode down the hallway beneath the glass-eye gazes of a dozen mounted big-game trophies, he slung on his shoulder holster with his .44 Magnum revolver.

Hewitt had briefly wondered who had been responsible for the blink of red brake lights he'd seen an hour before in the distant trees on the golf course. It was too early in the morning for the maintenance crews and too late in the season for golf course greenkeepers. Trespassers—locals, mainly—sometimes sneaked on the property to poach, steal things that weren't nailed down like lawn furniture and outdoor grills, or just go where they weren't normally welcome. Sometimes, one of the more ostentatious homes was vandalized simply for the reasons of jealousy and resentment.

But whoever had been on the grounds had apparently left. And if they hadn't, he'd arrest them for trespassing and haul their asses into the courthouse while reminding them that he was an officer of the court. He'd done it before.

Hewitt silenced his phone before slipping it into the zipper pocket on his shell, then strode down the sidewalk to the golf cart path. As always, he bent his head forward and swung his arms from front to back as he walked.

His brisk pace was useful not only for warming up in the morning but for burning calories as well. He walked every day no matter the weather. He had for years.

Judge Hewitt's morning routine was well known, as was his wrath if anyone tried to reach him while he was on his walk.

A FEW MOMENTS later, Soledad spoke with an urgent whisper: "Here he comes. Bearing south."

Cates sat up in his seat and LOR shinnied to the side of Zeus II, between the device and the topper wall. As he did, he readied his laser and range finder, one in each hand.

Cates studied the framing for the shot, which should have been straight out through the open rear topper window toward the cart path. It was a few degrees lighter now, and for the first time he could see a wall of pine trees bordering the other side of the fairway.

He could also see the bottom of an overhanging branch stretching across the top of the opening. It looked like a crooked arm with a bent elbow and it hung in clear view of the framed opening. Cates cursed quietly to himself, wishing he had known it was there and wondering how he'd maneuvered the truck into the alcove without hitting the branch in the first place. If he'd known, he could have repositioned the vehicle.

It was too late for that now.

JUDGE HEWITT POWER walked down the golf cart path. It was a straight shot down the fairway to the distant green, and it was light enough now that he could see the limp red flag at the pin.

When his phone vibrated, Hewitt cursed and drew it out while he walked. It was Jimmy Newman, the campaign manager for Governor Rulon. He *had* to take it.

"Damn it, what?" he said.

"I wanted to go over some scheduling with you—"

"I'll call you back," Hewitt said, cutting him off. "I'm on my walk."

Then he disconnected the call and strode on.

CATES HEARD A snatch of the phone conversation and was surprised how close Hewitt was. The man could really *move*.

LOR heard it, too, and thumbed on his laser pen and pointed it out the back. In the distance, Cates could see a pinprick of red on the trees on the other side of the fairway. He hoped Hewitt wouldn't notice it, that bastard.

With his other hand, Ogburn-Russell raised the range finder to his eye and aimed it toward the cart path, where he guessed the beam and his distance-reading device would intersect at exactly fifteen feet.

"FEARLESS" FRANK CARROLL, the newest deputy in the Twelve Sleep County Sheriff's Department, eased his just-assigned SUV from the county road toward the main gate of the Eagle Mountain Club. He was excited.

Although just twenty-four years old, Carroll had been a dedicated and passionate trout fisherman since he was eight and growing up near the Encampment River in southern Wyoming. He embraced the rudimentary training he'd received thus far in Saddlestring, finding it less rigorous than he'd received at the Wyoming Law Enforcement Academy in Douglas. What was more challenging, though, was learning about the geography, the locals, and the county itself. He had already met more colorful characters than he thought could actually be concentrated in a single area, and he'd heard stories from other deputies that were wild and hard to believe. After his second week on the job, he had started to wonder if he was in over his head, and that he'd never be up to speed on all the local miscreants and the extended lineage of so many notorious ranch families.

What had snapped him out of his doubts, though, was when he was given the key code to the front gate of the Eagle Mountain Club and when he'd been asked to patrol the hallowed grounds at least once a shift. He'd learned the layout of the place and that was when he saw big fish rising in Lake Joseph. The private, members-only lake was stocked with rainbow, brown, and tiger trout that averaged twenty inches or more. In his life, Carroll had only caught a few fish that big.

And now that the club was closed and virtually empty, he knew he had his chance. Yes, he was well aware that he didn't have permission to fish there. But fish belonged to whoever caught them, right? Sneaking onto the grounds before anyone was awake and still being present at the county building an hour later for the morning briefing with no one the wiser? What could be better?

His fly rod was assembled and rested on the top of the headrests of the SUV from front to back. His vest and waders were in the backseat.

It was a good plan and he was excited. He took his job seriously, but there had to be perks, right?

There was a reason they called him Fearless Frank, he thought.

THE BURNER ON Cates's lap vibrated, and he glanced down and flipped the screen toward him.

> A Sheriff's Dept. truck just came through the gate!
> Headed your way.

Cates took a deep breath. He didn't have time to answer Johnson. He could hear footfalls outside.

JUDGE HEWITT SENSED something different in the thick copse of trees and brush to his right as he approached it. It seemed darker than usual, as if there was a large object inside.

He slowed his pace and reached across his body for the grip of his .44 as a red beam of light hit him squarely in the eyes and blinded him, stopping him cold.

THE LASER BEAM appeared on the bridge of Hewitt's nose directly in front of Cates. The judge clamped his eyes shut while he drew his weapon. Cates said, "*Asshole,*" and jammed the joystick button down. The jaws of Zeus II exploded out the back of the truck but glanced off that underhanging branch, which slightly altered its trajectory. The pickup shuddered from the release and Cates hadn't seen the exact point of contact because he was distracted by the explosion of falling bark and pine needles from the damaged branch.

"He's down!" LOR cried. He had a better angle. All Cates could see was that the scissor jib was bent down toward the path due to the weight of the target in its teeth. "He's fucking down," LOR shouted. "Grab the bat and finish him off."

"We don't have time," Cates said. Then to Soledad, "Get us the hell out of here—*now.*"

"Roger that," Soledad said while turning the ignition. Cates was grateful the man hadn't asked why and delayed them any further.

FEARLESS FRANK CARROLL cruised along the eighteenth fairway and marveled at the huge empty houses. The house he'd grown up in, in Encampment, could fit into one of their garages, he thought.

He made the turn at the end of the golf course and could see Lake Joseph glow with dawn light through the trees to the right. Even though he wasn't close yet, his heart skipped a beat when a big trout rose and created a pattern of concentric ringlets on the surface.

"Damn," he said aloud.

For reasons he couldn't later explain, Carroll looked up the golf cart path that ran along the side of the fairway to his left.

On top of the hill, a pair of red taillights blinked out as a vehicle crested the rise and vanished down the other side. Then he noticed the heap of dark clothing sprawled across the path halfway up the hill.

Like the reflection of the dawn sun on the surface of Lake Joseph, a stream of dark liquid glowed on the concrete path as it poured from the victim.

AT HOME, JOE sat up suddenly in bed. He was instantly wide awake and checked the clock on the nightstand. It was six a.m.—he'd slept in.

Marybeth stirred beside him. "Joe, are you all right?"

He shook his head. "I just had a bad dream. I dreamed that grizzly came back."

As he said it, his phone on the nightstand lit up with an incoming call.

CHAPTER NINETEEN

Saddlestring

JOE ARRIVED AT the crime scene at the golf course at 6:35 a.m. to find a scrum of vehicles already parked on the eighth fairway halfway up the long green slope. There were three Twelve Sleep County Sheriff's Department SUVs, a Park County Sheriff's Office pickup, two Saddlestring PD cruisers, a dark Chevy Suburban with the logo of the club on the driver's-side door, and a white panel van that was driven by the area forensics technician, Gary Norwood. Several of the law enforcement vehicles had their wigwag lights on and their blue and red beams flashed across the walls of trees on both sides of the fairway and made the location look oddly psychedelic.

Rather than drive up the golf cart path, Joe used the tire tracks already pressed into the grass by the first responders on the side of it. As he ascended the rise, he could make out Elaine

Beveridge, the interim sheriff, standing and gesticulating with Jackson Bishop, the candidate for sheriff from Park County; Ruthanne Hubbard, the dispatcher and candidate for sheriff herself; and Judy, the longtime administrative director of the club. Norwood stood apart from the group, looking down at his shoes and acting as if he'd rather be anywhere but where he was. The remaining law enforcement personnel milled around between the vehicles and near the dense stand of trees.

It was a familiar sight, he thought. Whenever there was a serious incident, the location was flooded by LEOs, who largely stood around bullshitting with each other with not much else to do.

It was Norwood who noticed Joe's arrival first, and the tech quickly broke away and approached him as Joe turned off his truck and climbed out.

"This is a clusterfuck of the worst kind," Norwood said. "Judge Hewitt got attacked and now I've got three different people telling me what to do."

It was obvious where the attack had taken place. The path to the right of the trees and brush was painted with blood, and a lot of it. Fingers of dark crimson ran down the length of the path and pooled in a slight depression about four feet from where the body had been.

"Is he dead?" Joe asked Norwood.

"He was breathing, but really torn up. The bear got him right here," Norwood said, placing his left hand on top of his right clavicle. "I saw holes in his chest as big as any large-caliber bullet I've ever observed."

"But not his face and head?" Joe asked, surprised.

"Not that I saw."

"That's a little unusual."

"I wouldn't know," Norwood said. "Anyway, the EMTs bundled him up and transported him to the hospital. I think they've already called Billings MedFlight to take him to a real hospital."

Joe nodded. The county facility was fine for routine injuries, but severe trauma cases were flown to Montana. He'd made the flight himself several times over the years.

"Did you happen to take any photos?" Joe asked Norwood.

"Of course, but they're pretty grisly. No pun intended."

He handed Joe his cell phone after activating the photo app. The shots weren't as clear and crisp as the evidence photos Norwood usually presented with his professional camera.

Joe scrolled through them with a grimace. It was bad enough to see the results of a bear attack on unfamiliar victims, much less a man he'd known and worked with for years.

In the photos, Judge Hewitt lay on his side on the cart path. His left arm was flung out and his head rested on it. His knees were bent and parallel as if he were sleeping. Hewitt's face was pure white and his eyes were closed. A large-caliber handgun lay on the pavement next to him. There was a lot of blood on the path, but the damage itself seemed isolated to Hewitt's right shoulder, breast, and neck.

"Who found the victim?" Joe asked.

Norwood chinned toward the LEOs. "The new guy," he said. "Deputy Carroll. Everybody calls him 'Fearless Frank.'"

"Then I think I need to talk with Fearless Frank."

"Stay away from those wannabe sheriffs," Norwood cautioned.

"I intend to," Joe said.

"You might want to suggest that all those people stay the hell off the path and out of the trees," Norwood said with a pained wince. "I have a job to do here."

JOE KEPT HIS head down as best he could and gave a wide berth to the candidates for sheriff, Elaine Beveridge, and Judy. They appeared to be in a heated discussion about what steps should be taken next and who was in charge of them.

He heard Beveridge, who had a helmet of dark hair that never blew out of place, say, "I'm just not sure. This is my first grizzly bear attack . . . ," and Ruthanne Hubbard say, "When this gets out, there's going to be panic in the streets. *In the streets!* And wait until they find out it was Judge Hewitt . . ."

"I'll need to notify our membership," Judy said while shaking her head. "Nothing like this has ever happened here before. We've had golf balls go through windows and an older member got run over by a golf cart, but this is just insane."

"Ladies," Bishop said with a raised voice, "just forget it was a bear and forget it was a member and forget it was your judge. We need to treat this like any crime scene and start by sealing off the scene and starting the forensics."

"Hear! Hear!" Norwood chimed in.

"Do not '*ladies*' us, Jackson," Hubbard hissed at Bishop

while jabbing him in the chest with her index finger. "We don't need to have things *mansplained* to us—especially by a cop outside his jurisdiction."

"Hey, game warden—what are you doing here?" Beveridge called out. Joe cringed.

"My job," he responded.

"Maybe if you'd done your job in the first place and killed this grizzly bear, we could have avoided all of this," she said. Joe got the impression she was simply taking out her frustration on the nearest target, which was him. He thought that he wouldn't mind it when Elaine stepped back into her role as county commissioner.

"WHICH ONE OF you is Fearless Frank Carroll?" Joe asked a group of two deputies and one patrolman who were leaning shoulder to shoulder on the grille of an SUV.

"That would be me," said a light-haired, fresh-faced officer as he pushed himself to his feet, uncrossed his arms, and held out his hand. When he did, Joe noticed that the deputy's beige uniform was stained with blood.

Joe shook Carroll's hand. "I understand you found the victim."

"Affirmative," Carroll said. "I was patrolling the grounds and I looked up on the cart path and saw him lying there."

"Did you see the bear?"

Carroll shook his head. "Nope. He must have taken off when I showed up. At least I hope I scared him off."

"Did you see anything at all?"

Carroll reached up and rubbed his chin. "There was a vehicle driving away at the top of the hill near the tee box. I saw taillights for a second and then it was gone."

"A *vehicle*?" Joe said, puzzled. "Did you recognize the make or model?"

"Negative. It was still pretty dark out and I didn't get a good look at it. I thought about giving chase, but I couldn't leave the injured party. I didn't realize he's the judge around here."

"He is," Joe said.

"I rolled him over from his back to his belly, which is something I probably shouldn't have done," Carroll said. "But when I saw that he was still breathing, I was afraid he'd choke to death on his own blood. He had a wound right here"—the deputy indicated the right side of his own neck—"and it was pouring out blood."

"You probably did the right thing," Joe said.

Carroll nodded, but he was obviously unsure that he had.

"I hope he makes it," Carroll said. "If I'd been two minutes earlier, I might have been able to take a shot at that damned grizzly and saved the guy's life."

"I'm more interested in the taillights you saw," Joe said. "Tell me, do you patrol the club every morning?"

Carroll looked away and Joe noted the tell.

"Not every day," he said.

"When you do, are there any vehicles about? Especially now, when the place is closed?"

"I never see anyone," Carroll said. "It's too early, I think."

"Have you ever seen Judge Hewitt out on his walk before?"

Carroll hesitated for a moment, then took a deep breath. "I'll be honest," he said. "I wasn't really patrolling. I was going to sneak out here and catch a couple of big trout out of Lake Joseph. I was hoping to get in and get out in time for the end of my shift."

That brought a snigger from the town cop and a smile from the other deputy.

Joe said, "I assume you have a fishing license."

Carroll's face went pale, which Joe took as his answer.

"We can worry about that later," Joe said. "Let's retrace your steps when you found the judge."

Carroll led the way. Joe followed him.

GARY NORWOOD AND Jackson Bishop joined them as they crossed the cart path above the bloodstains and approached the stand of trees and brush adjacent to it.

"Please don't charge in there," Norwood said while taking the lens cap off his camera. "I haven't processed the area yet."

"Let's get it taped off first," Bishop said.

As if already taking orders from the inevitable new sheriff-to-be, Carroll and another deputy responded. They tied off one end of the yellow crime scene tape to the trunk of a tree on the side of the opening and extended it out and around the bloody path.

Joe stepped back to let them secure the tape to plastic posts that had been driven into the ground.

"I'd bet he never saw it coming," Joe said to Bishop while studying the shadowed opening in the trees.

The stand was hollowed out in the middle and the floor was a carpet of crushed twigs and pine needles. Foliage surrounded it on three sides and over the top. It was a perfect place for a bear to hide and wait for prey, Joe thought. It looked like a cave opening.

"This is really bad," Bishop said, standing next to Joe. "Judge Hewitt was showing me the ropes around here during my run for sheriff. He's my main man here in Twelve Sleep County. My sponsor, so to speak. Plus, he's my father-in-law."

"Yup," Joe said.

"I hope he makes it."

"We all do," Joe said.

Bishop turned to Carroll and said, "Good work, Deputy."

"Thank you," Carroll responded, and glanced over at Joe to see if Joe would add to the exchange and possibly reveal the real reason he'd been at the club. Joe kept quiet.

"We're sure the bear's gone, right?" Norwood said as he faced the opening.

"We *think* so," Bishop said with a wink.

At that moment, cell phones erupted in the pockets of all the law enforcement officers on the scene at the same time, and the local police officer nearest to Joe responded to his shoulder mic. Joe had no idea what was going on, although he heard the urgent voice of the dispatcher from the county building. The phrase he overheard several times was "drive-by." It sent a chill through him.

Elaine Beveridge held her cell phone to her face and threw her free hand into the air. "At the middle school playground?" she shouted. "Do we know who did it?"

Joe's immediate reaction was horror, followed by gratitude that he no longer had children in local schools.

"On my way," Carroll said into his phone before disconnecting. "There was a drive-by shooting at the middle school," he told Joe. "A thirteen-year-old girl was playing basketball outside before school started when she got hit. I've got to go."

"Of course you do," Joe said.

"Everybody," Bishop called out. "All of you need to respond *right now*." Then: "Norwood, follow me."

The forensics tech jogged to his van as the officers dashed toward their vehicles. Within thirty seconds, the only people remaining at the scene were Joe and Judy. Sirens wailed in the distance as the caravan of cop cars roared through the club en route to Saddlestring.

"How can this all be happening?" Judy asked. She looked genuinely distressed.

"No idea," Joe said. "It's a really bad day."

"I've never heard of a drive-by shooting in Saddlestring."

"There's never been one."

"That poor girl."

"Yup."

"I hope they find out who did it."

Joe was grateful that Jackson Bishop seemed to be taking charge, even though the man had no official brief to do so—yet. Maybe, Joe hoped, Bishop would turn out to be a good sheriff after all. It would be a welcome change in Twelve Sleep County.

He realized that Judy had asked him a question that he hadn't heard.

"What's that?"

She pointed toward the crime scene perimeter. "I said, what am I supposed to do with all of this?"

"Leave it," Joe said. "Norwood still needs to process it."

"Am I supposed to leave all the blood on the cart path?"

"Yes, for now. And please tell your maintenance folks to stay away from here for the time being. I realize they might be curious, but they need to stay away. Same thing for any locals who may want to come out and look. Please keep them away for now."

"What if that bear is still here somewhere?" she asked. "There are plenty of places to hide."

"Do you and your people have bear spray? I'd suggest that you advise them to carry it with them for the next few days."

"They'd rather carry guns," she said.

"Those will work, too."

She placed her hands on her hips and looked straight down. Joe assumed she was trying to wrap her mind around all that had happened in the last hour.

"Judy, are you doing okay? Is there anything I can do?" he asked.

"I don't know what that would be."

"Are you in good enough shape to check on something for me?"

She looked up. "I wouldn't mind a distraction."

"Who accessed the club this morning? Do you have the video from the gates?"

"I do, in my office," she said.

"Could you please go there right now and call me with what you find?"

She agreed and climbed into the Suburban she'd parked on the fairway. "I'll call you in a few minutes," she said.

"Thank you. And if you have a vehicle on tape, please send that to me, Elaine, and Jackson Bishop."

"Where are you going?" she asked. "To the school?"

He shook his head. "No, I think they've got enough bodies on the scene and they probably don't need another one. I'm going to go to the hospital to check on Judge Hewitt's condition."

"I'll pray for him," Judy said. "And I'll pray for that thirteen-year-old girl."

"Me too," Joe said as he strode toward his pickup.

MARYBETH CALLED AS Joe exited the Eagle Mountain Club through the main gate. She was driving to work.

"Did you hear about the shooting at the school?" she asked.

"Yes."

"Have they found who did it?"

"I don't think so."

"I saw on Facebook that a couple of the kids said they saw a white SUV with California plates on the street outside the play-ground. I think that's what they're looking for."

"That should be fairly easy to find," Joe said. "But I'd cau-tion against putting too much stock in that information this early."

"Of course," she said. "I'll find out more when I get to the library."

He had no doubt that she would.

"What's Judge Hewitt's condition?" she asked.

"I'm on my way to find out now."

"Was it the same bear that got Clay Junior? And Dulcie?"

"We don't know anything yet," Joe said.

Before he could continue, another call came in. It was Judy.

"I'll call you back," he said to Marybeth.

"Good, because I have a lot of questions."

Joe disconnected the call and punched up Judy.

"No vehicles entered the gates of the club until Deputy Car-roll came in this morning," Judy told Joe.

"You're sure?"

"I'm positive. I'm looking at the footage as we speak. It's time-stamped."

"Good. Please don't delete it for the time being."

His head was spinning. Then: "Is it possible that any of your maintenance people were out on the course early this morning?"

"I highly doubt it," Judy said. "I'd have seen their cars on the videotape when they came in to work. And they usually don't show up until eight or eight-thirty during the months when the club is closed."

"Deputy Carroll said he saw a vehicle," Joe said. "Do you have any cameras on the course itself?"

"Our members wouldn't stand for it," she responded. "Especially the ones who cheat."

He asked, "Is there still that old river road access?"

"Yes. We close it in the winter after they're done moving cows, but we don't tell the members about it at all because it washes out in the spring and it's not safe."

"Are there any cameras on it?"

"No."

Joe thanked her. The old river road was known only to locals who had intimate knowledge of the layout of the club. Did that suggest that the vehicle Carroll had seen that morning belonged to someone in the area?

He made a mental note to check the road for fresh tire tracks.

ON THE WAY into town to the hospital, Joe punched up Jennie Gordon on his cell phone. He had no idea where in the state she would be.

She answered by saying, "I just heard." She sounded weary and depressed.

"I'm not sure it's our bear," Joe said. "It's something else entirely."

There was a long pause. Then: "*What?*"

"This attack is different from the others, not to mention that it's over two hundred and seventy-five miles from the last one two days ago."

"How is it different?" she asked.

"From the photos I saw, there was only one big bite on the victim and the wounds were on his breast, clavicle, and neck. The bear didn't go for his head and face like the others.

"Also, I didn't see any claw marks or ripped-up fabric. I got the weird impression that the bear attacked and *missed*, then took off before finishing the job."

"That's bizarre," she said. "Do you think it got scared away before it was done?"

"It's possible but unlikely," Joe said. "A deputy sheriff found the victim immediately after the attack, but he didn't see the bear. He said he saw taillights in the distance, but no bear."

"Taillights?"

"I said the same thing. And no, we have no idea who was in the vehicle or how they got there. Or if it has anything at all to do with the attack."

"Let me think for a second," she said. Then: "Maybe the mystery vehicle drove up on the bear as it charged the victim and spooked it."

"I hadn't thought of that," Joe said. "I suppose it's possible. But whoever was in the car didn't stop to render aid or make a call to law enforcement. They just hightailed it out of there."

"Wouldn't you do the same if you were trespassing on the Eagle Mountain Club?" she asked rhetorically. "Nevertheless, we need to find that driver, Joe. We need to find out what he saw."

"I'm working on that," Joe said. "All I can tell you is that he didn't use the main gate to get in or out."

"I'll assemble the team and get up there as soon as we can," she said. "But given the distance between our attacks, that bear could be halfway to Utah by the time we arrive."

"Which is something I still can't wrap my head around," Joe said. "The mileage between the attacks is just incredible. This bear seems to have some kind of supernatural powers.

"I'm pulling into the parking lot of the hospital now," he said. "I'm going to try and talk with Judge Hewitt before they fly him out of here. I'll fill you in on everything after I do."

"I'm completely confused, Joe."

"We all are," he said. "But this doesn't look like our bear."

"I think you're trying to make my head explode," she said.

"You and me both," Joe said as he disconnected the call.

JOE COULD SEE the MedFlight chopper arriving in the clear blue sky from the north, looking like a huge black damselfly, as he pushed through the double doors of the hospital into the lobby. There was an attendant out on the helipad to help guide it in.

"Where can I find Judge Hewitt?" he asked the receptionist behind the counter. As he did so, she held up her hand to caution him against proceeding any further.

She was a dark, severe woman, with readers hanging from her neck on a chain.

"He's being transported to Billings," she said.

"I know that. I need to see him before they fly him out of here."

The receptionist frowned and said, "Judge Hewitt is in no shape to—"

Joe didn't let her finish her sentence. Instead, he turned to the right and shoved the push bar on the door with the heels of his hands and entered the emergency wing of the hospital. He knew that the staff used the ER as a staging area for patients being prepped to depart on the helicopter. The receptionist called to him to come back, but her voice was silenced when the doors closed behind him.

Judge Hewitt lay on his back on a gurney covered by white sheets. Fluids flowed into him through tubes from elevated stands with wheels next to him. A physician's assistant, a young man whom Joe recognized as being from the same high school class as his daughter April, said, "Hi, Mr. Pickett. I'm not sure you're supposed to be in here."

"I'll be quick. Is the judge conscious?"

"He's deeply medicated."

A male attendant who looked to be prepared to wheel Hewitt out to the helipad said nothing.

Joe approached the head of the gurney and sidled up next to it. Hewitt's face was like a death mask of pure white and his cheeks were hollow. His eyes were half open but unfocused, and a string of saliva hung from his slack lips to the top of his pillow. The side of his neck was heavily bandaged, as well as the top of his right shoulder. A spot of dark blood the size of a quarter had seeped through the binding from the wound on his neck. If it weren't for his chest slowly heaving under the sheets, Joe would have guessed he was gone.

"Judge, can you hear me?"

Hewitt's eyes moved across the ceiling but didn't settle on Joe's face.

"Judge? I need to know what you saw before you were attacked."

There was no recognition of the question in Hewitt's expression. His eyes continued to wander.

"Judge? Help me out here, please."

The roar of the helicopter outside increased in volume as it settled onto the helipad.

"Mr. Pickett, we've got to go," the PA said.

"Judge," Joe said sharply. "Look at me."

"Mr. Pickett . . ."

Joe knew that the judge disliked shaking hands or just about any form of physical contact, so he reached under the sheets and grasped Hewitt's hand. It was cool to the touch and it instantly recoiled.

Hewitt suddenly grunted and his eyes focused on Joe.

"He knows I'm here and I think he can hear me," Joe said. "Judge, what did you see?"

"Please," the PA said, shouldering Joe aside. "They're waiting on us."

Joe was frustrated, but didn't want an altercation, so he stepped back. The attendant moved to the foot of the gurney to push it outside. The PA opened the double doors and kicked wooden wedges under each one to keep them agape. Outside, the chopper idled on the helipad as its rotors spun ineffectually.

As the gurney passed by him, the PA suddenly leaned down

and turned his head so his ear was close to Judge Hewitt's mouth. He stood back up after the gurney rolled outside.

"Did he say something to you?" Joe asked.

The PA blinked. "He said what sounded like 'red dot.'"

"Red dot?"

"That's what I think he said. It could have been something else, though."

"Like from a rifle scope?"

"I don't know, Mr. Pickett. Now, if you don't mind . . ."

"I'm going, I'm going," Joe said. "Thanks for your help."

Red dot?

CHAPTER TWENTY

Cates Compound

DALLAS CATES PACED the length of his former house with an angry stride while firing out occasional air punches and mumbling, *"Fuck, fuck, fuck . . ."* His route was so familiar to him he could have done it with his eyes closed: from the front door, through the living room, into and out of the kitchen, and into the back mudroom until he reached the door. Then spinning on his boot heel and doing it again.

"Fuck, fuck, fuck . . ."

As he did it, Cates recalled episodes of his boyhood when he'd paced the same route before or during significant events in his life. He remembered doing it as a freshman in high school while wearing a wrestling team singlet, psyching himself up to take on the varsity wrestler in his weight class, which he did. Then again, two years later, as he prepared to win his first state championship in wrestling. He recalled nervously pacing a year later as he waited for the local cops to show up because of that sexual assault claim that had been made by a female hanger-on who had accused the entire wrestling squad.

He'd done the same routine in cowboy boots and chaps the day before winning the local rodeo and qualifying for his Professional Rodeo Cowboys Association card, and again when he had to win a go-round to get into the National Finals Rodeo in Las Vegas.

Back then, Eldon and Brenda had sat passively in their recliners watching him pace and shaking their heads. Eldon shook his head because he thought Dallas was wasting his energy. Brenda shook her head because she was just so darned proud of her youngest boy.

THIS TIME, THOUGH, Cates was cursing himself for the epic screwup an hour before. He was especially angry that it had been his fault, and his fault alone. He'd been so concerned that Bobbi would mess up and let a vehicle cruise through the main gate without alerting him, or that LOR's aiming scheme would give them a false reading, or that Soledad would do something stupid and impulsive, that he hadn't paid enough attention himself to that ridiculous overhanging branch that had altered the trajectory of the shooting head.

Had that Barney Fife in the sheriff's department vehicle actually seen them leaving the scene?

And had the shooting head, although slightly diverted, done fatal damage to that bastard of a judge?

CATES WAS SO consumed by his anger and self-recriminations that he almost didn't notice that Bobbi Johnson had entered the house through the mudroom door and now stood quietly with her back against the wall inside the living room. She watched him pace for a while, but he had no doubt she had come in there for a reason, that she had something she felt she needed to say.

"What?" he finally asked, putting his hands on his hips and glaring at her. He was out of breath from exertion.

"Dallas, I . . ." Her voice faded out. Or her nerve.

"What? Spit it out."

"Dallas, you need to get control of Axel before he gets us all arrested or killed."

"What about him?" Cates asked, momentarily confused. He hadn't even seen Axel since they'd returned to the compound and all of them had gone their separate ways with their own separate thoughts about what had just happened.

"Have you been in the bedroom?" she asked, chinning toward the closed door of what had been Eldon and Brenda's room.

"No."

"That couple last night, they're in there. They're dead. He shot them in the head this morning. Unless it was you who did it."

"It wasn't me," Cates said. "I wasn't sure what to do with them, but no, it wasn't me."

"Did you know about it?"

"Not until it was over."

Tears formed in Johnson's eyes and she swiped at them angrily with the back of her hand. "We're in too deep, Dallas. *I'm* in too deep."

"It'll be fine, Bobbi," he said as he moved in close to her and placed his hands on her shoulders. "Believe me, it'll all be fine. We're going to get to the end of this and no one will suspect a thing. Nobody's going to arrest us or hurt you."

She melted into him and buried her head in his chest. He wished she wouldn't cry like that. He wished she was tougher.

"I did my job this morning," she sobbed. "I called you the minute that guy came through the gate."

"You did your job," he said. "None of it was your fault. *I'm* the one who screwed up. Not you, not LOR, and not Axel."

As he'd paced through the house, he replayed the events of that morning over and over in his mind, wondering if he should have made different decisions.

Should he have just held off firing the shooting head and waited for another shot the next morning? That had flashed through his mind at the time, but he'd rejected it. Not with the laser point on Hewitt's face and the revolver coming out.

What if, instead of telling Axel to get the hell out of there, he had waited for the deputy to show up and taken *him* out? He could have possibly created two grizzly bear fatalities at the same location. Then he could have finished the job on the judge with the bat. But Dallas had rejected that scenario as well. For one, the tanks couldn't have been recharged in time for a second strike. Second, if the deputy had called for backup before he arrived at the scene, that could have been a catastrophe for them as well.

No, it all came down to not seeing that goddamned branch in the dark. And the unlucky break it had been that the deputy just happened to show up at *exactly* the wrong time.

Cates was ninety-five percent sure the judge was dead. He'd not only felt the power of the crushing mechanical bite through the metal arm of the telescopic scissor jib, but he'd glimpsed the still body of Judge Hewitt on the cart path. There had been a lot of blood. The grizzly bear teeth in the steel jaws were crimson with it.

"We don't need him," Johnson said, pulling him out of his musings. She was back to Axel. "We were doing just fine before he showed up. I mean, I know why you have to keep LOR around. I fucking hate him, but he can fix the Zeus II machine if it breaks down. But Axel? What good is he to you? To us? He's a loose cannon.

"I mean, he just killed those two people in there," she said. "What if somebody misses them and shows up? Will he just kill them, too?"

Probably, Cates thought but didn't say out loud. She didn't even know about what had happened to the attendant in Thermopolis.

"I mean, what are we going to do with those bodies?" she asked.

"Don't worry about that. I grew up here on this property and I know there are places to hide bodies where they'll never be found. My mom . . ." he said, but let it trail off. There was no need to get into those stories now.

She asked, "What if those people in there had a meeting in town and they don't show up for it? Wouldn't that raise suspicions? What do we do if one of their cell phones ring?"

"Those are good questions," Cates said. "My only answer is that the only way to avoid those problems is to work faster than I'd planned. Speed everything up so we can get out of here before any of that happens. We'll go see your sister," he said, having no intention of ever doing that.

"He's going to screw everything up," she said. "I don't trust him and he scares the shit out of me. Do you trust him?"

"I don't trust anyone except you," Cates said soothingly. Which was a lie, of course. He didn't trust her, either. "I'll tell you something I learned in prison, though. When the situation turns all raggedy-assed, it never hurts to have somebody crazier than you on your side. That can freeze your enemies in place."

She said, "He's a psycho. I thought LOR was bad, but he's not on the same level as Axel."

"Maybe that's what we need for the time being," Cates said. "Someone so unpredictable and ruthless that they'll think twice about coming after us."

"Axel isn't worth all that," she said. "I'm afraid he'll turn you against me. He wants new recruits for his stupid plan."

"Impossible," Cates said, squeezing her. He nuzzled his face into her and wished her hair smelled better. While he did, he contemplated that, within the group, Soledad wanted Bobbi gone, Bobbi wanted Soledad gone now and LOR gone as soon as possible, and LOR wanted to go home to Jeffrey City and be rid of them all the minute his obligation was fulfilled. And how he held all the cards for the moment on not only keeping them all together, but completing his goal. He was grateful he was a natural leader of men—and women. But it couldn't last forever. He was grateful Johnson couldn't see his smile while he held her.

Then, looking up, Cates said, "Where is Axel, anyway?"

"He's gone," she said. "I saw him driving away in that dead couple's car a few minutes after we got back."

"Really? I wonder where he went."

"Let's hope he never comes back," she said. "It would be all right with me if he just kept driving."

"Maybe he went to get breakfast," Cates said.

Johnson gently pushed away from Cates. She seemed reassured by him, and no longer at a breaking point. She caressed Cates's left hand, but he flinched when her thumb made contact with the fresh *X* tattoo that filled box number four of his kill list. He'd made it using a needle and ink from a ballpoint pen.

"Just three more," she said.

"Just three more," he echoed.

"Please don't tell him what we talked about," she said.

"You mean, what *you* talked about," Cates said with a chuckle, to confuse her.

"I mean, you have to agree with me, right? That we need to cut him loose as soon as we can?"

Cates whispered, "When the time is right."

"Isn't it right now?"

"Not yet," he said, noting movement outside through the living room window. He let go of her and brushed the curtain back. Soledad was behind the wheel of the dead couple's white SUV and he drove it into the open garage and parked it.

"Speak of the devil," Cates said.

AXEL SOLEDAD GLIDED through the front door on his crutches, grasping a large greasy paper bag with BURG-O-PARDNER printed on the outside of it. Like a sniffing puppy, LOR appeared behind him.

"I got us some food," he announced.

"Good, because I'm starved," LOR said.

"I haven't had a good breakfast sandwich from the Burg-O-Pardner for a long time," Cates said.

They all gravitated toward the kitchen table, even Johnson. Soledad placed the bag on the tabletop.

"Is that it?" Cates asked Soledad, wondering if the man would offer more information on his recent whereabouts.

"I also got us coffees," Soledad said, choosing not to understand Cates's real question. "I couldn't carry it all in one trip."

"I've got it," Cates said, going outside and walking toward the white SUV. He hadn't noticed before that it still had California plates.

Inside the vehicle, Cates found the box filled with lidded coffees on the front passenger seat. The interior smelled of fried food, hot coffee, and something acrid. He recognized the smell of gunpowder.

As Cates leaned over to pick up the box, he noticed two small brass casings on the driver's-side floor mat. And before he closed the car door with a bump from his right hip, he saw a semiautomatic .22 rifle laying across the rear bench seat.

He turned to find Soledad in front of him. Cates marveled once again how swiftly—and how silently—the man covered ground.

"I'm sure you saw the rifle," Soledad said.

Cates nodded.

"When we got back from the club this morning, I got to thinking. We left that golf course in such a damned hurry. I know it couldn't be helped under the circumstances."

"Yes."

"So we had no time to finish the job properly, and we didn't have time to cover our tracks. And when I say cover our tracks, I mean exactly that."

Cates felt a chill go through him. Not only were there probably tire tracks from Johnson's pickup in the soft mulch, but he'd walked around in the alcove himself.

"*Fuck, fuck, fuck . . .*" he whispered.

Soledad said, "Don't worry about it, Dallas. We're golden."

"But how? Did you go back to the club?"

"Of course not," Soledad said. "I figured the place was crawling with cops. So I borrowed a rifle from our California friends and took their car into town. Let's just say I created a diversion serious enough to pull all those cops straight off the golf course."

Soledad said, "Random violence screws them up, and they run around like chickens with their heads chopped off. I know about this from experience in the field. If you want to create an absolute clusterfuck, you do something with no motive, no rhyme or reason.

"The cops will start with the victim and work out from there. Who was she? Did she have enemies? Is there some kind of gang war going on at the school? Did the shooter have another target in mind? Those are the questions they'll ask. Then they'll chase their tails around like puppies and get absolutely nowhere fast. But what they won't do," Soledad said, "is think to go back to the original crime scene right away."

"She?" Cates said. "The *school*?"

"I'll give you all the details later," he said with a cold smile. "Just be happy that it worked like a charm."

As Cates started to put it together with equal measures of horror and admiration, Soledad said, "We'll need to get back up to the club tonight and take a couple of rakes. Then we can finish this thing in one fell swoop and get the hell out of Wyoming."

CHAPTER TWENTY-ONE

Never Summer Ranch

For Sheridan, breakfast was very uncomfortable and not just because she'd arrived late to the Never Summer Ranch. She'd been held up because it took longer than she'd estimated to feed and load all her falcons into her vehicle, as well as to pack up her belongings. And when DeWayne Kolb wasn't behind the front desk like he'd told her he'd be, she'd had to go out and find him at a diner down the block to return the room key and get his assurances that he'd adjust the cost of the room to reflect her stay.

"I hope that lunatic Bottom didn't drive you away," Kolb said, mainly for the benefit of the other local men at the table. "You were barely here long enough to experience the place."

"I finished my job," she told him. "Now I'm going home."

"Come back," Kolb said. "You should see this place in the summer."

"All five days of it," another man said with a chuckle. "It's wonderful."

LEON BOTTOM WAS a little cool at first when Sheridan arrived, but his mood improved rapidly when Katy Cotton delivered plate after plate of steaming food from the kitchen adjacent to the dining room. He dug into fried eggs, bacon, hash browns, pancakes, syrup, wheat toast, strawberry jam, and fresh-squeezed orange juice.

Cotton retreated to the kitchen after the first round and eased the door closed. She'd made a point of not making eye contact with Sheridan as she served the food.

Sheridan was fascinated with watching the man eat. He did so with total focus, his fork working from the plate to his mouth like a piston, and not until he cleared his plate did he look up at her.

"I went into the barn this morning," he said, going for seconds. "There wasn't a starling in sight."

"Excellent."

"Where do you think they all went?" he asked. "Not that I care, but I'm curious."

She said, "By now, those starlings have found a new place to invade. I'm pretty sure they won't come back, but I thought it made sense to hang around here until about noon. There might be a few stragglers who return, not knowing the big group was chased off."

"You can stay longer than that if you'd like," Bottom said.

"I already checked out of the Alpine Motel."

Bottom snorted and said, "No wonder you don't want to hang around. That place is a dump and the owner, Kolb, is one of those mouth-breathing locals I was warning you about."

"It's okay, really. Mr. Kolb was fine."

"You wouldn't say that if you stayed there much longer. Did you look carefully for peepholes and such?"

Sheridan stiffened in her chair. She was shocked.

"Seriously?" she asked.

"I've heard things," Bottom said, but not convincingly, Sheridan thought.

"Anyway, we have plenty of room here," he said, gesturing to the staircase that led, she guessed, to several bedrooms upstairs. "I won't even charge you."

Sheridan got a warning vibe that she'd learned over the years to take seriously. He was a little *too* insistent. And a man who thought about peepholes might know something about them, she thought.

"No," she said. "I really need to get back."

It was almost true, but not quite. But Sheridan wanted to maintain good relations with her customer while firmly declining his invitation at the same time.

"You're not eating," he said, pointing to her empty plate with the tines of his fork. "Dig in. Katy is a great cook. That's one of the biggest reasons I insisted she come with me."

"I don't usually eat breakfast," Sheridan said. "But it does look good."

She'd learned from going on ride-alongs with her dad that it was always a good policy to accept meal invitations from hunters, landowners, or, in this case, clients. It might be construed as insulting to refuse, he'd told her. He claimed that he sometimes ate three breakfasts in a row while patrolling elk camps and was therefore miserable for the rest of the day.

"If drinking bad coffee and eating dry eggs is what it takes to be neighborly, it's worth it," he'd said.

So she took the platter of pancakes and slid two onto her plate, followed by two slices of bacon.

"Katy makes the best pancakes," Bottom said with approval. Then his cell phone chimed and he looked at the screen. "My bankers," he said. "I need to take this."

"Sure, no problem."

Bottom rose from the table and turned to the door that led to the front porch. He called toward the kitchen door, "Katy, come on out and give Sheridan some company. You need to eat, too."

Then he stepped outside and closed the door behind him.

COTTON PUSHED SLOWLY through the door with her eyes down and didn't say a word. She slid into the chair opposite Sheridan. Her mouth was pursed into a scowl and she came across as either angry or very tense.

As Cotton took two pancakes for herself, Sheridan lifted the handle of the syrup container and handed it across the table to her. The ceramic container was the shape of a bear and the syrup poured out of its open mouth. Cotton glanced up at it and quickly looked away.

"Okay," Sheridan said, taking the syrup back.

Without staring overtly, Sheridan observed as Cotton generously buttered her pancakes and then lifted the top one and slid a fried egg between them. Then another on top of the stack. As Cotton did it, Sheridan again felt the curious pang of discordant familiarity that she'd noted before. Something about Cotton's eyes, features, or mannerisms unnerved her. When had she encountered this old woman who refused to look at her or speak to her? And why the brazen animosity?

"There's something I wanted to ask you before I leave this ranch forever," Sheridan said.

After a beat, Cotton said, "Mmmmm?"

"Look, I think we somehow got off on the wrong foot and I'm not sure why. What I'm wondering is if we ever met each other before. Or maybe you're confusing me with someone you had a bad experience with?"

Cotton shook her head almost imperceptibly.

"So we haven't met?"

Again the headshake.

"Then what is it? I'm really curious to find out."

"It's nothing. Kindly eat and leave."

"Wow," Sheridan said, pouring syrup on her pancakes. "Right to the point."

As Sheridan ate her first mouthful, she said, "I can see why

Mr. Bottom likes his breakfast. These pancakes are delicious."
And they were: fluffy, slightly sweet, with a sour buttermilk
tang.

"Leon likes his breakfast, even though he eats it like a pig,"
Cotton said. Her tone was bitter and dismissive, but for the first
time she'd actually said something to Sheridan that wasn't
passive-aggressive or downright hostile toward her.

Sheridan wasn't sure how to respond, so she didn't. She
watched as Cotton broke the yolk of the first fried egg and let
it run off the crisp white edges until it painted the surface of the
top pancake. Then she lifted it and pierced the yolk of the middle egg.

Sheridan was startled, and at first she couldn't put her finger
on why. Then it hit her.

"My dad eats pancakes like that," she said. "You're the only
person besides him I've ever seen who uses that . . . method. No
syrup at all, just egg yolks soaked into the pancake."

Cotton seemed to freeze. Again, she refused to make eye
contact.

"He also makes the best pancakes I've ever had until these,"
Sheridan said. "What's your secret?"

"No secret," Cotton said, deadpan. "It's just Bisquick, but I
add sugar, baking powder, buttermilk, oil, eggs, and a teaspoon
of vanilla."

Sheridan sat back. "That's *exactly* what my dad does. He
used to make them for us every Sunday morning. I grew up
eating these exact pancakes. Isn't that a strange coincidence?"

"It is," Cotton said with no enthusiasm.

"What are the odds? The same pancake recipe."

"I don't find it all that interesting," Cotton said. "It's a recipe right off the side of the box. Nothing special."

"Still . . ."

Cotton ignored her. She was eating more quickly, as if in a hurry to get it all over with as soon as possible. Sheridan used the moment to slip her phone out of her back pocket, activate the camera app, and raise it from her lap until the lenses barely cleared the table.

"Did you make your kids pancakes when they were little?" Sheridan asked. While she said it, she snapped several photos of Cotton, then lowered the phone back out of view.

Cotton flinched at the question. "Why do you ask?"

"I guess I'm just making conversation."

"Yes, I made my boys pancakes. No big deal. Why do we need conversation?"

"I guess we don't," Sheridan said. "Boys, huh? How many?"

"Two," Cotton sighed.

"Do they live around here? Do you get to see them?"

For the first time, Cotton looked up. Her eyes flared. "The younger one is dead. The older one I never see."

"That's sad for you, I'm sure," Sheridan said.

"It's the way it is. I don't want to talk about this."

"Okay. I didn't mean to pry."

Sheridan returned to her breakfast, but something was still nagging at her. The feeling was getting stronger.

"I've had only three men in my life," Cotton said, surprising her. "The first one was very bad. The second was very good. The third is Leon. I'm not sure what he is."

Sheridan didn't interrupt Cotton. The woman seemed to have something to say finally. And Sheridan didn't want to steer the conversation to her own recent loss. There were still too many conflicting emotions over that and she didn't feel prompted to share them with an odd old woman.

Cotton said, "I regret things that I did in my life before I met the very good man, Mr. Cotton. When I cut that bad man out of my life, I cut out everything about him. Everything. It was like I had a tumor removed that also took some healthy tissue. It is what it is."

"Do you mean your sons?" Sheridan asked.

"I said I don't want to talk about it and I won't."

"What was your married name before you met Mr. Cotton?" Sheridan asked. "I might be crazy, but I can't get over the feeling that we've run across each other before, somehow."

"We haven't," Cotton snapped. "Now, go."

With that, she pushed her chair back and rose from the table. Sheridan watched her carefully as she hurried to the kitchen door.

Before she slammed it shut, Cotton looked back at Sheridan with angry eyes. From behind the door, she shouted, "Go away and never come back."

SHERIDAN SHOULDERED BY Bottom on the front porch. He seemed to be arguing with his bankers and his face was bright red.

She was in a fog and her stomach hurt. Her vision seemed clouded by her sudden thoughts and feelings.

The very bad man. Two sons, the younger one dead and the older a stranger to her. Healthy tissue removed along with the tumor. Katy Cotton was in her mid- to late seventies and Leon had alluded to the fact that she had some kind of ties to Wyoming in her past.

But most of all, it was the *pancakes* and the way she cooked and ate them.

Sheridan drew her phone out of her back Wranglers pocket and speed-dialed her mother. Marybeth answered on the first ring by saying, "Hi, honey. How are things going in Colorado?"

"Great, actually. I'm ready to head back."

"This place is a nightmare right now," Marybeth said. "Wait until I catch you up."

"I look forward to that, but there's something I really need to run by you."

"What's that?"

"Are you sitting down?"

"I'm at my desk. What is it?"

"What was Dad's mother's first name?"

Marybeth hesitated for a beat. "Her name was Katherine. I never met her, and your dad never talks about her, because she walked out on the family when he was ten years old and his younger brother, Victor, was eight. Why do you ask?"

"Was she known as Katy?"

"Yes, she was," Marybeth said. "Katy Pickett."

Sheridan turned around and stared at the house on the

Never Summer Ranch. Leon Bottom paced and gesticulated on the front porch, arguing with his banker. Behind a lace curtain on the second floor, a figure looked back at her.

"I think I just met my grandmother," Sheridan said. "And she's a nasty piece of work."

CHAPTER TWENTY-TWO

Twelve Sleep County Library

M Y *MOTHER*?" JOE said incredulously to Marybeth. "In Walden, Colorado? Can that even be possible?"

They were in Marybeth's office in the Twelve Sleep County Library. Marybeth was seated behind the desk and Joe had taken the hardback chair across from her. His hat was crown-down on a side table and he'd come to fill her in on everything that had happened that morning and to find out what she'd heard as well. The door was closed and Marybeth had disconnected with Sheridan just a few minutes before.

For Joe, it was the last bit of information he would have dreamed of receiving at the moment, and he felt like he'd been gut-punched.

"She goes by Katy Cotton now," Marybeth said. "Apparently she married a man named Cotton and they moved to Michigan years ago, but now it appears that she's turned up on this ranch in Walden where Sheridan had a job."

Joe looked at the ceiling tiles. He was speechless.

"When is the last time you saw her?" Marybeth asked.

He grunted instead of responding. He didn't want to think about it.

"Joe?"

"I don't know. Over forty years ago, I guess. Victor woke me up and told me Mom was gone. George was in the kitchen drinking coffee and trying to get over his usual morning hangover. It's not like she said goodbye or left a note or anything."

Marybeth raised her hands and placed them on the sides of her cheeks. "I'm so sorry, Joe," she said. "You never talk about her."

"There's nothing to say. She was just gone from our lives, just like that. I barely remember her."

"She was there for your first ten years. You have to remember something."

Joe shook his head. "She and my dad were bad news together, I've told you that. It was like they had their own thing going and they didn't let anyone else in, including Victor and me. They loved each other like teenagers one minute and hated each other's guts the next. They were very loud about both. My brother and I sort of raised ourselves, anyway, so when she left I guess it wasn't all that different."

"Do you miss her?"

He shifted uncomfortably. "I haven't really thought about it."

"You might want to think about that now."

"Why?"

"I'm not really sure," Marybeth said. "I guess because now we know she's out there. At least, Sheridan thinks she met her."

"Sheridan might be wrong, though," Joe said.

"It's possible. Here, she took a couple of photos."

Marybeth slid her phone across her desk. Pained, Joe picked it up and scrolled through all four shots. They were hurried and not in sharp focus.

"She looks like a mean old lady," Joe said. "I can't be sure of it." But it was jarring to see her face, her white hair, the pinched mouth. She looked *familiar*, he thought. Like she could still easily lurch across the table and smack his ear with a cupped hand like she used to do when she was drinking or angry with George, which was most of the time.

"Sheridan said she was mean," Marybeth said.

"That tracks with what I remember," Joe responded. "Still, I hope it isn't her. Sheridan doesn't deserve to get sucked into this stupid thing. She's got enough on her plate."

"Your daughters are naturally curious about their relatives on your side," Marybeth said. "They've always kind of wondered how their parents came to be."

"They should know we aren't the product of our parents," Joe said, without mentioning his mother-in-law, Missy, by name. "Of all people, you should know that. When I think about what you went through growing up . . . I still can't believe you made it through."

He sat back in the chair and sighed. He said, "I'm not sure I even care about this right now. I don't want to focus on it. There's too much going on."

"I understand," Marybeth said. "But I'm going to fire up my database programs and start doing some research. I want to see if I can confirm Katy's trail from Wyoming to Michigan to Colorado. Aren't you just a little bit curious?"

"Nope."

"What if you have half brothers or sisters out there that you've never met? Wouldn't it be interesting to know about that?"

"Nope."

He said, "All these years we've done real well on our own, haven't we? We've got your crazy mother, and now mine might have crawled out from under some rock in Colorado. But we've got three great girls and we've got each other. That's pretty good, right?"

Tears filled her eyes. "Yes."

"We've done all right," he said.

"We have," she responded.

"Why muck it up now if we can help it?"

"I understand."

Joe reached up with an imaginary eraser in his right hand and moved it in a circular motion, as if to remove the previous exchange from the fronts of their minds.

"So tell me about your morning," she asked. "What have you found out about that bear?"

He said, "I'm working through a problem and I'd love your

thoughts on it. Either we've got a bear with magical powers, a bunch of bears acting in unison, or we've got something else entirely."

WHEN JOE WAS done recapping the events of that day, Marybeth squinted across the desk at him. "Does Jennie Gordon have a theory on how this is all possible?"

"Not really," Joe said. "It's all new ground. We're both bumbling around in the dark, with no clue when the next attack will come or where it could happen.

"Think about it," he said. "This grizzly—if it is one creature—has covered hundreds of miles in a huge loop around the state of Wyoming, picking off people along the way and not displaying any kind of normal bear behavior. It's not protecting its territory, food supply, or cubs. It's hunting lone humans and tearing them to shreds and not caching the bodies—except for Clay Junior—or even feeding on the remains. Judge Hewitt was the exception to the pattern this morning, of course, but the grizzly was apparently spooked away before it could finish the job. Other than that, the attack was similar."

"Thank goodness it didn't finish the job," Marybeth said.

"Hewitt said something about seeing a red dot before they loaded him on the helicopter," Joe said. "It doesn't make any sense. I associate red dots with scopes on firearms, not with bears. I wish Hewitt could have explained what he was talking about, but it's very possible he was hallucinating at that point.

There were plenty of drugs in his system and that attack had to be traumatic.

"All sorts of scenarios go through my head when I consider the factors in the attack," Joe said. "What if someone has trained a grizzly to kill on command? What if someone is driving around the country with a trailer and a grizzly in the back and unleashing it on people in random places?"

"But why?" she asked.

"I don't have a clue. That's where my speculation falls apart. Every theory I have falls apart if you look at it real closely."

"So you're injecting a human element into the attacks?" she asked.

"I guess I am. But I can't get it to square with anything that seems remotely plausible. No one has attack bears at their disposal. And I sure never saw any evidence of that when I actually saw the grizzly in person on the Double D. No, that bear was acting entirely on its own when it went after Brodbeck in the river."

"So we're back to the lone bear theory," she mused.

"I don't know *what* we're back to," he groused.

"What if the bear is still here?" Marybeth asked.

Joe shrugged. "It could be. Or it could be twenty miles away on a dead run looking for its next target. We just don't know, and that's the frustrating thing."

"Just like we don't know anything about that drive-by shooting at the school," Marybeth said with a shiver. "They still haven't found the car or anything else, from what I understand."

Joe said, "A white SUV with California plates? That almost sounds like projection instead of reality."

"You need to stay out of that investigation, Joe," Marybeth cautioned. "I'm serious. As awful as it may sound, you can't get distracted right now."

Joe grudgingly agreed with her.

"There is something that occurs to me," Marybeth said after a full minute of silence between them. "It's crazy, but it's not crazier than the theories you've laid out."

"Please tell me," Joe said. "That's why I'm here."

She put on her readers, as if they would help her see more clearly, then said, "You're looking at all of this from the perspective of the grizzly bear. You and Jennie as well. You're trying to establish a behavior pattern based on what you know about bears and what motivates them to attack or run away. You're looking at times and distances—logistics. And you're trying to guess what the bear will do next based on what it's already done."

Joe encouraged her. "Go on."

"What maybe you haven't done is look at the pattern of attacks based on the *victims* instead of the bear."

"I don't follow."

"And I'm not sure this even makes any sense once I really think about it," she said. "But isn't it just bizarre that we know three of the victims personally? Clay Junior, of course. Then Dulcie—and now Judge Hewitt? How do you square that, since I know you don't believe in coincidences?"

"I don't, usually," he said. "But maybe this time I do. We

don't have much population in Wyoming, and the longer we live here the more people we know. It isn't crazy to think that we're acquainted with the victims in some way. Tell me: When is the last time someone in this county or the area died and we didn't know them, or at least know of them?"

"I'll grant you that," she said. "But still . . ."

"We didn't know that prison guard, whoever he was," Joe said. "Right?"

She agreed.

"So how do we square that? It breaks the pattern, right?"

"It does," she said. "But maybe we need to learn a little more about that prison guard. Who knows? We may find something that links him to the others in the same way."

Joe thought about it.

"You're not buying it, right?" she asked.

"I'm not rejecting it entirely. But like my theories, it may not hold up. Why would someone target people we know? Do you think a bear keeps a list of our friends and acquaintances? And where does that corrections officer from Rawlins fit in?"

"I don't know," she said. "But I can do some digging into him. I know who I can call who might be able to shed some insight into him."

"Who?"

"Dick Weber," Marybeth said. "He's the deputy warden at the prison. He's been there a bunch of years and he probably knows all of the COs."

Joe rubbed his jaw. "How do you know *him*?" It always took him off guard when Marybeth brought up names in conversation he'd never heard before, because he doubted there was a single person on earth Joe knew that his wife wasn't aware of.

"I met him through his wife, who runs the food bank in Carbon County," she said. "I met him last year when we did an event down there."

Marybeth was on the executive board of the Wyoming Hunger Initiative, which had been formed prior to the pandemic to feed children, but had grown in dollars and influence to become a primary source of nutrition for poor families throughout the state.

"Ah, gotcha," Joe said.

"Dick seemed like a very solid guy. Old-school, military type. I think he could help us out here with Officer Winner."

"I suppose it can't hurt," he said. "Meanwhile, I've got to gather up Gary Norwood and get back to the Eagle Mountain Club as soon as he can shake free. We still have to process the crime scene and find out if we can learn anything about that mystery vehicle and who might have been driving it around the golf course this morning."

"What if it turns out to be a white SUV with California plates?" she asked with arched eyebrows.

He chuckled and said, "Well, that might make things easier. But I doubt it."

"So do I."

JOE ROSE FROM his chair and retrieved his hat. He realized that Marybeth was observing him more closely than usual.

"I'm okay about the Katy Cotton thing," he said.

"Really?" she asked.

"Yup."

"We can talk about it later. Maybe when Sheridan gets back. I know you'd prefer she wasn't involved," Marybeth said. "But she's the one who brought this to us."

He groaned.

"I have a suggestion for when you go out to the club with Gary."

"Yes?"

"Take Nate along with you," she said. "I can tell that you're much more married to your grizzly behavior theories than mine, and that's okay. But who do we know who can actually get into the heads of alpha predators more than Nate?"

It was true, Joe knew. And it was something he could never explain or rationalize. Joe never talked about Nate's unique gift to anyone but Marybeth. He knew that no one in his world of wildlife biologists and professionals would believe him.

"Gary can find bear prints if they're at the scene," Marybeth said, "but only Nate can get into the *mind* of a grizzly bear. He'd be good to have along."

"Agreed," Joe said. "And having his .454 Casull at the ready isn't so bad, either. Especially if that grizzly has decided to hang around."

CHAPTER TWENTY-THREE

Eagle Mountain Club

NATE WAS VERY pleased with himself as he rappelled down the cliff face near the Staghorn Creek campground. He'd caught and hooded two young peregrines that had flown into his bow net traps during the day, and the birds lay calm and inert in a mesh bag attached to his harness. The hoods had calmed them down immediately, which was important, because they could have injured themselves or broken off feathers by thrashing in his hands.

He was interrupted when he felt the phone in his breast pocket vibrate with an incoming call.

Nate drew the phone out to see a square-jawed graphic of Dudley Do-Right on the screen. Dudley Do-Right had been depicted in the cartoons of his youth as conscientious, cheerful, and somewhat dim-witted.

"Hey, Joe," he said.

"Hey, Nate. Where are you?"

"Staghorn Creek. I caught two peregrines today and Sheridan will be beside herself when she sees them. They are *great* young birds."

When Joe paused too long, Nate said, "Don't worry. I'll file all the proper paperwork on them at some point. I always do."

"You *never* do," Joe growled.

"Anyway, you called for a reason," Nate prompted.

"I did. Hey, I could use your help if you've got the time. I'm headed back to the Eagle Mountain Club and I'm waiting for Gary Norwood to get freed up so he can process the crime scene. I was hoping you could join me."

"Is that where Judge Hewitt got whacked this morning?" Nate asked.

"Yup."

"I'm not sure I can provide much help, to be honest. I don't process crime scenes, Joe. I create them."

"Very funny. We don't know the current location of our bear right now and I could use your help keeping lookout. Plus, there are some strange things going on around here. Oh, and it was Marybeth's suggestion," Joe said.

"Why didn't you say that in the first place?" Nate asked while quickly freeing the climbing rope from the belay device and plummeting down the face of the cliff. "When do you need me there?"

"See you in an hour."

———

It was dusk when Joe and Nate observed Norwood pulling on a pair of nitrile gloves before entering the hollow in the trees. Nate arrived after the others once he'd secured his two new acquisitions in the mews at his compound and fed them. Deputy Frank Carroll showed up last.

"There was just an arrest on that drive-by," Norwood reported. "But it sounds kind of hinky to me."

"Me too," Carroll added.

"Why?" Joe asked. He'd heard nothing about an arrest on the mutual aid channel over his under-dash radio.

Carroll said, "The highway patrol spotted a white SUV with California plates on I-25 headed south with two subjects, a young male and female. The subjects refused to cooperate, and they were arrested for resisting. When the troopers searched the SUV they found twenty pounds of weed.

"But no gun," Carroll added. "And no way to tie them to cruising around Saddlestring this morning. The troopers will sweat the suspects and try to get them to turn on each other. And we'll check all the cameras in town to try and put them there, but I think it'll all turn out to be a false alarm. Elaine and Ruthanne took off to Kaycee to help with the interrogation."

"Probably not a good idea," Joe said.

"Elaine Beveridge wants them to be the shooters *so bad*," Norwood said. "She wants this thing to be over, but I think she's in over her head."

"Jackson Bishop tried to tell her to calm down and not make any announcements until we know for sure," Carroll said, "but she wouldn't listen to him. She was all over social media this afternoon saying we found the perps who did this."

"Not good," Norwood said. Then to Joe: "I think Bishop might actually be a good sheriff if he wins. He seems like a straight shooter."

Joe nodded, acknowledging Norwood's sentiment.

"But you're not sure yet?" Norwood asked Joe.

"I've learned to wait and watch," Joe said.

"Enough with the local politics," Nate said. "Let's get this over with."

A FEW MINUTES later, Norwood entered the shadowed alcove with his evidence bag. Joe and Carroll watched from the cart path and Nate moved into the trees twenty yards north to watch and listen. The forensics tech stayed near the base of the tree trunks on the northern wall so he wouldn't trample the soil in the middle.

As was his habit, Norwood called out what he saw into a digital recorder that hung from a lanyard around his neck.

"I'm entering the hole in the trees from the direction of the golf cart path," he said. "The opening is about ten feet wide and twelve to fifteen feet deep."

Norwood's camera clicked and whirred as he snapped a stream of photos.

"I don't see bear tracks on the ground at first glance," Norwood said. "And I don't see bear scat or hair, either. I need to comb every inch in here."

Joe saw the interior of the alcove light up as Norwood turned on his headlamp.

"There appears to be some bark on the floor of the opening. That's weird." Then Norwood backed halfway out and rocked back on his haunches. He looked straight up. Joe followed his gaze and noticed an overhanging tree branch with damage to it. The branch looked partially skinned and pale on its underside.

"Bark is missing from the branch, but I don't know whether the bear clawed it or what," Norwood said. "I don't see any claw marks."

With that, Norwood photographed the branch from several angles, then squatted back down and lit up the floor of the hollow with a flashlight. Joe watched the beam move methodically across the surface of the mulch and he heard Norwood say, "Hmmm. This is goofy, too."

"What's goofy?" Joe asked.

"Like I said, I don't see any signs of a bear. This ground is pretty soft and you'd think there would be impressions of its paws, right? But that's not what I see."

"So what do you see?" Carroll asked impatiently.

"Tire tracks," Norwood said. "Two sets of fresh tire tracks that crushed down the pine needles. That, and boot prints."

His camera clicked a few dozen times while Joe held his

breath and considered the implications of what Norwood was reporting. It was mind-boggling.

"How do you know they're boot tracks?" Carroll asked.

"Because the heels make deep impressions and the toes are squared off," Norwood said. "You know, like the cowboy boots they wear these days."

"This makes no sense," Carroll said. "Are you saying somebody drove a bear here in the back of their truck and let it go on Judge Hewitt?"

"I'm not saying anything at all," Norwood stated. "I'm just telling you what I see in here."

Carroll turned to Joe and screwed up his face. "I'm totally confused," he said. "What are we dealing with here? A man and his trained pet grizzly?"

"I don't want to think that," Joe responded.

"But he doesn't see bear tracks," Carroll said.

"I can hear the man."

WHEN NORWOOD WAS through, he packed up his equipment in his evidence bag near the opening of the trees under the light of his headlamp.

"We need to check out the river road," Joe said. "I'm guessing we'll find similar tire tracks on it."

"What river road?" Carroll asked, and Joe told him about it.

"Locals know about it," he said. "But very few other people. I'm guessing that the vehicle you saw this morning used it to access the club and get away without being caught on any of the gate cameras."

Carroll made a pained face. "We don't know of any locals with a trained bear. I can't wrap my mind around this."

"Neither can I," Joe said. "But we'll go where the evidence leads us."

"This is getting crazy," Carroll said. "I'm gonna call Bishop and let him know what we found here. He'll shit his pants. And I'm *not* going to call Elaine."

A MOMENT LATER, Nate appeared from the line of trees fifty yards south of where he'd gone in. As he approached, Joe touched his hat brim to him, indicating that he wanted to speak to him out of the earshot of Norwood and Deputy Carroll.

"Did you hear or see anything?" Joe asked.

Nate shook his head. "Just you and the yokels yapping away like magpies."

"We found no bear tracks," Joe said. "But we did confirm that a truck was parked in the trees this morning and someone was walking around it before the judge got hit."

Nate narrowed his eyes and leaned close to Joe. "I don't know what it means that you found vehicle tracks, but that grizzly bear is still around."

"You're sure about that?" Joe asked. "Did you find sign of it?"

"No," Nate said. "Don't ask me to explain it, but your bear is still around. It's just not here at the moment."

"You're kidding."

"I can feel it."

Joe didn't know what to think.

"Do you need me to stick around?" Nate asked.

Joe thought about it for a moment. "Nope."

"Call me if you need anything more," Nate said, patting Joe on the shoulder.

"Will do," Joe said. "I'll head home myself as soon as Gary is done on the river road." To Nate's wide back, Joe said, "Thanks, Nate."

Nate stopped and looked over his shoulder. "For what?"

"For watching our backs and then scrambling my brain and making me even more confused about everything than I already was."

"My pleasure."

THREE-QUARTERS OF A mile away, Dallas Cates made the turn on the river road toward the Eagle Mountain Club with his headlights off. Suddenly, he hit the brakes. Soledad reached out to brace himself against the sudden halt and Johnson cursed from the backseat as she was thrown to the floor.

"Christ," LOR exclaimed from the back of the pickup through the open rear-window slider. "What's going on?"

"Look," Cates said, pointing through the windshield to the north.

In the distance up a long manicured slope, on the left side of the eighth fairway, was the location where they'd attacked the judge. It was bathed in light. Three vehicles were parked astride the cart path with their headlights aimed into the alcove. A figure passed through the beams, then another.

"They're up there now," Cates said. "Shit. They'll be on to us."

"I wonder who it is?" Soledad asked. "I can't see them clearly enough in the dark."

As he said it, a man wearing a red uniform shirt and a cowboy hat walked through a set of headlights and disappeared again in the gloom.

"That was the game warden," Cates said. "Joe Pickett."

"Well, that son of a bitch," Soledad said. "I thought he'd be home by now."

"I've learned not to underestimate him," Cates said, smacking the steering wheel with the heel of his hand. "But it looks like I did it again."

Soledad took a deep breath and expelled it slowly. He said, "There's no reason to panic. No reason at all. We'll just have to change the order of things tonight."

"Change the order?" Johnson asked from the backseat.

"We won't go to his place first like we talked about," Soledad said. "We'll go there second."

Cates saw the logic immediately. He turned in his seat and said to LOR, "Keep the compressor on and let me know when the cylinders are full."

Then he carefully backed the truck up without using his brakes until it was fully hidden in the dense cottonwoods next to the bank of the Twelve Sleep River, where he did a precise three-point turn.

"They'll probably find and study our tracks," Soledad said.

"Maybe take impressions. That's fine—finding our tracks will slow them down. It'll give us plenty of time to move to our alternate destination and get set up."

Johnson said, "I'm confused about what's going on. Aren't we going to the game warden's house?"

"Don't you worry your pretty little head about it," Soledad said dismissively.

AT THE SAME time, Marybeth swung into her van in the parking lot of Valley Foods with a grocery bag. She liked the idea of making a big pot of spaghetti with elk burger red sauce for dinner, along with garlic bread. That way, she could get it prepared and let the sauce simmer and they could eat at whatever time Joe got home.

She dug her phone out of her purse to call Sheridan to see if she'd like to join them for dinner when she got back to town from Walden. As she lifted the phone, it lit up in her hand. The screen read: WYOMING DEPARTMENT OF CORRECTIONS.

"Yes? This is Marybeth Pickett."

"Marybeth, Dick Weber from the DOC. We met last year, if you'll recall. I'm sorry for calling so late."

"Not a problem at all and I do remember meeting you. Thanks for calling me back."

As she spoke to him, Marybeth pictured the man she'd met in Rawlins at the food bank: crew cut, square jaw, icy blue eyes, military bearing, no-nonsense.

"First, I really have to apologize to you," Weber said. "I've been out on a two-week hunting trip in the Wind Rivers and I'd assigned a list of tasks to my staff, but it seems the ball got dropped around here. I really had to chew some asses today and it didn't make me very popular, as you can imagine."

"Really," she said, "there's no reason to apologize. I just left the message a few hours ago. I didn't expect you to be at your desk."

Weber hesitated before responding. "To be honest, I didn't hear your message. But I understand that you're probably pretty upset. It's all my fault."

"Now I'm confused," she said. "The message I left was to ask if you could provide some background on the CO who was killed by the grizzly bear. His name was Ryan Winner, I believe."

"Yes, Ryan," Weber said with a note of sadness. "He'd been here as long as I've been around. It's a real shame, and a terrible thing to have happen. I didn't even know about it because I go radio silent when we're in the elk camp. For two wonderful weeks, I'm away from the phone. And look what happened."

"It was a tragedy," she said.

"I mean, these guys face threats all the time," Weber said. "They deal with some of the nastiest men in this state, and anything can happen if they let their guard down even for a second. In fact, Ryan worked in E pod, which is the worst of the worst. He was there for seven years, I think. But what happens to him? He doesn't get shanked by an inmate or rushed by a gang. He gets attacked by a grizzly bear as he gets ready to come to work. It's just insane."

"It is," she said.

"There aren't supposed to be any grizzly bears in Rawlins. How did that happen?"

"A lot of people would like to find out," she said. "Including Joe, my husband. He's a game warden up here. I think I told you about him."

Weber chortled. "Yes, I've heard of Joe Pickett. Everybody has by now, I think. All of us in state government get memos about him. He's kind of the poster boy for what not to do with state property. Doesn't he hold the record for the most damage done to state vehicles?"

"That's him," Marybeth said with a roll of her eyes.

"Winner will be a tough one to replace," Weber said. "We're chronically short-staffed down here as it is. I'm afraid that until we can get the legislature to offer significant pay raises, it'll continue to be tough for us to hire new COs.

"I'm sorry," Weber said. "I got off track completely. What was it you wanted to know about Ryan?"

"How well did you know him?" she asked.

Weber took a few seconds to reply. "Well, we got along pretty well, I'd say. I can't think of any serious disciplinary issues, although a few inmates complained that he was too much of a hard-ass. But they say that about all the COs. In fact, if an inmate says nice things about a CO, I get suspicious, if you know what I mean. Yeah, Winner could be a little petty and vindictive and he had some feuds with a couple of guys, but nothing that was so serious that a disciplinary hearing was held. And I know a lot of the younger guys looked up to him."

"Did you know him well outside of work?"

"Not really. I went to a barbecue out at his house once to celebrate his divorce, which I thought was kind of weird. This would be the house outside of town where the bear attacked him, by the way. For the barbecue he only invited prison staff. No neighbors or friends. He didn't have any kids that I know of. I can't say I knew very much about the man outside of his job. Why do you ask?"

"Well," Marybeth said as she cleared Saddlestring and turned onto the state highway toward her home, "Joe's investigating these bear attacks and I'm trying to assist him. There was another attack just this morning around here."

"Another one?" Weber said. "Jesus. They're happening all over the damned state."

"Yes, they are, and no one can figure out why, how, or who might be next. And frankly, we're grasping at straws at the moment. We're wondering if there is any connection between the victims other than the fact that Joe and I knew three of them. But we didn't know Ryan Winner at all. I guess I was hoping that you might know if he was connected in any way to the other people who were attacked. Specifically, I mean Clay Hutmacher Jr., from here, Dulcie Schalk from Laramie, or Judge Hewitt?"

"I really doubt that," Weber said. "Winner came here straight from the pen in New Mexico, where his people are from. I don't think he knew his way around this state and, like I said, he didn't seem to have many friends. If he knew them, he never mentioned it to me, but I can ask around. It's possible he might have said something to a couple of his coworkers, especially when those other attacks were in the news."

"Thank you, I'd appreciate that," Marybeth said. "I knew this was likely to be a shot in the dark, but I appreciate your time."

"Are you saying this bear has a hit list?" Weber asked with a chuckle.

"I don't know what I'm saying. I was just following up on a line of thought that I think we can now dismiss. So again, thanks for your time."

"Of course," he said. Then: "So you're not upset with us?"

For the second time during the conversation, Marybeth was puzzled. "Why would I be upset with you?"

"Because we didn't call you when Dallas Cates was released."

"What?"

"It's in the file that you were to be notified, but like I said, that ball got dropped while I was away."

Marybeth pressed hard on the brake pedal and pulled her van to the side of the road. She was instantly furious and she couldn't see straight. The road ahead of her seemed to tilt in her headlights.

"When did this happen?" she said through gritted teeth.

"Um," he said, while audibly tapping at a keyboard. "It looks like October 15. I went hunting on the twelfth and—"

"I don't care about your hunting trip," Marybeth seethed. "You're telling me that Dallas Cates, the man who has threatened my family's life more than once, was released from prison twelve days ago?"

"I'm sorry you have to hear it this way," Weber said. "I really am. But when we got to talking about Ryan Winner, it got me on the wrong track."

She could barely hold the phone because her hand was trembling.

"Where did he go when he got out?" Marybeth asked. "Who picked him up?"

"I don't know. Once they're out, they're out. And, like I said, it happened while I was gone."

"What was the relationship between Dallas Cates and Ryan Winner?"

"Like I said, Winner worked E pod. That's where Cates was housed last. I don't think they got along, but Dallas didn't get along with most folks. Cates was always trouble, with a capital *T*, and Winner didn't coddle types like that. It probably didn't help that Cates was one of the big WOODS guys."

"Hold it," Weber said. "Are you suggesting . . ."

"I don't know what I'm suggesting," Marybeth said, disconnecting the call. She angrily tossed the phone onto the passenger seat.

She sat back and hugged herself while she looked around where she was parked. The highway was empty, and her headlights lit up the yellow grass in front of her on the side of the road. The only movement was the moonlit branches of the river cottonwoods swaying in the evening wind.

Beyond her headlights, all was dark and empty.

Twelve days. *Twelve days*. Her mind raced as she reviewed what had happened in the last twelve days.

She snatched the phone off the seat and called Joe. He answered on the first ring, which meant he was close enough to be in cell range.

"Joe—where are you?"

"About ten minutes from home."

"Good. I'm less than that," Marybeth said as she put the van in gear and floored the accelerator. The vehicle fishtailed in the loose soil of the borrow pit before her tires bit on the asphalt and launched her back onto the highway.

"Marybeth, are you okay?" he asked.

"No, I am not. Hurry home, Joe."

He found Marybeth at the kitchen table with her laptop open and a Wyoming Department of Transportation state road map unfolded on the surface. A plastic bag of groceries had been haphazardly tossed on the kitchen counter, its contents strewn across the Formica.

There was a frantic look on her face when she turned from the screen to greet him as he entered through the mudroom.

"Dallas Cates was released from the penitentiary," she said.

The words stopped him cold. "When?" he asked. "They were supposed to notify us."

"They didn't, those bastards." she said. Beneath the table, Marybeth shoved a chair free with her foot and it slid across the floor. "You had better sit down," she said.

Joe did, although he felt like he'd had the breath knocked

out of him. It wasn't that he hadn't seen it coming at some point. For years, they'd both kept track of the ongoing incarceration of Cates. And since the offenses he'd been convicted of were flimsy at best, they'd known the time would come when the man was released.

Joe remained conflicted about the circumstances that had put Cates away, even though he firmly believed that the former rodeo cowboy had done much worse and deserved punishment. Cates was an evil man, the spawn of an evil family. Unfortunately, he hadn't been convicted of the murders and kidnappings he was involved with because the evidence wasn't there and they couldn't pin it all on him. Dallas was diabolical and calculating and he had the ability to involve others in his crimes and insulate his own role in them. Since he was a youngster, he'd perfected the act of instigating wrongdoing and then stepping back when accused and claiming, "Who, me?"

The fact was that the combined law enforcement forces in Twelve Sleep County had overtly targeted Dallas, Joe included. He'd participated in a kind of conspiracy to get Dallas Cates off the streets. No one knew at the time that their effort would result in the deaths of the entire Cates family, one by one. Even Brenda, the matriarch and actual brains behind the malevolent actions of her clan, had recently died in prison.

No, it wasn't a shock that Dallas Cates had been released. Joe just wished they'd had notice of the event and could have made efforts to track his movement.

The map was open in front of him and he saw that certain locations in the square state of Wyoming were marked with sloppy black marker. The circles, if joined, looked to Joe like a poorly rendered sketch of the Big Dipper, or a child's drawing of a kite with a tail.

"What's this?"

Marybeth took a deep breath to calm herself, then jabbed her finger at a circle around Rawlins in the bottom center of the map.

"Two things happened on October 15," she said. "That's the day you found Clay Junior's body after he was attacked by a grizzly bear on the Twelve Sleep River. The second is that Dallas Cates was released from prison. No one seems to know who picked him up or where he was headed."

Her finger slid eastward along I-80 and then north to Hanna. "October 16, a body is found at the scene of a local museum that was burned to the ground. The body is later identified as Hanna town marshal Marvin Bertignolli. That's the same day Bill Brodbeck was attacked up here right in front of you and the Predator Attack Team."

"How are they related?" Joe asked.

"I don't think they are, on the surface," she said. "Except the second attack in as many days made a lot of news, as you know. Everybody in the state went on high alert."

"This museum fire," Joe said. "Why bring it up?"

"At first, I didn't see the significance of it," she said. "But when I dug into it just a few minutes ago I found something really interesting."

"What's that?" Joe asked.

Marybeth called up a previous window on her screen and

read from the *Cowboy State Daily* news item. "'Another victim of the fire was the twelve-foot mounted grizzly bear known as Zeus that had been a prize in the collection for decades.'"

"I don't understand," Joe said.

"Just stay with me here," she said, her eyes wild. He knew that when she looked like that it was best to listen and keep quiet, so he did both.

Marybeth ran her finger in a backtracking motion to Rawlins again.

"October 23, a full week later, Corrections Officer Ryan Winner is attacked by a grizzly bear outside his home. No one can explain how a bear got there or where it came from. You said that yourself."

She slid to the right again along I-80 going east. "October 25, two days later and a hundred miles away, Dulcie Schalk is killed on her ranch.

"Then," she said, drawing a long imaginary line to the north and west, "on October 26, yesterday, a high school student and part-time attendant is found murdered at Hellie's Tepee Pools in Thermopolis. Again, according to the *Cowboy State Daily*, the murder appeared to be a random act and no suspects have been identified. The cash register was not looted, and the murder weapon appears to be some kind of long daggerlike knife."

Joe sat back confused. He saw five hastily drawn circles with no obvious conclusion.

As if reading his mind, Marybeth's finger landed north of Thermopolis on the town of Saddlestring.

"Seven violent incidents in a matter of days," she said. "That alone is unusual in Wyoming and completely outside the norm.

"Which brings us to today," she said. "This morning it was Judge Hewitt. All of these incidents in a row lead to here, Joe. We couldn't see it or connect things in any logical way because we were blaming the mind of a grizzly bear. But what if it wasn't a bear? What if it has been Dallas Cates all along?"

Joe felt the hairs prick on the back of his neck and on his forearms. His belly went cold.

"Dallas had a list, Joe," Marybeth said. "We all know that. Dulcie was on that list, and so was Judge Hewitt. Sheriff Reed is out of the picture. But you're not, and neither is Nate."

"Clay Junior wasn't on any list," Joe said. "Brodbeck, either. And how does the CO fit into this? Or the pool guy?"

"Winner and Cates didn't get along in prison," Marybeth said. "Weber confirmed that. I think he was added to Dallas's hit list recently."

"What about the pool guy? And what about the marshal?"

"I'm not sure about the pool guy," she said. "His murder may not be related at all except that it falls within the pattern of movement. He might just have been in the wrong place at the wrong time, or seen something he shouldn't have seen. Or somebody. But I think your other question shouldn't be about the Hanna marshal, unfortunately. I think it's about Zeus."

"Clay Junior? Brodbeck?" Joe asked again.

"Think of Clay Junior and Bill Brodbeck as totally unrelated. Start with Hanna and Zeus instead, because I think that's what Dallas did. I don't know how he contrived this, but somehow he did.

"As you know," she said, "the bear attacks up here generated a lot of attention. They were all over the television, statewide radio, and the internet. There is no way Dallas wasn't aware of what happened, especially in his old hometown. We know how Dallas thinks and how cunning and opportunistic he can be. I think he saw the news about the bear attacks and somehow figured out how to take advantage of them for his own purposes. He had a week to prepare. I'm not sure how he's done it, but I think Zeus figures in somehow."

"Or Zeus's teeth and claws," Joe said.

They stared at each other for a moment, and both of them came to the same thunderous conclusion at the same time.

"Lock the doors," Joe said. It was the first time he'd *ever* said it to Marybeth.

"You call Nate," Marybeth said in a panic. "I'll call Liv."

CHAPTER TWENTY-FOUR

Yarak, Inc.

"Kill the lights and back up slowly," Cates whispered to Soledad through the open back-window slider of the pickup truck. "Complete silence from now on," he cautioned everyone. Then he gestured to LOR to proceed.

Cates was in the tractor seat at the controls. Soledad and Johnson were inside the cab with Soledad behind the wheel. LOR was bunched up at the foot of the bed near the closed tailgate. The man slowly opened the rear hatch and readied his range finder.

The front door of Nate Romanowski's home was illuminated under a lone porch light. Interior lights were on as well, but no one had looked out to see the vehicle approach the house and back up. So far, so good, Cates thought. He reached down and fingered the grip of the pistol that was tucked into the shaft of his cowboy boot.

Just in case.

The twin air cylinders were completely filled and the compressor had been turned off. The steel head of the mechanical bear jaws loomed in the open rear window, poised to lash out.

"Twenty-seven feet," LOR whispered.

Cates relayed the distance through the slider to Soledad.

"Twenty-two feet.

"Eighteen feet.

"Fifteen feet," LOR said, and Cates whispered, "*Stop*," to Soledad.

The pickup ceased moving. Soledad killed the engine.

Cates triggered the red-dot sight and trained it at eye level on the crack between the door frame and the door itself.

"Ready," he said. It was Bobbi Johnson's signal to get out of the truck.

Inside, Liv stirred a pot of green chili on the stove with a wooden spoon. When Kestrel said that she "wanted to do it"—something the girl demanded more and more—Liv picked up her daughter and balanced her on her hip and handed over the spoon.

Kestrel used the implement to thrash around the pot. "Gentle," Liv said.

"I'm helping," Kestrel said.

"Yes, you are," Liv smiled. "You're a good helper."

Nate was on his way home. She'd texted him earlier to ask him to stop at the grocery store in Saddlestring for a gallon of milk for Kestrel and a package of flour tortillas to eat with the chili.

That was when there was a light knocking on the front door. It startled Liv because visitors rarely came to their home, since it was several miles off the county road, and she hadn't noticed a vehicle outside.

"I'll do it," Kestrel said, wriggling to get free of Liv. She meant she wanted to open the front door to see who was there. Visitors to the house were a rare and exciting event in their household.

"No, you won't," Liv said, depositing her daughter in her high chair to keep her contained. Kestrel had yet to meet a stranger she didn't want to talk to, which was a trait Liv and Nate were getting concerned about.

"You'll stay right here, little bug."

Liv quickly untied her apron and hung it over the back of a chair. As she did so, her phone burred with an incoming call. Probably Nate, she thought, wondering what brand of tortillas to buy. She thought she'd call him back as soon as she dealt with the visitor.

Liv looked through the gap between the front-room window curtains and peered outside. A pickup truck with Wyoming plates was backed up to the front porch. A thin woman with straggly blond hair was standing in front of the door. The woman looked nervous, Liv thought.

"Probably lost," she muttered as she reached for the doorknob.

CATES WATCHED AS the shadow of a figure approached the front
window to his right, but he couldn't see a face. He didn't need
to. Nate Romanowski was seared into his memory.

The knob turned on the front door and it opened a crack.

Johnson rushed her words. "I'm sorry to bother you . . ." as
the door swung in.

A BRIGHT RED light hit Liv in the eyes followed by a blur of
open steel jaws and yellow teeth.

TWELVE MINUTES LATER, Sheridan drove along the gravel road
through the sagebrush toward the Yarak, Inc. compound. She
was tired and wrung out because it had been a long day in every
way. The falcons were restless inside the vehicle and they were
ready to eat. Feeding the Air Force was her first priority and
then she could leave them in the mews overnight.

She was surprised to encounter a vehicle coming the other
way, especially in the dark. She assumed it must be either Nate
or Liv, since visitors on the road were rare at any time of day.

Sheridan eased her SUV to the shoulder to make room in
case the other driver wanted to stop and chat. She whirred
down the side window and let the cool evening air rush in. It
felt refreshing on her face.

But the approaching vehicle, which turned out to be a white

extended-cab pickup with a topper and County 6 plates, didn't slow down. Instead, it accelerated as it passed by. All of the windows were tinted and in the darkness it was difficult to see the occupants clearly.

Sheridan caught a glimpse of what she thought were two figures inside the cab, but when it flashed by she could only see one. A man was at the wheel and he either deliberately or inadvertently turned his head away from her at the last second. The second occupant, if there had been one there at all, either ducked down or leaned away so as not to be seen.

She quickly closed the window before a roll of dust washed over her. Then she watched the red taillights recede in her rearview mirror until they blinked out when the truck took a turn in the road and entered a grove of aspen. She thought she saw a glimpse of red light through the tinted back topper hatch window, but she thought it may have been a reflection of her own taillights.

Wyoming folks weren't usually so rude, she thought, especially on an isolated road. If they didn't stop to say hello and state their business, they'd at least wave or nod as they passed by. County 6 was Carbon County in the south-central part of the state. What were they doing up in Twelve Sleep County? Maybe hunting?

Nevertheless, Sheridan eased back onto the road to the compound. After feeding the Air Force, she knew she had a decision to make. Both Liv and her mom had invited her for dinner. She wasn't sure which invitation to accept, or to punt on both and pick up something on the way to her apartment. As always, she wished DoorDash existed in her little town so she could order in.

If she accepted Liv's invitation, they'd inevitably discuss business and her first remote assignment. That was fine, but Sheridan was still sorting the experience in her mind and especially how it had ended. She wasn't sure how much to reveal and how she felt about it. Discovering that she had a second grandmother was hard to wrap her mind around. One nasty grandmother was enough, she thought.

Dinner with her parents was even more fraught. Sheridan wasn't sure what her dad's reaction would be to the discovery of his mother at the Never Summer Ranch in Colorado, and what she'd said. Sheridan didn't want to upset her father, who had more than enough on his plate at the moment.

She took the turn into the compound and drove past the outbuildings toward the mews. As she did, she glanced over at the house and slammed on her brakes.

The front door was wide open, and a human form was crumpled at the base of the threshold. Dark splashes were flecked against the light-colored exterior of the house as if someone had flung a mop through the air. A stream of what looked like blood flowed down the concrete steps of the porch.

Then she saw the flowing black hair, the pale reflection of an outstretched hand, and Liv's unique tooled cowboy boot flung aside and sitting upright on the top step of the porch stairs.

Sheridan screamed as she hurled herself out of the SUV and ran to the lifeless body in the open door. Beyond Liv, she could see Kestrel inside the kitchen near the table in her high chair. The two-year-old was struggling to get out and crying, "*Mom, Mom, Mom . . .*"

"WELL," SOLEDAD SAID to Cates through gritted teeth over his shoulder as he sped onto the county road, "you really fucked *that* up." Soledad had to shout over the *rat-a-tat* cadence from the compressor, which was in the process of refilling the tanks. They'd pulled over to the side of the road to allow for the recharging of the tanks, and the wait time was excruciating.

"What?" Cates yelled back. He leaned closer to the slider.

"You heard me the first time. I said you really fucked that one up," Soledad repeated. Then he mumbled something to himself that Cates genuinely couldn't discern.

Cates turned in his seat at the controls and nearly shoved his entire face through the opening so he could see and hear inside the cab.

Bobbi Johnson was curled up in the passenger seat, holding her bent knees to her face. She was crying and rocking from side to side. "That woman had a little girl in there," she wailed.

"Tell her to shut up," Soledad said to Cates. "I can't hear you over this compressor."

"You heard the man," Cates said to Johnson. "Keep it down."

"We didn't have to shake her like that," Johnson said. "And LOR didn't have to hit her with that bat."

"Shut up," Soledad commanded. "I mean it." He reached

over and gripped the back of her neck and squeezed it until she squealed. Cates did nothing to stop him and she continued to weep, but more quietly.

Soledad looked up and saw Cates's face filling his rearview mirror. "What were you thinking?"

"I was thinking that I'd hit whoever opened the door first."

"What if Romanowski was inside?"

"Then I would have shot him when he ran up to check on her," Cates said. "I was ready for that. We could have messed his body up so bad with the bat afterward that it looked like a double bear attack."

"And you're just telling me this now?" Soledad said.

"That was his lady," Cates said from the back. "She was on my list, too. And in some ways, this is even better. This will tear him up when he finds out. He'll know what it's like to lose a member of his family, just like I did."

"That's not what I'm concerned about," Soledad said. "I'm afraid it'll make him go nuclear."

"Nuclear and sloppy," Cates said with a short laugh. "That's okay with me. He'll be more vulnerable if he's reckless."

Cates caught Soledad rolling his eyes. It was disconcerting. Was Soledad really questioning his judgment now? Was the man losing his grip and threatening to break their pact?

Instead of acknowledging the gesture, Cates said, "You know how to get to that game warden's house, right? This is his new one I'm talking about. I burned down his old one."

"I know where it is."

"Then *go-go-go*," Cates said. "Fucking floor it, man. The

tanks will be charged by the time we get there. We can do this quickly now that we've got the timing and distance down."

Soledad said, "What about that SUV we saw on the way from the compound? I didn't view the driver clearly, but I know the silhouettes of hooded raptors in the back when I see them."

"Let's just get out of here," Johnson wailed. "Let's get the hell out of this place."

"Bobbi, be quiet," Cates said. "Please. We've got a job to finish."

"That poor woman," Johnson said. "That poor mama . . ."

"Jesus," Soledad said with disgust to no one and to everyone.

"Okay," LOR announced. "We've reached maximum capacity."

Cates glanced at the air pressure gauge. It was at two thousand PSI.

"Okay, go," he ordered Soledad.

Five minutes later, through the windshield, Cates could see as the headlights swept across a brown wooden sign that read GAME WARDEN STATION. Next to it was a turnoff that led into heavy timber and eventually to the Twelve Sleep River and the house next to it.

He was surprised when Soledad eased off the accelerator and let the pickup roll to a stop, but also grateful that the man hadn't slammed on the brakes and thrown Cates and LOR around the back like rag dolls.

"What are you doing?" Cates asked through the slider.

"I'm getting out," Soledad said while checking the loads on the shotgun he'd pilfered from the old Cates place. Cates knew

Soledad also had a handgun tucked into his waistband, as well as the long blade concealed inside his crutches.

"Getting out?" Cates asked. "Why?"

"Nate Romanowski will be coming after us," Soledad said. "That girl in the SUV will give him a description of our truck. I'm going to hide here in the trees and take him out when he gets here. I'll find the best place to ambush him."

Cates thought it over for a moment. Was Soledad bugging out on him or volunteering to take on Romanowski by himself? He wasn't sure. But if nothing else, creating a confrontation with the falconer two miles from the target house would at least slow the man down. And if Romanowski got the best of Soledad, another problem was solved. It was to Cates's advantage, however it went.

"Thanks for watching our back," Cates said.

Soledad nodded and slipped out the door and slammed it shut. Cates watched the man clamp the shotgun under his right arm, mount his crutches, and glide away into the gloom.

Cates took a long breath, then said, "He's gone now, Bobbi. You can relax."

He observed her body language as she seemed to uncoil in the seat.

"Are you sure?"

"After we cut LOR loose, it's just you and me. Just like you wanted," he said. "I doubt we'll ever see Axel Soledad again."

"I hope not," she said as she flopped her head back and sighed.

"But I need you to calm down and step up. Then it'll all be over."

She looked at him with a wary expression. But she was willing to listen. Cates didn't dwell on his once-again-proven ability to persuade individuals to do his bidding, and he almost loved her for it.

"Slide over and drive," he said gently. "All you'll need to do is drive to the Pickett house and back up to the front door, just like Soledad did. I'll tell you when to stop, baby. That's all there is, and I know you can do it."

Johnson started to raise her leg over the center console when she stopped and looked into his eyes. "Then it'll all be over?"

"It'll all be over," he said.

"And we can go get my sister?"

"We can go get your sister."

"And . . ." she said, tilting her head toward the back of the truck, meaning Lee Ogburn-Russell.

"That, too," he said. "I promise."

With that, Johnson wiped the tears from her face with the back of her hand and slid behind the steering wheel. The pickup lurched forward and Cates swung around into the tractor seat.

LOR looked back at him expectantly. "We good?" he asked.

"We're good."

"Is that prick Soledad gone?"

"Yes, sir," Cates said. LOR nodded his pleasure.

"Get ready," Cates said. "This is going to happen fast once we get there."

CHAPTER TWENTY-FIVE

Game Warden Station

A FEW MINUTES LATER, Joe paced the floor of their house with his cell phone in his hand. "It's not unusual for Nate not to answer his phone, but still. He won't pick up," he said to Marybeth.

"Neither will Liv," she said. "And she's really good about picking up. I'm worried that something bad has happened. Do you think you should go over there?"

"Maybe," Joe said. "But I don't like the idea of leaving you alone in the house."

"We should both go," Marybeth said while kicking off her slippers and stepping into a pair of shoes in the mudroom. He followed her and gathered up his holster from where he looped it on a peg next to parkas and other heavy coats.

"Crap," Marybeth said as she looked at her phone. "Sheridan

tried to call twice in the last ten minutes and I missed her while I was calling Liv."

Although it was better than it used to be, cell phone service was still notoriously unreliable in the Twelve Sleep Valley, especially away from town. Notices were often delayed, messages sometimes arrived days after they were sent, and individual calls simply didn't go through. Which was another possible reason why Nate and Liv hadn't responded, Joe thought.

He buckled on his holster, pulled on his jacket, and clamped his hat on his head. The familiar *I am going out* actions roused Daisy, who padded into the mudroom from where she'd been curled up in the kitchen. Tube and Bert's Dog watched Daisy go but apparently had no interest in getting up and around so late in the evening.

That was when there was an insistent knock on their front door.

Joe and Marybeth exchanged looks. Neither had heard a car outside.

It wasn't unusual for visitors to simply show up, even at night. Their house was a game warden station, after all, funded by taxpayers, and considered by many to be as public as a local police station. Hunters, fishers, hikers, landowners, and law enforcement personnel who happened to be in the area stopped by from time to time.

This seemed different, though.

"Is your pistol handy?" Joe asked Marybeth.

She patted her handbag, indicating that it was inside. Joe

had purchased a five-shot Ladysmith revolver for Marybeth years before for self-protection. He was grateful that for once she had it handy.

"It won't do us much good in your bag," he said.

She reluctantly drew the weapon out and held it loose at her side.

"Good," he said while retrieving his own weapon. "I'll see who's at the door."

When Joe leaned into the peephole all he could see was blond hair. Whoever was out there was so close to the lens that there was no broad perspective of the visitor.

Then he heard, "Mom! Dad! It's me. Open up. I can't find my key."

"Sheridan," he said to Marybeth over his shoulder as he threw the bolt and holstered his gun.

Their oldest daughter blew in as he swung the door back. She had Kestrel in her arms and there was blood on the sleeves of her shirt and on her pant legs. The baby appeared to be un-hurt and she exclaimed, "Unka Joe!" as she was carried past him into the house.

Joe stepped out onto the porch and peered through the gloom. Sheridan's SUV was parked sloppily to the right, but no one appeared to have followed her. He stepped back inside and closed the door and secured it once again.

When he turned around, Marybeth had taken Kestrel from

her daughter's arms and both were agitated and talking over each other so fast he could barely make out the conversation.

"My God," Marybeth said. "Are you hurt? Are you okay?"

"I'm not hurt, but I'm not okay, either," Sheridan said. "It's Liv's blood."

"Liv's blood!"

"That bear attacked her at their front door. It was horrible, Mom. I tried to give her mouth-to-mouth, but . . ."

"But what?"

"Her face was mutilated," Sheridan cried. "Her mouth was *hard to find*."

Marybeth winced and clamped her hands over Kestrel's ears. The toddler responded with a belly laugh because she assumed it was a game.

Sheridan leaned into Marybeth and said with a fierce whisper, "Kestrel might have seen it happen. I don't know. I found her inside in her high chair and I took her out of the house by the back door."

"I don't think she saw anything," Marybeth whispered back. "If she had, I think she'd be a lot more upset right now."

"It was so horrible," Sheridan said, holding herself.

Joe stepped over and took her into his arms. "You did the right thing bringing Kestrel here and getting away from that house," he said.

"Thanks, Dad," Sheridan responded.

"Did you see anyone on the county road headed here?"

"No," she said, shaking her head. "I came the back way along the river. I didn't take the county road because I wanted to get here quicker."

"Good thinking," Joe said.

"Was Nate there?" he asked her.

"No."

"Did you see the bear?"

"No. It was gone by the time I got there."

"You did everything right," he said.

Then she let out a loud sob. Now that she was in their home, what she'd seen and gone through seemed to be overwhelming her, he thought.

JOE LOOKED UP. Marybeth had settled down with Kestrel in her lap in a lounge chair in their front room. They were going page by page through a recent copy of *Wyoming Wildlife* magazine and Kestrel was pointing at photos of bears and prairie dogs as Marybeth complimented the child on knowing what species was what.

Joe was grateful that Kestrel seemed to be oblivious to what had happened to her mother, but it broke his heart that she'd have to find out. What would they tell her and how would they do it? How much, he thought, had Kestrel's life just changed in perpetuity?

Marybeth looked up from the magazine and met his eyes. Tears were pouring down her cheeks, but somehow she was able to hold herself together and remain cheery while Kestrel pointed out animals.

"Listen to me carefully," Joe said to Sheridan. "Did you see any vehicles near Nate's place?"

"No," she said. Then: "I'm sorry. My mind is blown. Yes, I did see another car. There was a pickup coming out on the road and I pulled over to let it by."

Joe felt his insides clutch. "Can you describe it?"

He felt her nod her head yes on his shoulder. "It was a pickup, like I said, with a shell over the back. I think it was white with Wyoming plates, but I can't tell you the make or model. It was just a normal pickup like you see everywhere here. I couldn't see the driver or the passenger, but I think there were two of them."

"Was it local?" he asked.

She indicated it was. "It had County Six plates. I didn't get the rest of the numbers, though. I remember thinking: Carbon County."

Joe let go of Sheridan and stepped back. "Help me make sure all the doors are locked. Then we'll shut off all the lights."

"Dad," Sheridan said, "you're scaring me. What's going on?"

"Dallas Cates was released," he said. "It wasn't a bear that attacked Liv. It was Dallas Cates."

Sheridan's eyes shot open and she covered her mouth with her hand.

"We'll tell you everything we know," he said. "But right now we've got to lock up and make this house completely dark."

Marybeth stood up with Kestrel and nuzzled the girl. She'd obviously heard the exchange. She said to her, "Let's get a blanket and a flashlight and we'll make a tent in the bedroom and look at the animals. We'll go *camping.*"

Kestrel squealed with delight and Joe's heart broke even further.

Five minutes later, under the muted light of a headlamp he'd fitted over the crown of his hat, Joe left their dark bedroom with Marybeth and Kestrel in their "tent" and Sheridan sitting on the bed with a loaded lever-action .30-30 rifle on her lap. He'd placed his service Maglite flashlight on the bedspread next to her within her reach.

"Text me if you see or hear anything," Joe said. "But don't open the door or look out the window."

"Where will you be?" she whispered back.

"Outside. That way I can see them if they approach the house. I'll text you when they get here."

In the soft yellow light of his headlamp, Sheridan's face looked like a blank mask. He knew how terrified she likely was, and he understood.

"Got that, Marybeth?" he whispered.

"Got it, Joe," Marybeth said with fake cheer from inside the tent blanket. She obviously didn't want to alarm Kestrel in any way and make her cry out.

Joe felt his phone chime in his hand and he looked down at the screen, both hoping and fearing that it would be Nate.

Instead, it was a text from Sheridan, who was ten feet away.

"I started a text thread between you, me, and Mom," Sheridan said. "That way we're all on the same page."

"Smart," Joe said.

"Dad," Sheridan said, "if you text us, don't worry about misspelled words or punctuation for once in your life. That'll take too long."

Joe nodded, duly chastened. "Got it," he said.

As he padded down the hallway toward the back door, Joe could hear Kestrel identifying an owl and Marybeth praising the child once again.

AFTER LOCKING THE back door behind him, Joe covered the ground from the house to his work shed in short mincing steps so he wouldn't trip over anything in the dark. His headlamp was off. Even though he hadn't seen or heard an oncoming vehicle in the trees, he didn't want to be spotted if someone was lurking in the shadows of the heavy timber.

Although he normally enjoyed the location of their state-owned home in a private and heavily wooded alcove of river cottonwoods with the river to the west, it bothered him that he wouldn't be able to see a visitor coming until they were less than a hundred yards away. The heavy brush and timber also muted sound, as did the musical flow of the river.

He eased the door of the shed open and stepped inside and placed his Remington Wingmaster twelve-gauge shotgun on the workbench. He'd loaded it with double-aught rounds and he jacked one into the receiver so it was ready. Double-aught buckshot was devastatingly effective at close range, with nine large-caliber pellets capable of penetrating car doors if necessary.

Because Sheridan had arrived via the two-track river road

from the Yarak, Inc. compound instead of the county road, she'd arrived at least ten minutes faster. If Cates was coming by the more conventional route, he could show up at any minute.

Joe drew out his phone.

> I'm in the shed with good views of the house and the road. Is everything okay in there?

Before he sent it, he recalled Sheridan's admonition and changed it to:

> I'm outside. Everything OK?

She instantly responded with a thumbs-up emoji.

JOE GAVE IT a few minutes to simply keep watch and let his heartbeat calm down so he could listen for approaching vehicles. It was a cold night and his breath puffed into clouds of condensation near his mouth and nose. He slipped on a thin pair of gloves so that his fingers wouldn't go stiff in the chill.

Assured that all was quiet outside, he raised his right hand and used his teeth to remove the glove. He needed help with the situation, and he needed it as fast as he could get it.

He tried once again to connect with Nate and once again there was no response. Instead of leaving a message, he sent a text:

> Liv was attacked and killed at your home. Kestrel is safe
>
> with us. Come as fast as you can.

Then Joe stared at the glowing screen of his phone for a moment, trying to figure out what he was going to do next. Call dispatch in Cheyenne and request assistance from any available law enforcement personnel in the vicinity? He discarded the idea quickly. His home was remote and it might take more time to explain the exact situation he was in to the responding officers than he thought he had.

He quickly ruled out calling either Elaine Beveridge or Ruthanne Hubbard. They'd want him to explain and justify his request, and he could only imagine how skeptical they'd be about his theories that the killings were caused by a man and not a bear. Plus, he didn't want to have to detail who Dallas Cates was and their long history together.

So he punched up Jackson Bishop's personal number and activated a call. It rang twice.

"Undersheriff Jackson Bishop," the man said in a clipped tone. "What can I do for you, Joe?"

Joe was grateful he'd connected with the likely next sheriff of Twelve Sleep County. Bishop exuded calm authority.

"I need you and as many guys as you can round up to come to the game warden station right away," Joe said.

"I know where it is. What's going on?"

"This is going to sound crazy," Joe said, "but I'm convinced that an ex-con named Dallas Cates has been using the bear attacks as cover to try to kill people he blames for ruining his life—including Judge Hewitt this morning. He killed Liv Romanowski less than an hour ago at her home and I think he's coming here."

Bishop hesitated and said, "That does sound crazy. How's he doing it?"

"I don't know. Either he's got a bear of his own or some kind of machine. It doesn't matter—we'll figure it out, eventually. But I'm guessing he's coming any minute and my family is threatened."

"Joe, are you saying that this Cates guy has figured out how to kill people and make it look like a bear did it?"

"That's exactly what I'm saying. I know it sounds far-fetched, but I'm convinced of it and I need your help."

"How many subjects are with him?"

"I don't know that, either. There's at least two of them, including Cates."

"What are they driving?"

Joe said, "Late-model white pickup with a topper on the back. Carbon County plates."

"Jesus, Joe . . ."

"I know."

"I can't just issue commands to a department I'm not even in charge of. I guess I can ask Elaine . . ."

"Do whatever you have to do," Joe snapped. "Just do it as fast as you can and get out here. I've got to get off the phone so I can be ready when they show up."

"Man, oh man," Bishop said. "I'm thinking . . ."

"My family is in the house with the lights off," Joe said. "I'm in my toolshed at the side of the house. Don't shoot me when you get here, okay?"

"Okay," Bishop said. Then: "I think I've got everybody's cell numbers and I can ask Ruthanne to dispatch as many deputies as we have on call."

"That's a good start," Joe said. "And, Jackson, keep in mind that Cates is likely armed and dangerous. Same with whoever is with him."

"Do you really think he has his own bear?" Bishop asked.

"I don't know," Joe said, exasperated. "Just hurry."

"I'll text you when we're near the scene," Bishop said.

Joe disconnected the call and placed the phone down on the workbench. There were no new messages from either Sheridan, Marybeth, or Nate.

Sheriff on the way, he texted them. Stay cool.

Sheridan responded with three more thumbs-up emojis.

IN THE SHADOWS of the heavy brush behind the game warden station sign on the county road, Axel Soledad felt the vibration of an incoming call on his cell phone. He was instantly annoyed. He turned his back to the road so the glow of the screen couldn't be seen from a passing motorist.

"I told you to never call me unless it's on a burner," Soledad hissed through gritted teeth.

"Pickett called me direct," Bishop said. "He knows you're coming. He asked that we scramble some guys and get out there. He knows all about Cates."

"Shit."

"I can slow-walk things on my end," Bishop said. "These rubes are completely incompetent, so that's easy. But you might want to wrap up and get the hell out of here."

Soledad nodded in the dark, well aware that Bishop couldn't see him. He said, "Delay as long as you can, then wipe your phone history and don't contact me again unless you use the encrypted app or you've got a burner."

"Gotcha."

"I'm detaching from Cates and his band of idiots," Soledad said. "I'm going solo."

"That's probably a good idea."

"You'll hear from me when we activate, *Sheriff Bishop*."

"Well, not yet," Bishop said. "But I like the sound of that."

Soledad stuffed the phone into his pocket. A car was coming, and rather than retreat farther into the brush, he quickly glided out onto the asphalt on his crutches until he stood astride the center line.

As the headlights of the car washed over him, Soledad slumped a bit and let his head loll slightly to the side. He needed to look damaged and unthreatening.

A dented 2012 Honda Civic with green and white Colorado plates slowed to a stop ten yards from him and the driver's window rolled down. A white-haired birdlike woman in her seventies stuck her head out and said, "Are you okay? I could have hit you standing in the middle of the road like that."

"Thank you for stopping," he said with a faux grimace. "They left me here on the side of the road. I don't even know where I'm at."

"Do you know where the game warden station is?" she asked. "I haven't been here in ages and I've got . . . business there with the game warden. My name is Katy Cotton. What's yours?"

"Dallas Cates," Soledad said.

"Who left you? Who would do something like that?" she asked.

"My friends," he said. "Or at least I *thought* they were my friends."

"That's just awful. Do you need a ride into town?"

"God bless you," he said. He clumsily made his way to the side of her car, as if he'd never used his braces before.

"Come around and climb in," the woman said.

With lightning motion, he slid the thin blade out from its brace sheath and drove the point into her eye.

Then he dragged her body to the ditch on the side of the road and climbed into the Civic and drove away.

THE MUFFLED *POP-POP-POP* of gravel under tires made Joe bend forward toward the open shed door to hear more clearly. He'd been in solid darkness long enough without any artificial lights that he could make out vague shapes and shadows outside.

He grabbed his shotgun off the workbench and moved closer to the opening and stood framed within it. The moon was a slice like a fingernail clipping in the clear night sky, but the stars were so clear and sharp they cast a light blue glow atop the dry grass.

He turned his head toward the bank of trees on the other side of the meadow where the gravel road emerged and he could see it.

A vehicle was very slowly coming through the dark timber with its lights off. It was boxy and there were no interior lights.

It was a pickup, for sure, with a camper shell or topper covering the bed. Joe couldn't see any figures inside.

The truck crept forward until it cleared the trees. It was barely moving, although there was no doubt it was headed for his home.

Joe stepped back into the shed so he couldn't be seen. He removed his gloves and let them drop near his boots while thumbing the safety off his shotgun with a barely discernible *click*. Locating his phone, he turned his back toward the open door so there would be no glow from the screen as he touched it to life.

He texted Sheridan and Marybeth: Truck outside the house. DO NOT LOOK OUT OR OPEN THE DOOR.

He watched from the shadows as the vehicle did an extremely slow three-point turn in the yard in front of his front door. As the pickup faced him, he felt his insides clutch up and he raised the shotgun and fitted the butt against his shoulder. The vehicle had County 6 plates.

Joe couldn't see the driver in the dark, nor a passenger if there was one. Reflections of the stars dotted the windshield and slid across it as the truck maneuvered. He *thought* he heard whispering from the vehicle as it executed the turns and began to slowly back up to the front door.

When a tiny red laser dot appeared at eye level on the door frame, it seemed incredibly bright in the darkness. Joe quickly looked away, but the red dot, like an angry apparition, lingered in his vision.

This would be a good time, he thought, for the sheriff and his men to show up.

That was when Joe detected movement in his peripheral vision far to his right in the direction of where the pickup had emerged from the trees. The form was big, pear-shaped, and low to the ground. It moved across the grass in an almost liquid flow. He recognized the hump on its shoulders and saw a shimmer of starlight undulate on the grizzly bear's thick coat.

The bear crossed the road quickly and kept moving until it reentered the woods on the other side without slowing down.

Joe was astonished and confused. Was this the bear Dallas Cates had somehow recruited? It was a preposterous notion, he knew.

Then, like a ghost, another figure emerged from the dark timber where the bear had come out of. It was over six feet tall with blond hair pulled back in a ponytail.

Nate's .454 Casull revolver was out and gripped in front of him in both hands as he walked silently and deliberately toward the front of the pickup.

———

THROUGH THE SLIDER in the back, Dallas whispered to Bobbi Johnson to kill the engine and get out.

"Make sure the interior lights are off when you get out," he said. "Knock on the door and say you need to talk to the game warden."

"Why are their lights off?" she asked over her shoulder. "What if they're not home?"

"His truck is right over there," Cates said. "Didn't you see it on the way in?"

"I guess I did."

"Bobbi, quit screwing around," Cates said. "We're in range and we're ready." He tried to keep his voice calm and friendly. This wasn't the place or the time to have an argument.

"Knock on the door and step to the side just like you did before," he said. "He'll have to answer. He's the damned game warden."

"You're sure?" she said. He knew he had her.

"Yes, baby," Cates said. "Then we can go get your sister."

Johnson turned and appeared to steel herself to the task. She was convinced, he thought. Her hands were on the steering wheel at ten and two like she was prepared to drive off, although he knew that wasn't possible with the engine off.

Then she raised her head and stared at something through the front windshield and he saw her mouth drop open.

The bullet punched through the windshield and took off the side of Bobbi Johnson's head. Blood, brains, and long dirty blond hair stuck to the glass on the inside of the open slider. The concussion of the gunshot rocked the pickup.

JOE SAW IT happen before he could call out or stop it.

Nate had approached the front of the pickup and, without any hesitation, raised his weapon and fired into it. The plume of orange from the muzzle of his revolver overwhelmed the lingering red dot in Joe's vision.

Joe heard a scream from the back of the pickup from under the topper. *There are people back there.*

He ran from the shed toward his house. Nate didn't respond when Joe yelled, "Nate, stand down. It's me."

Someone hurled themselves out of the open back window of the topper and fell in a heap near the rear bumper. Joe saw the man scramble to his knees and raise his hands over his head.

"I surrender," the man appealed to Joe. He was gnomish with a broad face and tiny wild eyes that reflected starlight. "I'm Lee Ogburn-Russell and I was forced by Dallas Cates to be here. I surrender, Officer."

Nate suddenly loomed behind Ogburn-Russell from the other side of the pickup and shot him point-blank in the back of the head. The man's lifeless body flopped forward into the grass.

Then Nate swung to his left and aimed through the open back window and his revolver barked three times in rapid succession.

Joe reached up and clicked on the headlamp fitted over his hat as he ran to his friend. Nate was now bathed in harsh light and in the midst of dumping his five spent casings at his feet and speed-loading fresh rounds into the cylinder.

When Nate looked up at Joe, he was almost unrecognizable. His face was a blank white mask and his mouth was turned down. His eyes were rimmed with red and his pupils were sharp black pinpricks.

"Nate, I . . ." Joe started to say, when Nate shook his head sharply and retreated around the back of the truck to the other side.

Joe peered into the back of the pickup and the first thing he saw in the beam of his headlamp was a set of massive open steel jaws less than a foot from his face. Inset along the jaws were long yellow grizzly teeth stained with dried blood.

He cried out and dropped as if his legs were cut out from under him. His glimpse of Dallas Cates, balled up and still in the front of the bed, registered almost as an afterthought.

Joe heard the pickup roar to life and a cloud of exhaust from the tailpipe choked him. Nate had obviously shoved the dead driver aside in the cab and started the truck.

He pulled himself back to his feet and caught a glimpse of the back of Nate's head through the gore-streaked rear window and slider.

"Nate!" Joe called as the vehicle sped away. "Nate, stop!"

JOE TURNED WHEN the porch lights came on at the front of his house, and Sheridan stepped out holding her rifle and watching the taillights of the pickup blink out as it rocketed through the trees.

"Are you okay?" she asked.

"Yup."

"Are we safe from Dallas?"

"Yup."

"Who is the dead man?"

"Said his name was Lee Ogburn-Russell."

"Was it Nate?" she asked.

"Yup."

"Does he know?"

"I'm pretty sure he does, honey."

Marybeth shouldered through the door holding Kestrel against her breasts. The little girl was crying.

"The gunshots upset her," she said.

Joe nodded dumbly. He had trouble unseeing the steel jaws, the three-inch teeth, Dallas's body, and Nate's terrifying face in the light of his headlamp. Joe slid on the safety of his shotgun and turned toward his pickup.

"Where are you going?" Marybeth asked.

"I'm going to find Nate."

"Are you going to bring him back?" she asked.

"Not if the sheriff is here," Joe said over his shoulder.

WHEN JOE ARRIVED at the former Cates compound, he found Dallas tied to a pole once used by his father and brothers to hang game animals. His hands were bound behind his back. Dallas's broken body was glowing pink from the taillights of his pickup positioned fifteen feet away. A red-dot laser hovered above his right eyebrow. Cates was conscious but badly hurt, with bullet wounds in both of his shoulders and his upper left thigh.

Joe pulled his truck in front of the pickup and climbed out, deliberately leaving his shotgun inside the cab.

He sidled up to the side of the pickup's topper, where an oblong slider was open, and he peered inside.

Nate sat on a metal tractor seat with his hands gripping the controls and his thumb poised over a red button on the right joystick. He looked straight ahead out the back of the pickup over the top of the telescopic scissor jib. Nate didn't acknowledge that Joe was standing right next to him.

"Don't do it, Nate," Joe said.

"Ah, go ahead and do it," Cates said, slurring his words. "Get it over with."

Joe said, "Let me cut him down before he bleeds out. He'll go back to prison for the rest of his life, unless they execute him."

"Like that will ever happen," Cates said with a grin. "When's the last time Wyoming executed anyone?"

"You're not helping your case," Joe said with annoyance.

"I ain't trying to," Cates said.

Joe turned back to Nate. He said, "Not like this, Nate. Not in cold blood."

"He killed Liv in cold blood," Nate said in a tight whisper. "Then he used a tool with bear claws on it to mutilate her body."

"I know," Joe said. "It was brutal and she didn't deserve it. He's a monster, but you don't have to be one."

"Axel Soledad was with him," Nate said.

Joe was shocked. "What?"

"Soledad didn't die in Portland and he still wants revenge."

Joe turned to Cates. "Is he kidding? Was Axel Soledad with you when you killed all these people?"

Cates nodded his head. "Right up until the end. Then he bugged out on me."

"Where is he now?" Joe asked.

Cates made a bitter face. "In the wind, I guess. Plotting his next move. The guy is a stone-cold killer and I can't say I miss him much." Then: "Come on, get on with it. You people wiped my family off the planet and sold our property. Then you bring me out here to rub salt in the wound. So you might as well finish the job. That's what you do, isn't it? You make sure the people you consider white trash stay beneath you?"

Nate didn't respond and Joe wasn't sure what to say to either of them.

"There's two bodies inside that house," Cates said, chinning toward his old home. "The interlopers. Axel gets the credit for that, too. Plus that middle school girl in town."

Nate turned his head to Joe. His face was still a white mask. "What if he gets out of prison, Joe? What if he escapes?"

"He won't," Joe said without conviction.

"We can't take that chance," Nate said. "Soledad is still out there and he'll be coming for Geronimo, you, and me. And he's probably got some of his true believers out there ready to deploy."

Joe felt a chill wash through him.

Nate said, "I've got to find him before he comes back, and I don't want to worry about Dallas here joining up with him again or getting in the way."

"What about Kestrel?" Joe said. "You can't just leave her."

"She's in good hands," Nate said. "Better hands than mine. I can't put her life in danger like I did with Liv."

"No," Joe said, shaking his head. "You can't blame yourself."

"I can blame myself for leaving my cell phone at the grocery store and not getting calls from you, Marybeth, or Liv tonight," he said.

"I didn't know about that," Joe confessed.

"I made a mistake getting back on the grid," Nate said. "I'm not you, Joe."

"Nate . . ."

"*Jesus*," Cates exclaimed. "Quit yapping like a couple of damned schoolgirls. Get on with it!"

Nate said, "I told you that bear was still here. I reached out to it and she answered and she guided me to your house. *That* is my world, Joe. Not this one."

Cates hollered, "I'm going to die here waiting to die, for fuck's sake!"

"Please, Nate," Joe whispered.

Nate ignored Joe and focused on the controls. Joe turned his head away as the jaws fired out of the back of the truck and struck home with a terrifying *crunch*.

OCTOBER 29

The killing beast that cannot kill
Swells and swells in his fury till
You'd almost think it was despair.

—Edwin Muir, "The Combat," *Collected Poems, 1952*

CHAPTER TWENTY-SIX

Double Diamond Ranch

Two days later in the midafternoon, Joe followed a Game and Fish Department SUV driven by Brody Cress and Jennie Gordon down a county road toward the Double D Ranch. The SUV was speeding and its wigwag lights were flashing red and blue. Joe kept his distance behind them in his pickup to avoid the dust cloud trailing the vehicle.

Clay Hutmacher had called thirty minutes before and reported that the grizzly bear was back on his ranch. He'd found it feeding on a freshly killed Angus heifer in a pasture just beyond the corrals. Hutmacher said he'd unloaded his .300 Winchester Magnum rifle at the grizzly and he was pretty sure he'd hit it at least once before it ran away.

Clay sounded both ecstatic and half mad as he explained what had just happened.

The day before, Bill Brodbeck had died in the hospital from his wounds. Somehow, Judge Hewitt was still hanging in there.

THEY FOUND HUTMACHER in the pasture next to the carcass of the disemboweled heifer. The rancher pointed to a rock outcropping halfway up a hill to the east.

"That's where he went," Hutmacher said, pointing with the muzzle of his rifle. "Up in those rocks. I've been glassing it since I called and I haven't seen him come out."

Cress raised a pair of binoculars and stood next to the rancher.

"I don't see him," he said.

"That don't mean he's not there," Hutmacher responded.

Joe found Gordon looking not at the outcropping but at him. She had concern on her face.

"Joe, are you okay?"

"I'm fine."

"I need you to be fully here with us when we go after that bear."

"I said I'm fine."

"You don't look like it," she said.

He didn't respond.

JOE HAD BEEN in a kind of fugue state the thirty-six hours since he'd found Nate and Dallas Cates on the compound once owned by the Cates family. The scene he'd happened on still chilled him, and the peripheral events surrounding it puzzled him because they were filled with unknowns that may or may not be connected.

Why had it taken Jackson Bishop over an hour to show up at his home that night? According to Sheridan and Marybeth, Bishop had displayed no sense of urgency at the scene, and he'd arrived without backup. He *claimed* he couldn't rouse the deputies quickly enough in time to respond, but that excuse came across as baffling to Joe. Wouldn't eager, young Fearless Frank Carroll have jumped on the chance to confront the bad guys who had earlier eluded him? It didn't jibe, and Joe had disturbing doubts about the man who would inevitably become the local sheriff.

Axel Soledad's involvement had come as a shock as well. Joe was all but certain the man had bled out in an alley in Portland, the result of Geronimo's and Joe's fusillade of shotgun blasts, but it appeared he'd somehow survived and joined up with Dallas Cates. And now he was in the wind.

Marybeth had asked her board for a leave of absence while Kestrel settled into their lives. The little girl still wasn't sure what had happened to her parents, and she looked expectantly at the outside door whenever it opened and she frequently asked for her mother. Marybeth put on a brave and cheerful face and she slipped easily back into the role of caretaker for small girls that she'd mastered dozens of years before.

Nate was gone, his house empty and his Jeep missing. He'd

assured Joe he'd be in touch once he "worked things out." But there had been no word from him and his cell phone had been apparently discarded.

The fact that Joe's estranged birth mother, Katherine Pickett/Cotton, was identified as the murder victim left on the side of his county road was baffling. Had she literally followed Sheridan back to Wyoming? Why? Was her purpose to try to reconcile? The thought of that both confused and chilled him.

The disappearance of Axel Soledad and the discovery of his mother's body in around the same location was more than a coincidence.

The story, whatever it was, was bound to be continued.

THEY FOUND THE dead grizzly bear wedged between two large boulders in the center of the outcropping. A weathered telemetry collar was around its neck, the battery long ago depleted. The grizzly was splayed out as if sleeping, its rear paw pads facing up and legs stretched out.

"It's over," Cress said as he shouldered his rifle. "It sure looks like the bear we saw in the river."

"She never left the area," Gordon said with quiet awe. "We chased her all over the state and she never really left."

Joe arched his eyebrows. "She?"

"It's a female," Gordon said. "That kind of surprises me."

"Are we sure it's the same bear?" Joe asked.

"We'll do some forensic testing, but I'd guess the odds to be ninety-nine-point-nine percent it's the same bear that attacked Clay Junior and Brodbeck.

"See here," Gordon said, bending back a tuft of thick long hair on the far left thigh of the animal to reveal a scabbed-over bullet wound. "One of us hit her like we thought. Maybe that's why she didn't go very far. She must have hunkered down in the woods until she felt good enough to move again."

"That poor old girl got blamed for a lot of bad acts," Cress said. "I kind of feel sorry for her. Almost."

"Now for the moment of truth," Gordon said as she bent down next to the bear's massive head.

Joe was confused for a moment until he saw Gordon pull on a pair of nitrile gloves and reach down to the grizzly's snout and peel back the thick upper lip.

There, on the pink underside of her lip, he could clearly see the numbers *4-1-3* stenciled in dark ink.

"Oh, no," Gordon sighed. "*Oh, no.*"

"Tisiphone," Joe said. "The Mama Bears were right."

Gordon looked up at Joe and implored him with her eyes to never speak of this again. She did the same to Cress, who nodded his agreement.

"Let me get my knife," Cress said. "We need to get rid of that tattoo."

ACKNOWLEDGMENTS

The author would like to thank the people who provided help, expertise, and information for this novel.

Dan J. Thompson, PhD, the large carnivore section supervisor for the Wyoming Game and Fish Department, provided invaluable in-person experience and research about grizzly bears in and around Wyoming.

Special kudos to my first readers, Laurie Box, Molly Box, Becky Reif, and Roxanne Woods.

A tip of the hat to Molly Box and Prairie Sage Creative for cjbox.net, merchandise design, and social media assistance.

Congratulations to Doug Wick, Lucy Fisher, John Dowdle, Drew Dowdle, Michael Dorman, and Julianna Guill for bringing Joe and Marybeth to life on television.

It's a sincere pleasure to work with the professionals at Putnam, including the legendary Neil Nyren, Mark Tavani, Daphne Durham, Ivan Held, Alexis Welby, Ashley McClay, and Katie Grinch.

And thanks once again to our agent and friend, Ann Rittenberg.

C. J. Box is the author of twenty-four Joe Pickett novels, eight stand-alone novels, and a story collection. He has won the Edgar, Anthony, Macavity, Gumshoe, and two Barry awards, as well as the French Prix Calibre .38, the Western Heritage Award for Literature, and two Spur Awards. An avid outdoorsman, Box has hunted, fished, hiked, ridden, and skied throughout Wyoming and the Mountain West. He has been executive producer on television series based on his books, including ABC TV's *Big Sky* and *Joe Pickett* on Paramount+.

VISIT C.J. BOX ONLINE

cjbox.net
AuthorCJBox
CJBoxAuthor
CJBoxNovels

C. J. BOX

"One of today's solid-gold, A-list, must-read writers."
—Lee Child

For a complete list of titles and to sign up for our
newsletter, please visit prh.com/CJBox